"The magic's here!

"Daddy, you got to go get Merry!" Sean cried.

"Get Merry? Why?"

"Because the magic's here!" Sean was tugging urgently at Peter's hand. "Merry said the rose would bloom and the chickens would come back and then the Christmas magic would be here and it would let me live with you. You got to get her so that the magic can give *her* little boy back."

Peter stooped down, taking his son's hands in his own. He didn't understand everything the boy was saying. Okay, the rose had sort of bloomed, and he was seriously trying to figure out how to have Sean live with him. But what was all this about Merry and a little boy? And how did Peter convince his son that there was no magic, just...

Snow in Death Valley.

Pigs that flew.

And giant chickens back in Mentone....

Dear Reader,

Welcome to Silhouette *Special Edition* . . . welcome to romance.

Last year I requested your opinions on the books that we publish. Thank you for the many thoughtful comments. Throughout the past months I've been sharing quotes from these letters with you. This seems very appropriate while we are in the midst of our THAT SPECIAL WOMAN! promotion, as each of our readers is a very special woman.

This month, our THAT SPECIAL WOMAN! is Lt. Callie Donovan, a woman whose military career is on the line. Lindsay McKenna brings you this story of determination and love in *Point of Departure*.

Also this month is *Forever* by Ginna Gray, another book in the BLAINES AND THE McCALLS OF CROCKETT, TEXAS series. Erica Spindler brings you *Magnolia Dawn*, the second book in her BLOSSOMS OF THE SOUTH series. And don't miss Sherryl Woods's *A Daring Vow*— a tie-in to her VOWS series—as well as stories from Andrea Edwards and Jean Ann Donathan.

I hope you enjoy this book, and all of the stories to come!

Sincerely,

Tara Gavin
Senior Editor

QUOTE OF THE MONTH:

"I have an MA in Humanities. I like to read funny and spirited stories. I really enjoy novels set in distinctive parts of the country with strong women and equally strong men. . . . Please continue to publish books that are delightful to read. Nothing is as much fun as finding a great story. I will continue to buy books that entertain and make me smile."

—T. Kanowith, Maryland

ANDREA EDWARDS

THE MAGIC OF CHRISTMAS

Silhouette®

SPECIAL EDITION®

Published by Silhouette Books
America's Publisher of Contemporary Romance

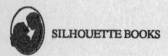 SILHOUETTE BOOKS

ISBN 0-373-09856-1

THE MAGIC OF CHRISTMAS

Copyright © 1993 by EAN Associates

Printed in U.S.A.

Books by Andrea Edwards

Silhouette Special Edition

Rose in Bloom #363
Say It with Flowers #428
Ghost of a Chance #490
Violets Are Blue #550
Places in the Heart #591
Make Room for Daddy #618
Home Court Advantage #706
Sweet Knight Times #740
Man of the Family #809
The Magic of Christmas #856

Silhouette Intimate Moments

Above Suspicion #291

Silhouette Desire

Starting Over #645

ANDREA EDWARDS

is the pseudonym of Anne and Ed Kolaczyk, a husband-and-wife writing team that concentrates on women's fiction. "Andrea" is a former elementary schoolteacher, while "Edwards" is a refugee from corporate America, having spent almost twenty-five years selling computers before becoming a full-time writer. They have four children, two dogs and four cats, and live in Indiana.

Dear Santa,

My name is Sean MacAllister and I am five years old. I've been living with my grandma in Mentone, Indiana, since my mommy died last year. I like Grandma a lot, but I would really like to live with my daddy again. For Christmas, could you please make him want me with him?

Your friend,

SEAN

P.S. I'd really like a new mommy, too, if you have an extra one.

Chapter One

The room was empty, just as every other room had been. No furniture, no light, no laughter. Peter crossed over to the other room, the sounds of his steps echoing in mockery. He reached out to turn the knob, his heart filling with hope as it had so many times before. But there was no Kelly, no Sean, no life here. . . .

A phone began to ring somewhere, and the empty room faded into nothing.

The ringing continued, and Peter opened his eyes to the night. He looked through the shadows toward the other side of the bed. It was empty. It had been empty since Kelly had died over a year ago. He snatched up the phone.

"MacAllister," he barked.

"Huh?"

"MacAllister," he repeated.

This time he was greeted by silence. What the hell was this, some stupid kid prank? His eyes went to the digital clock on his nightstand. Just past five-thirty. No kid would be up this early.

"This is Peter MacAllister," he said. "What do you want?"

"Daddy?" a tiny voice asked.

"Sean?"

"Of course, it's Sean." Peter's mother's voice came briskly over the telephone lines to scold him. "Who else would be calling you Daddy?"

"Is something wrong?" Peter asked.

"There has to be something wrong for a son to call his father? Honey." The softening of her voice made it clear she was no longer talking to Peter, but to Sean. "Go ahead now."

"I don't wanna," Sean said. "He's mad at me."

"He's not mad at you, dear."

"Of course I'm not mad at you, Sean." Peter sighed and tried to regain his senses. "What're you doing up this early?"

"We wanted to get you the very first thing this morning."

"The very first thing in the morning is too early for a five-year-old," Peter said.

"Indiana's an hour ahead of you folks in Chicago," his mother replied. "And if you spent more time with your son, you'd realize that the younger they are, the earlier they like to get up."

"Mom." He didn't need another lecture. He would spend more time with Sean if they weren't a hundred-fifty miles apart. And they wouldn't be so far apart if he and his mother hadn't both agreed that Sean was too young to bounce around between day-care and an assortment of nannies.

"So, Sean." Peter forced joviality into his voice. "What can I do for you?"

His son screamed out his silence.

"Go ahead, dear," Peter's mother said.

"Happy birthday," Sean mumbled.

Oh, God. So it was.

Peter pushed aside his own sinking awareness and concentrated on his son. "Thank you, Sean," Peter said. And thank you, Mom. He'd been doing his best to suppress all his little anniversaries. There seemed to be a zillion of them, full of memorable moments. Like the fact that Kelly always used to serve him breakfast in bed on his birthday.

"And what else were you going to do, honey?" his mother gently prodded Sean. "You were going to sing your daddy a birthday song, remember?"

His son stayed silent. Peter knew that between the two of them, he and his son couldn't carry a tune in a bucket. "That's okay, Mom. There's no need to—"

"Yes, there is. You two are family and rituals help keep a family together, especially when the members are apart from each other. Go ahead, Sean."

"Happy birthday to you. Happy birthday to you. Happy birthday, dear Daddy. Happy birthday to you." The words were spoken rapidly and totally without melody.

"Thank you, Sean," Peter said. "That was great."

"Can I have my pancakes now?" Sean asked.

"Of course, sweetie," Peter's mother replied. "Go wash your hands."

There was a pause, then the sound of a receiver slammed into its cradle. Peter's mother sighed heavily. "He should have said goodbye."

"That's okay, Mom," Peter replied. "Don't worry about it. He's just a little kid."

"He gets nervous around you," his mother said. "You only see him a few times a month, and he's just not sure how to please you."

"He doesn't have to do anything to please me."

"You and I know that, but he's just a little boy."

Peter leaned back against the headboard and closed his eyes. His mother with an agenda was like a Sherman tank, undeterred by any logic or facts that might fall in her way.

She felt he should spend more time with Sean, but his job was here in Chicago and his son was in Mentone. And that was best for the kid. Sean needed to be around happy people, not a widower still subject to fits of depression.

"You want me to bring you anything from Chicago?" he asked, trying to divert the conversation to lighter channels.

"Just yourself."

"That's easy enough."

"When will you be in?"

"Sometime this evening. I've got a presentation this afternoon, but I should be able to get out by three. Nobody wants to work late the day before Thanksgiving."

"You shouldn't be working today at all. You should have come down yesterday and spent your whole birthday here with your family."

"Mom, I'll be home for two weeks over Christmas and New Year's. We'll have plenty of time to visit then."

"I guess." There was a long pause. "There are a lot of people moving back home these days."

"Oh?"

"Yes," his mother said. "Denise Wharton just moved back, along with her two children. You remember her. She used to be Denise Nance. She was a few grades behind you."

"When did she become Denise Wharton? I thought she'd married some guy named Gustafson."

His mother cleared her throat. "Things didn't work out and now she's single again. Used to live around Washington, D.C. someplace. Just got plumb tired of the big city and all those crowds. Now she's back home in Indiana."

Peter rubbed his forehead, feeling a dull ache building. He knew where she was headed. "Mom."

"I'm glad that we cleared up when you're coming in. Maybe I'll have some people over for cake and coffee this evening."

Her ploy was transparent as glass. "Mom, don't go counting on me. Something could happen and I could get tied up."

"That hasn't happened yet, in all the times you've made the trip."

"That doesn't make my arrival time a given. As an actuary and a statistician, I can tell you with absolute certainty that what happened in the past does not guarantee the future." In fact, he would make sure of it.

"You've been working too much, Peter. You should try spending some time with people who talk plain, ordinary English."

A huge ice ball formed in his stomach causing him to break into the shivers. His mother and her agendas. Damn. He wasn't up to any more disasters. He knew that it was over a year since Kelly died, but just barely. The thought of dating or even man-woman small talk made his blood run cold.

"Mom, don't fix me up with somebody again." How was that for plain English?

"Oh, my goodness. Sean is ready for his pancakes. Blueberry ones. Remember how you used to love them?"

She'd made up her mind and was charging full steam ahead. There had to be a way to derail her. "Mom, I mean it. Don't start shopping around for a girlfriend for me."

"For goodness sakes, Peter. I'm not doing anything of the kind."

"Then there won't be any guests?"

"How would I know? People are always dropping by. That's what friends and neighbors do. Especially over the holidays."

His hand tightened on the phone as he remembered the previous casual "meetings" his mother had arranged. "Mom, don't. It could embarrass everyone."

"Embarrass?" She sounded puzzled, then laughed suddenly. "Oh, you mean you're bringing somebody with you for the holidays? Why, Peter, that's wonderful."

It wasn't wonderful. It wasn't anything close to what he'd meant. "No, I—"

"What's she like?"

He stopped and consciously closed his mouth on the explanation he wanted to make. What would be more effective in keeping his mother from matchmaking than convincing her it wasn't necessary?

"Just a friend," he said and felt the ensuing silence weighing on him. "Actually, a pretty good friend, but still just a friend." He cleared his throat, trying to force his brain to think fast. "I met her after work and…and we sort of got to be friends."

"That's such good news. What's her name?"

"Uh . . ." He should have known his mother would give him the third degree. "Mom, I really can't talk now. I have an early morning meeting and I haven't even taken my shower yet."

"A name is one word, Peter. If you have time to make that speech, you have time to say one word."

"We'll talk when I get down there."

"Skip goodbye and say her name."

"I really gotta go, Mom."

"Peter." She took an audible deep breath. "Fine, so don't tell me. I'll just call her Miss Mystery when I meet her tonight. See you." And then she hung up.

Peter listened to the dial tone in stunned paralysis for a long moment. Tonight? When had he ever said he was bringing someone tonight? He slowly hung up the phone. His mother was in for some disappointment when she found out he was coming alone, but she should learn not to jump to conclusions like that.

But then his mother was good at jumping to things. Like jumping in to take care of Sean when Kelly died.

Suddenly warring with his pain and absolute revulsion of relationships was his realization of all his mother had done for him in the past year. She'd buried her own hurt, put aside her own life to take care of Sean. Any pestering she did was only because she loved him and Sean and wanted them to live like a real family again.

Peter got out of bed and walked to the glass wall of windows, pulling back the drapes. A sweeping view of Lake Michigan lay before him. He stared down from his perch on the twenty-third floor, letting his vision blur out to where the lake met the sky. It was a humongous expanse of space. Like standing on the edge of a rolling Indiana cornfield, except the corn varied in shades of green, where the lake varied from blue green to gray. And in the early morning stages of awakening today, the lake was gray, preparing for the gloom of winter.

Peter watched the choppy waters below him, whitecaps high and rolling over the cement walkways lining the shore, and suddenly felt himself shivering. The apartment was cool, but his body wasn't reacting to that. The surface of the lake twisted and turned as if fighting off the oppressive weight of an even grayer sky. The scene before him awakened the seeds of his own dark mood.

It was more than a year now since Kelly had plunged off the road in that thunderstorm up in McHenry County. She'd been scouting out country homes for them, looking for a place full of trees, fresh air, horses and all the other things her city-girl fantasies had told her were part of the good life. Fortunately, Sean had had the sniffles and had been with a sitter that day.

More than a year, and the world decided it was now time for the widower to move on with his life. And for a widower with a child that meant getting into another relationship, one that his mother would define as a serious relationship.

His mother meant well, but . . .

Peter rubbed his face and eyes. First, she'd found him a divorcée with a four year old daughter. They'd been introduced during his Fourth of July visit at Cousin Bob's lake cottage. Sean and the girl hated each other at first sight and it had taken an effort by both of them for Peter and the woman to part on civil terms.

The next catastrophe occurred over Labor Day weekend. His mother's bridge partner had had her unmarried niece visiting. Peter had taken her to the Lakeview in Warsaw for dinner where she'd smoked continuously. They spoke no more than ten words the entire evening.

Shaking his head, Peter pushed himself away from the windows. He couldn't take another arranged meeting. He couldn't make small talk with a woman, he couldn't smile and laugh with her, and he couldn't possibly be part of a couple again, not even for an evening. He would do whatever he had to to keep his mother from fixing him up again.

He stalked into the bathroom and jerked back the shower curtain. It ripped off the rod. Damn. He wanted to scream, but he just closed his eyes and leaned his forehead on the cool tile.

What a day. He had two reports to finish up. He had to pack. And then he had a three-hour auto trip to Mentone. And on top of it all, he had to find a make-believe girlfriend to bring home.

"Merry, aren't you out of the shower yet?"

Merry Roberts paused in drying her hair to glare at the door. What was this nonsense? She thought that her roommates were sleeping in today. Sandi was flying to Tucson with her boyfriend and ZeeZee was going to Minneapolis with her sister's family to visit relatives, but neither was leaving until this afternoon.

"I'm drying," Merry called out.

"You don't have to do that in the bathroom," ZeeZee shouted.

True. Merry didn't have to, but she wanted to. Then, grimacing, she admitted to herself that for a girl who'd never seen a flush toilet until she was six, she was getting mighty fussy in her old age. In another five years, she'd hit the big three-O. At the rate she was going, she'd really be cranky by then.

"Dry yourself in your room," ZeeZee said. "I need to get in there."

In her room? Right, Merry thought to herself, but only if she stood on her bed. If she faced the window, she wouldn't be able to stretch out her arms. Her room wasn't quite six feet wide and the width of the single bed took up a good bit of that.

But that was nothing to complain about, she realized as the album of her childhood she always carried in the back of her mind pushed forward a snapshot. Growing up, the only way she could take a shower in Four Corners, Tennessee was if it was raining. And since she slept in the living room with her five brothers and sisters, the only way she could get any privacy was to go into the woods. Her present room might be small, but it had a window and she had it all to herself. Life could be a lot worse.

"Just a minute," Merry said. She wrapped the towel around her body and gathered up her toothbrush and toothpaste. "It's all yours," she said as she stepped through the doorway.

"Oh," ZeeZee said, touching Merry's hair as she walked by. "I'd kill for red hair like yours. Why can't they put color like that in a bottle?"

"My momma said an angel has to come down and paint your hair for it to be this red."

"Aw, that's sweet."

"Yeah." Merry opened the door to her room. "She had her moments."

"Oh, hey, Merry." ZeeZee dashed up to Merry's open door. "JoJo's got this really big van."

Merry just looked at ZeeZee.

"I mean, she wouldn't mind if you came along. I know you don't like kids, but hers are really great. I mean, they aren't brats or anything."

Merry winced and tried to sound not quite so crotchety. "It's not that I don't like kids," she said. "I'm allergic to them."

"But you're going to be here all alone and on Thanksgiving."

"That's the best part. I can spread my papers out as much as I like, stay up all night reading and get lots done."

"It's no trouble. Really."

"ZeeZee, I don't want to go anyplace. I have a sociology paper due in two weeks and I need to work on it. Being here by myself is the best way to get it written."

ZeeZee nodded her head rapidly. "I dig it." Then she gave a quick wave and was gone.

Merry closed her door, threw her towel over the chair and slipped into a robe before plopping down onto the bed. There were a lot of things her roommates didn't understand. The main one being that not everyone was comfortable around kids. She didn't dislike them—no, just the opposite. But she also feared them, feared their power to awaken memories best left hidden. It was safest for her to just stay far away from kids.

The other thing her roommates didn't understand was that the holidays meant different things to different people. Merry didn't have any Kodak moments of the family gathering around the turkey. The closest she'd come to a real Thanksgiving meal as a kid had been when some do-gooders brought turkey and the trimmings to church, but being somebody's charity case tended to suck the flavor out of the food.

No, to Merry, Thanksgiving was just an annoyance. The restaurant would be closed two extra days because of it and that meant losing two days' wages. It was hard enough to scrape together tuition money without having the holidays screw up everything. Oh, well. Wouldn't be the first time she had to stretch a nickel.

Merry plugged in her hair dryer and settled on the corner of her bed with the dryer in one hand and her brush in the other; then she propped a book up in front of her. It was about this weird guy who turned into a bug, but it had made Number 26 on the list of Harvard's All-Time Classics that *USA Today* had published, so she figured it had to be good.

This education business was a lot of work, but then if it were easy, everybody would be smart, and being able to discuss Kafka wouldn't impress anybody.

She glanced almost without choice toward a faded newspaper clipping tucked into the edge of her mirror. It would all be worth it, though, when she finally was somebody. Jason Byron O'Connell was one smart cookie, and she was determined to be worthy of him.

Peter walked the length of the restaurant to his usual booth in back and dropped his body into the seat with a sigh. He put his face down in his hands and rubbed at his eyes. What a crappy day this had been so far.

He'd gotten to the office even earlier than usual and had accomplished absolutely nothing. After talking with Sean, being reminded of his birthday and the victim of his mother's maneuvering, he'd been tense before the day had even started.

What was he going to do about this girlfriend thing? If he showed up alone, with only a lame excuse in tow, his mother would start arranging dates again. And now that his allotted year of mourning was over, there was no way to avoid future potential disasters. He had to find somebody to play his girlfriend. But how?

An employment bureau had hung up on him and a talent agency had just laughed. The two dating services he'd called had given him long spiels about filling out forms and providing references before being allowed to check through the notebooks of available women.

Peter raised his head from his hands and looked around for someone to take his order. If he didn't get a sandwich, and fast, he'd eat the tablecloth.

He signaled to a waitress sitting at the bar as she glanced his way. She smiled and nodded before turning her back to him. From the movements of her body, Peter guessed the woman was slipping her shoes back on.

A sigh eased from his lips as his mind danced back to his lazy days of youthful summer. He was down by the creek, his bare feet dangling in the water as tension flowed out of him. He could almost feel the warm sun caressing his body.

It was a time when everything was so simple, and so possible. No goal was too great, no achievement unattainable. It was . . .

"What can I get you?" the waitress interrupted his thought.

Peter looked up. The overhead lights hit the waitress's head just right, bringing out the dark cherry color in her hair. Her blue eyes were sparkling and her wide, generous mouth was ready to overflow with joy. She was medium tall, with a curvy body and words that came wrapped in a soft twang.

"Would you like to order?"

She was the nice one. The young one. The fast, efficient one with the wisecracking mouth. She was one of the few who Peter remembered by name. Merry.

"Sir. What would you like?"

Peter sighed and rubbed the back of his neck, his mind suddenly filled with fuzz. *What would he like?*

"A woman. I really need a woman."

God, no. He hadn't really said that, had he?

He had been working hard the past several weeks and the dreams were haunting him again, but he'd never, ever talked so stupidly. Never in his whole life.

"Sorry," the waitress said, the laughter in her voice tickling his ears. "All we've got is burgers, BLTs and stuff like that."

"I—" His cheeks were hot, but his tongue was frozen. Peter tried to force some words out. Words of apology, explanation, anything.

"Now if you still want something hot—" her grin spread wide across her face, forcing a dimple into each cheek "—there's our regular chili. Large bowl or small. With or without mac."

The flame in his cheeks flared into a white-hot heat. His tongue tied itself into a double step-over slipknot. She was laughing at him just like Kelly used to when he got too technical answering Sean's questions.

"But if a lady's what you gotta have, then that's what you gotta have." Merry put her hands on her hips, a saucy grin on her lips. "Now I don't know this for a fact, since I've never been in the need myself, but I've heard that the Pink Pussycat is the place. Folks say a body can find most anything they want there."

He could feel the tension in his neck slowly ease up. He started to shake his head.

"It's over on Clark Street," she said. "About three blocks north of the river."

"It came out wrong. That's not what I meant." Peter wasn't really sure she was buying it. "I'm just hungry. I haven't eaten all day."

"Oh. Poor baby."

There might have been a flicker of sympathy in her eyes, but Peter didn't feel up to a close examination. He hurried on. "I've been working hard for more than a month. Lots of overtime, that kind of thing. And then my—" He stopped and changed direction slightly. "I got this call at five this morning. Denise Nance is divorced again."

"Not again? Poor, old Denise." The waitress shook her head in pretend sadness as she pulled out her notepad. "You want your regular?"

"Regular?"

"Turkey sandwich, chips, coleslaw and soup of the day," the waitress said. "You have it all the time."

He did? Peter had a momentary glimpse of a gray-haired old man gumming his sandwich and slurping his soup, but he sent that image packing in a hurry. So he'd fallen into some ruts since Kelly had died, it was just that other parts of his life were more important than lunch, requiring all his energy and attention.

"That's fine," he said briskly. "And—"

"Hot tea to drink," she finished for him.

Peter just nodded as the waitress hurried off to place his order. Would he have to find another place to eat now? He really didn't want to, but if this waitress started to talk . . .

Nah, she wouldn't do that. Servers in a place like this made good money. And he was usually quite generous. A momentary cloud of concern passed before his eyes as he hoped that the waitress shared his definition of generous.

"There you go."

She set his cup of soup before him along with his pot of tea. "Your sandwich'll be right up. Need anything else?"

"Not right now," he murmured. "Thank you."

"Give me a holler if you do," she said with a wink and then went back to her seat at the bar.

The wink bothered him momentarily, but then Peter decided that it was a signal that everything that had been said before was their little joke. This waitress was always joking around with the patrons. Young and lively as she was, she probably got all kinds of propositions. And a few could even be weird. Given the way things were today, they had to be.

His soup was hot and he slowly stirred it, staring out the window at the city scene passing before him. It looked like it was starting to snow. He hoped that bad weather wasn't on the way.

The thought of his trip took the taste out of his food. He looked at his watch. Great. He had only two hours left to find a girlfriend, and he sure as hell wasn't going to the Pink Pussycat.

"Here you go."

He looked up as Merry put his sandwich down in front of him. Her smile seemed to comfort, to say that she could handle anything.

"Need any mustard?"

Peter shook his head. "No, this is fine, thank you." He bit into his sandwich as she walked away.

This was Chicago, a big city. All kinds of services were available to meet members of the opposite sex. A professional escort service might be the thing. Those women were probably more up to handling the unusual. It would probably be an easy gig for most of them.

Except that he'd seen a number of those women, especially in more expensive restaurants with older men. They were good-looking women. But they looked so... so professional. Yeah, that was the word. Professional.

That type of woman would fit in at Mentone about as well as some exotic animal from the jungles of Asia. He needed someone more down to earth.

"How's it going?"

His eyes looked into a broad smile, bright enough to drive the gray back out over the lake. "Fine," he replied.

"Little slow eating there," she said as she poured more hot water into his tea.

Peter shrugged. "I got a lot to think about."

"Denise Nance?" She shook her head. "My momma always said it's best to run with your fuel gauge on full."

He smiled, an idea taking shape, and pushed his dish back. "Things are probably going to be a little slow around here for a few days."

"Yeah," she agreed. "Most of the offices around here are closed Thursday and Friday for Thanksgiving. We're closing at three today and won't open until Monday."

"Going anyplace over the holidays?"

"Yeah," she said with a laugh. "But I haven't decided where yet. It's a toss-up between laying on the beach at Cancun or skiing in the Alps."

He smiled himself. A working girl who couldn't afford to go to either.

"Maybe I'll just go to both."

Everyone had a right to their fantasies. "Gonna be tiring, hopping back and forth."

"Yeah, but what's a vacation for if not to get worn out?" She broadened her smile. "Actually. I've got a lot of work to do."

"Oh? I thought you said the restaurant would be closed."

"I go to school," she replied. "Columbia College. I'm studying acting."

Peter nodded. "They have a good program."

She looked down at his plate. "Can I get you anything else?"

He slowly shook his head. She was good-looking, with a pleasant personality. Obviously intelligent. And she was cool. Handled that stupid remark of his just as if it were an everyday kind of request. A country girl like this would fit right in with the folks in Mentone, his mother, the whole nine yards.

"Actually, I would like something else," he said.

"Apple, custard and pumpkin pie, chocolate cake or vanilla, chocolate and strawberry ice cream."

"I need someone to go to Indiana with me," he blurted out.

"You mean a bodyguard to protect you from Denise?"

He gritted his teeth. What he had was a business proposition. If she'd stop being a smart aleck for a minute, he could lay it out.

"Look," he said, trying to be patient. "What I need is a woman to go with me and visit my mother in Indiana."

Merry didn't reply. Instead, she turned her attention to the check and totaled up the tab. Then she placed it face down on the table and patted him on the shoulder. "I really think you should try the Pink Pussycat. And if that don't work, try a bell captain at any of those big hotels along Michigan Avenue."

"Damn it!" Peter sent his fist crashing down on the tabletop. "If I don't produce my own girlfriend, I'm going to get fixed up with Denise, and I don't want to be."

Merry stepped back, but continued looking at him full in the face. "Ever hear of the word no?"

"It's not that easy," he said and took a deep breath. "Look, I'm willing to pay for your time. How about a hundred dollars? Two hundred?"

She edged away slightly. "I've already got plans."

"How about five hundred?"

She stopped edging.

Chapter Two

Dumb. Dumb. Dumb! This was the absolute dumbest thing she'd ever done. And she'd done some real dumb things before this.

"Pretty soon we'll be in the real Indiana."

Merry stared and glanced quickly at Peter, then back out the window. They had just left Interstate and the area around the interchange was ordinary white-bread suburban America. Strip malls, office buildings, motels and fast-food joints as far as the eye could see, all surrounded by a hundred zillion acres of gray asphalt.

"Great. This fake stuff is really depressing." Merry said.

Peter just laughed. "The real Indiana is small towns," he said. "With grain elevators and flat, open farmland stretching from one end of the earth to the other."

"Oh."

Great response. Bet he was really impressed with that. He was probably thinking the same thing she was—that this was the dumbest idea ever.

She was actually surprised that he was making small talk with her. He was obviously much better educated than she was. He probably had a master's degree from some high-class Ivy League University.

"And train tracks," Peter added. "Most of the grain used to be transported by train. Now they use trucks."

"Things are always changing," she murmured while staring out her window.

Silence returned to their midst, taking up the space between the two of them, pushing them farther apart into their respective corners. Merry scrunched down in her seat and let her peripheral vision take in Peter as he drove the car. He was a tallish kind of guy. Husky, with strong hands. Sort of rugged looking, but it was obvious that he hadn't come up in the world chopping cotton. And once he started talking, the upper-class background and education came spilling out.

She forced her eyes forward and concentrated on the road before them. Peter was the type of man that girls like her got into trouble with. Of course, she had let that happen once in her life, but that little mistake had been a whamdoozer.

Merry sat up straight and clenched her jaw. She was a big girl now. Been around the county a few times and was taking care of herself. Like her granny used to say, first time a mistake, second time stupid.

This little deal had potential for disaster, no matter what way she looked at it. Peter could be a tremendous actor, hiding a heart full of evil behind a cool, gentle facade. Then all she'd have to look forward to was a fight and a hike back to civilization. But it wouldn't be the first time. Growing up in Four Corners, fighting came natural to a kid. And she was wearing a good, solid pair of hiking boots, so she was well prepared.

More likely, Peter was exactly what he looked to be—an upper-class kind of a guy with a good job and a family full of upstanding citizens in some small town hidden away in the cornfields of Indiana. Then what she had to fear was somebody breaking through her pretense and finding out what she really was—a dumb, illegitimate girl from the backwoods of Tennessee.

But it was too late to back out now. She was just going to have to concentrate and play her part. Then, when the curtain came down, she would run like the devil was after her.

"I went to school there," Peter said, nodding toward a cluster of red-brick buildings interspersed among the trees. "That's Valparaiso University. It's a small liberal-arts college, although they do have a law school and some graduate departments."

She would have guessed that he was an Ivy Leaguer. "What did you study?"

"Math."

"You look more like a Harvard M.B.A. type."

A smile split Peter's face. "A real snob type, huh?"

"No." Merry felt her cheeks starting to glow. "No. I didn't mean that at all. I meant..." She shrugged helplessly.

"Actually, I do have an M.B.A.," he said. "But I got it from the University of Chicago."

"They're sort of the same thing, aren't they?"

"Yeah," he agreed. "Graduates from either school think rather highly of themselves."

They were out in the country now, flat, open fields filled with nothing but empty. Houses were few and far between. Mostly just filling stations and restaurants at the major crossroads.

"I did go to Harvard." Peter cleared his throat. "But it was to get a Ph.D. in statistics. I had very little to do with the business school there."

Jeez. Merry's stomach sank. She'd thought he was educated, but three college degrees had been beyond even her wildest guess.

"And I have a master's in actuarial science from the University of Michigan."

Oh, damnation. No wonder he talked the way he did. He didn't have a reason or need to talk like regular folk.

"You sure spent a lot of time in school," Merry said.

"It was either go to school or go to work. And I'm on the lazy side."

The words were backed by that smile again. Broad like the Indiana landscape. Right, as if he were just a simple country boy. Uh-huh. Merry turned to stare out the window again.

They passed a sign for Hanna, Indiana. The towns had nice, cozy names, almost like down home, but the land wasn't anything like Tennessee. It was flat. There were none of the hills and hollers that made up the coal country, dips in the land where a body could hide.

There'd be no place for her to hide in Mentone. Merry knew that for an absolute fact. She'd be onstage tonight, Thursday, Friday, Saturday and part of Sunday. Almost four days, counting them off on her fingers. She prayed that she would make it. It was going to be tough.

"We probably ought to cover some background for each other."

She turned to look at him. His gaze was shy, almost sheepish. The man's smile had more variations than the Chicago weather.

"Want to go first?"

Merry swallowed hard. "Not much to tell." She'd used this same story for years now, but for some reason her tongue seemed frozen stiff. She took a deep breath. "I'm just your average kind of gal. I grew up in the suburbs, went to public schools and moved around a little bit."

"Where did you grow up?" he asked.

"Near Atlanta," Merry fibbed. "Just north of the city."

"That's surprising," he said. "I thought you were more of a country girl."

A moment's panic washed over her, but she fought it back. How did he know? "Nope, not me."

He let it pass. "Any brothers or sisters?"

"Nope."

"What did your father do?"

"He was in business. Worked for a restaurant-equipment company." For all she knew, that could be true.

"Your mother?"

"She stayed home when I was little. Then she worked as a secretary." That sounded so nice, so maternal, so "Ozzie and Harriet."

They were heading east into the dusk that had fallen on the Indiana countryside. The flat fields were clothed in the drab colors of the Midwest's late autumn garb. Black to dark brown earth, interspersed with yellow stubble, mostly corn or soybeans. Merry knew that she should talk more about herself or Peter would think that she was holding back, but her fabrication only went so deep. She'd learned the first rule of lying long ago; don't include too many facts, it makes it easier to keep things straight.

"So, what's your story?" she asked him.

He frowned into the growing shadows. "Well, you know about my educational background. Otherwise, I grew up in Mentone. I was a good student, top of my class and good at baseball and basketball. The expectations were the hardest thing about growing up."

Merry nodded, pretending she understood. Nobody had expected anything of her when she was a kid, and she didn't know which was worse.

"I was close to my grandparents, and they really helped me keep things in perspective. Grandma always had a plate full of cookies. And Gramps always had a fence to fix, a barn to paint or just a stick that needed whittling."

Merry wondered for a moment whether she should lay out some sweet, little memory for herself, but she quickly discarded that thought. "I didn't really know what to do when high school ended," she said. "So I just moved around a bit, taking up odd jobs like waitressing wherever I went."

"That must have been a bit of a challenge," he said. "I mean, suburban life is usually fairly protected."

Merry shrugged. "I guess. So what did you do after college?"

"Got my job as an actuary and got married."

Whoa. This was a new wrinkle to the scheme. She opened her mouth to ask for an explanation, but then closed it again when she saw how tightly his hands were gripping the steering wheel.

"Kelly died last year," he said slowly. "It was an automobile accident."

"I'm sorry." The words seemed so inadequate when faced with his obvious pain. She didn't know how to deal with the thick silence that descended upon them.

He did, though. "Where do your parents live now?"

"My parents?" She was startled, and her mind rolled about in confusion. "Uh, they're dead. They died a while ago." At least, that was true. Her mother had died when Merry was twenty. And her father—well, since she had no idea who he was, he'd always been dead to her.

"I'm sorry," Peter murmured.

"You've only mentioned your mother," she said. "Does your father live in Mentone?"

"No," Peter said. "He died—" he paused a moment "—fifteen years ago. He was the town doctor."

"So your mother lives alone?"

Peter did not reply, and as she waited Merry could feel the silence grow heavier. She turned to look at him. Maybe it was her imagination, but in the dim lights of the oncoming cars he looked grimmer.

"Not exactly. There's a lot of family around." He nodded toward a green-and-white highway sign that announced it was only one mile to Etna Green. "Almost there."

Damn. That was pure cowardice. She was going to find out about Sean soon, anyway, so why was he playing stupid games? It was just that he'd seen how women changed when they found out about Sean, turning all sympathetic and motherly in the blink of an eye. And he didn't want this to be anything but a business relationship.

"How do you pronounce that?" Merry asked, pointing to the sign announcing that they had left Marshall and were entering Kosciusko County.

"Most folks around here pronounce it Ka-zee-osco," Peter replied. "Although I went to school with a guy from South Bend whose grandparents came from Poland, and he said that was wrong. But I could never make my tongue say it the way he did."

"Was the county settled by Polish immigrants?"

The turn for Etna Green came up and he slowed down, making a right onto State Road 19. Another eight or ten minutes and they'd be in Mentone.

"I'm not much into any kind of history," Peter replied. "Ask my mother. That's her thing."

Ask my mother anything you want, he wanted to say. Ask her a million questions. Keep her busy. If you don't, she'll start prying into your life. And his mother had a way of getting people to spill their guts. Must be a skill they worked on at teacher's colleges back in the old days when his mother was a college student.

They were through Etna Green in a flicker of an eyelash, and open country stretched before them. There was no turning back now. Sean was probably watching television, but his mother would be on the window seat in the library, staring out into the night.

He couldn't even fake a flat tire. As was his practice, Peter had called from the gas station, just past Bourbon. His mother always said it made her feel better to know that he was close to home. If he turned back now and called again from that station, his mother would just send one of the neighbors out after him. He could run, but he couldn't hide.

Peter took his left hand off the steering wheel and wiped his palm on his pant leg. Then he did the same for his right. As he did so, he fervently prayed this harmless little scam wouldn't blow up in his face.

If it did? Well, that was just the way it was going to have to be. He couldn't face up to his mother's matchmaking. He was well aware that widowers, especially those with small children, were supposed to mourn for a year, then jump right back into the thick of things. But he didn't give a damn what custom dictated. He wasn't ready yet. He might never be ready.

Bringing Merry along was actually doing everyone a favor. His mother wouldn't feel pressured to push women at him. They could all relax, including Sean. Besides, Merry would do just fine. Hell, if she could handle that crowd at the restaurant, she should be able to handle anybody in Mentone.

"It's just like you said."

"What?" Peter snapped the question out. He'd been in his own little world there. "What's just like I said?"

"There's the railroad track," Merry said, pointing up ahead of them. "And right alongside are the grain elevators."

Peter glared down the street. Damn. He'd been daydreaming. He turned the car around. "Yeah, and here's Main Street."

They drove slowly down the quiet, almost deserted street. Now what? Did he point out the hardware store as the place

Sean got his new sled last winter? Or Teel's Restaurant as the boy's favorite place to eat?

Peter made a left and drove north through the old residential district. Some folks had moved into new houses on the edge of town, but his mother wasn't about to leave the old homestead.

"My parents moved in here soon after they married," he told Merry. "Dad used to walk the two blocks downtown to his office. When he worked, which was almost all the time, Mom would make soup and sandwiches. Then we would go down and eat lunch with Dad."

"That's nice," Merry said, and the softness in her voice made it obvious she meant it.

"There it is." Peter pulled into the driveway and around to the back by the garage. "This is where I grew up."

Merry looked at the house. The light from the back porch softened her features, giving a glow to her face. "I like old houses."

"Then you should love this one," Peter said. "It's very old."

His mother was already out on the porch as they stepped out of the car. She and Belle, their old springer spaniel, waited at the top of the stairs. "Mom," he said. "You're going to catch a cold standing out here with no coat on."

"Nonsense, Peter," his mother snapped. "Coddling just weakens a body."

If standing out in the chilly night air was so great, then where was Sean? No doubt sitting inside the warm house where his grandmother would have told him to stay.

Their old dog gave a couple of woofs, as if to second his mother's opinions. Both of them, Belle and his mother, were super ornery.

"Mom," Peter said as they came up the steps. "This is Merry Roberts. Merry, this is my mother."

"Hello, Mrs. MacAllister," Merry said putting out her hand. "I'm pleased to meet you."

His mother took Merry's hand, a wary look in her eye. Merry had a broad, easy smile on her face, but it always took his mother a while to warm up to somebody new.

"How do you do, Miss Roberts?"

"Just call me Merry. No one calls me Miss Roberts, and I might forget you're talking to me."

"Very well, Merry," his mother replied with a short nod. "Welcome to Mentone. I hope our quiet little town doesn't bore you to death."

"It'll be a nice change from Chicago," Merry replied. "I'm glad to be here."

Peter could see a softening in his mother's posture and relaxed.

"And that's Annabelle Lee," he said. Merry was already on her knees, eliciting grunts of pleasure from the dog as she scratched behind its ears. "We call her Belle for short."

"Hello, Belle," Merry said, kissing the dog on the nose and getting her face slobbered in turn.

"Peter, get the luggage, please. Belle, mind your manners." His mother took Merry by the arm and led her toward the door. "Let's get on in the house, Merry. It's getting a touch bitter out here."

Merry and his mother were starting up the stairs to the second floor when Peter entered the house with the suitcases. He paused to peek into the living room and the den. Sean wasn't in either room. Could he be in the kitchen having a snack? That was doubtful. His mother wouldn't let the kid eat this close to dinner.

"Quit lollygagging, boy," his mother said from the top of the stairs. "We need to get Merry settled in. Supper's waiting."

Sean was probably upstairs, playing in his room. Maybe they could get Merry settled in first. Then he could introduce her to his son. Peter made his way up the stairs. Belle, panting encouragement, waited for him at the top.

The difference this time was that Merry was there to flash him a sympathetic smile. He noticed the bags seemed lighter than usual, even with the addition of Merry's stuff. Those thrice-weekly workouts at the gym were starting to do the job.

"I'm putting you in this room, Merry," his mother said.

Peter stepped through the door after them and stared about the room, his face wrinkled in thought. Something wasn't right. "This has always been your sewing room," he finally blurted out.

"Land sakes, Peter," his mother snapped. "The world doesn't stand still and wait for nobody. A body's got to change, improve themselves."

Blinking, Peter looked around the room again and wondered what he'd done to bring on that little sermon.

"This is your bathroom," his mother was saying to Merry as she turned on the lights. "Your towels are peach."

"Thank you," Merry murmured.

"You'll have to share the bathroom with Peter," his mother said. "His bedroom is on the other side through that door."

"That's no problem," Merry replied.

"I figured as much," his mother said with a snort. "From what I hear, young folks these days no sooner get their how-de-do's out of the way and they're sharing a lot more than a bathroom."

"Mother—" But his protest went no further as his mother ignored him and continued talking to Merry.

"You can lock this door from inside your room," his mother said, pointing at the old-fashioned flip latch.

"Oh, good," Merry said.

Peter was about to give Merry a supercharged glare, one that would knock her back into a respectful type of silence, but his mother turned just as he was ready to fire up.

"Peter, put Merry's bag on the bed. No reason for her to be all bent over just to unpack."

Storing his controlling force for later, he put the bag on the bed, where he was greeted by a complaining meow/growl.

"Oh, good heavens." For one of the few times in his life, Peter saw his mother flustered. "Zachary, I told you your new room is over in the back corner."

She looked at Peter. "He doesn't adapt well to change."

"Hi, Zachary," Merry said. She reached out to scratch the Burmese cat under the chin, who gave her a purr of regal acceptance. "My goodness, look at all that gray. You're an old feller, aren't you?"

"He's twenty years old," his mother said. "And he's blind now."

"Poor guy," Merry crooned, kissing the cat lightly on the top of the head.

Zachary just grumbled, and Peter frowned. He bet there were a lot of guys in Chicago that would like Merry to treat them like that. The cat should appreciate what he was getting.

"That's why he doesn't like change," his mother said. "Here, let me take him."

"That's okay," Merry said. "He can stay."

"No, no," Peter's mother insisted. "He should be in his own room."

"I think as far as he's concerned, this is his room," Merry replied. "I'm only going to be here a few days. I've got no right to push him out."

His mother looked thoughtful and seemed about to say something when a shout from downstairs seized their attention.

"I'm home!"

His mother poked her head out into the hallway. "We're upstairs, dear."

Small footsteps stomped up the stairs, sounding as if they carried the weight of an elephant. Peter felt his heart beat to the tune of the rapidly advancing noise. He sure missed the little guy.

Sean stepped into the room, giving them all the open, wide-eyed stare of a five-year-old. "Hi, Daddy," he said.

"Hi, Sean," Peter said softly, squatting down. God, it was so good to see him. And so painful, too. Kelly's eyes looked back at him from Sean's face, and he had to swallow away the hurt. "How are you?"

His son shrugged. "Okay."

They stared at each other a long moment, stared until his mother broke the silence.

"Sean, give your father a hug."

Peter held his arms open. Sean paused a moment to examine Merry, then came forward and gave the required greeting. Freeing himself after a quick moment, the boy turned to face his grandmother.

"I thought you said Zachary was gonna sleep in your new sewing room."

Peter glanced at Merry. She was just sitting there, staring at Sean as if he were a creature from a faraway planet.

"Zachary needs a little more time," his mother was telling Sean. "But Merry said he could stay here. Isn't that nice of her?"

Merry wasn't even blinking. Her face was pale and her eyes were wide. She looked as if she had stepped into hell.

"Finding out you had a son kind of threw me for a minute," Merry said with a laugh.

Peter thought she had seemed a little more than just "thrown," but he said nothing. By the time they'd sat down to dinner, she'd seemed almost normal, though she hadn't said much to Sean. And after the boy had gone to bed and Peter suggested taking an evening stroll down toward Main Street, she had been herself, laughingly warning him not to show her too much excitement the first evening.

"I worked for a few years at the Abracadabra Café on the north side," she said. "We had to do magic tricks for the kids, and I guess I just got kind of overdosed on them."

Her laugh seemed shakier this time and, though he wasn't sure why, he took her hand in his. "I should have told you about Sean. It's just…" His reasons seemed lame and silly now.

"That there wasn't a chance," she finished for him. "It's not like we had time to cover our whole lives in that three-hour drive down here."

The existence of a son could be covered in a few seconds, Peter thought, but allowed Merry to believe her excuses. At least she hadn't turned into a motherly, simpering female, ready to take over his life.

They turned onto Main Street. The buildings filled the shadows while empty circles of light dotted the sidewalks. No one else was in sight.

"We'd best not stay out too long," Merry said. "I don't think my heart can take all this excitement."

He let her turn him from his thoughts. "It looks like we're the only two people left on earth."

"Well, that ain't all bad," Merry said as she squeezed his hand. "Don't need but two folks to have a little fun."

"Depends on the folks involved," Peter agreed. "Some twosomes seem to have a whole lot of fun."

Merry laughed, and Peter felt his ears warm. He couldn't believe what he'd said. Was it this woman who inspired some hidden persona to come to life or was it the clear night air?

"So when is Denise going to jump out of the bushes at you?" Merry asked.

"What?"

"You know, the one I'm supposed to be protecting you from."

"Oh, that Denise." He relaxed as they strolled down toward the post office, their steps sounding softly in the night. The breeze held a slight chill, but it felt good, invigorating.

"I think I'm probably safe from her," he said. "But you'd be surprised at the reactions a widower inspires in women. They all assume that I'm looking for an immediate, serious commitment because of Sean. So either they run away like a scared rabbit or they jump on me. I get the feeling some of them view my ready-made family in the same vein as buying a mature dog instead of a puppy."

"So, in other words, you've got all the women coming or going."

He laughed, and the sound seemed to echo around them. "I guess. Trouble is my mother encourages the 'coming' ones."

"So that's where I come in. I get to pounce on any woman who comes too close. God, I can see it now—bodies flying all over the Indiana countryside."

"Uh, I don't think you'll be quite that busy."

"Don't be too sure. I'm taking this job seriously. We go to the grocery and some little old lady pushes her cart too close to you, and she's history."

"Jeez, I've created a monster."

"I'm just making sure you're getting your money's worth."

"So I'm getting a bargain?"

"You'd better believe it."

Peter chuckled. He'd been right to hire her. She had a great sense of humor.

"Are you going to show me the grain elevators?" she asked.

"Nah," he replied as they crossed the street and went back in the direction they'd come. "Don't want to show you everything in one night. Then what will we do the rest of the weekend?"

They walked in silence for a block or two, letting the darkness lay like a cloak around them. The stillness felt good, comforting. He relaxed, letting the tension slip from his shoulders like rain off a windshield.

"I take it that you haven't started dating again," Merry said softly.

"Oh, I've made a few forays into that alien territory," he admitted. "I tried a single's bar a few times about six months after Kelly's accident."

"Rough place to start."

"You aren't kidding. I thought I could handle dating again, but learned pretty fast I was wrong." He wasn't sure why he was telling her all this, but it felt right. Maybe it was the night that seemed to offer anonymity, or maybe it was the open way she listened. He felt he could tell her anything.

"Single's bars aren't dating, they're a meat market."

"So I found out." He agreed. "Then friends fixed me up a few times."

"With the widows and divorcées?"

He nodded. "My mother's favorites."

"I guess I'm lucky I don't have any family around. Nobody but my roommates to bug me about dating."

"They think you ought to, or they don't like your current flame?"

She laughed, the sound rippling comfortably around them. "They think I'm too serious."

"You?"

"Not jokewise, but lifewise. They say I do nothing but go to work and school."

"Do you?"

"Once in a while," she admitted. "But it's not easy to attend college piecemeal. It doesn't leave you much free time. Besides, my plans don't leave room for worrying about somebody else."

"Oh, no?" He wondered just what her plans were, but it felt like it would be prying to ask.

"Goodness," Merry exclaimed and screeched to a halt. "That certainly is a big rock."

He looked ahead of them at the six-foot shape hulking at the edge of the parking lot and smiled. "That's not a rock. That's an egg."

"An egg?" she repeated, doubt hanging heavy in her tone. "You mean like the kind laid by a chicken?"

"Yup."

"Well, I hope she was a big, old bird. Otherwise, she probably had a serious case of hemorrhoids."

Peter found himself laughing out loud, something he hadn't done for ages, as he took her arm to lead her forward. He'd have to get together with Merry once they got back to Chicago. Take her out to some nice restaurant and maybe a show.

Then it hit him, like the proverbial bolt of lightning. He was a single parent and he was going to stay a single parent, but that didn't mean he had to be a monk. He could date and do all the other things a normal single man did. The key was to limit himself to the proper kind of women. Women who were intelligent and had a sense of humor but no desire for any major commitments. A woman like Merry.

They stopped in front of the stone egg, and Merry bent close. "It says here that Mentone is Egg Basket of the Midwest."

"I'm sure I told you that," Peter said. "And I never lie."

"Never?" She straightened up to look at him, and suddenly her eyes weren't laughing anymore.

A warmth moved and stirred inside him. It was a slow, lumbering sensation, like something waking up stiffly from a long sleep. It felt good, welcome even, but at the same time worrisome. He didn't want to feel anything; he liked the numbness he'd been living in.

"We better get back," Peter said and took her arm again. "Mom will think we got lost."

"Did your mother worry about you when you were a kid?" she asked.

"Nah. Not in a place like this."

"Yeah," she agreed. "This isn't like Chicago."

"I walked all over this town when I was a little kid. To school, to the library, to the store, everywhere. And I didn't have a baby-sitter, a nanny, or some other adult constantly dogging my steps."

"Sounds good."

"It was great. Oh, I know now that a whole bunch of adults were keeping an eye on me. But as far as I was concerned, I was a big shot, off on my own, exploring the big world around me."

He paused. "And that's how I want my son to grow up," Peter said. "Free, with a strong sense of self and independence. He couldn't do that in Chicago or its suburbs. I'd have to hire some adult to act like a bodyguard for him."

"I'm sure he likes it here," Merry said.

"I miss him," Peter said. "But I have to think of what's best for him."

They walked the last block in silence, Merry's body brushing up against his own. That sensation came back, stronger this time and less alien seeming. Being attracted to Merry wouldn't hurt him. She was one he could be attracted to and stay safe. He was definitely going to ask her out once they returned to Chicago.

The front-porch light was on when they got back to the house. Peter paused at the bottom of the steps and turned to face Merry. "I really appreciate you helping me out," he said. "Especially on such a short notice."

"Hey," Merry replied. "I've never been to the Egg Basket to the Midwest before. I couldn't let the opportunity pass."

Peter laughed and put his hands on her shoulders. "Seriously. Thank you." He held her for a long moment. She felt warm and soft beneath his touch and hungers grew suddenly within him. "Maybe we can do something together once we get back to Chicago."

"Maybe," she replied.

Her lips drew him closer and closer, mesmerizing him until he had no will of his own. He leaned forward and kissed her lightly. Her lips were softer than he expected and radiated passion that filled him to overflowing. A lightness seized his heart; a smile wanted to take over his lips. He let her go with a strange reluctance in his heart and led her up the stairs.

The blind, old cat gave a low, growling meow, and Merry put him in front of his water dish. "There you go, old feller. Have yourself a tall one before we get in bed." She leaned against the doorway to the bathroom and listened to the *lap-lap* of the cat's tiny tongue.

"He never told me he had a kid."

The old cat continued drinking.

"Not that it mattered," Merry said. "Sean seems really nice. I just wasn't expecting it." She shrugged. "I don't like being around kids."

The cat quit drinking and turned away from the water dish. Merry picked up Zachary and carried him to the bed. She placed him near the foot where he'd been sleeping when she'd come into the room.

"Oh, who am I fooling?" she said. "I'd like being around one certain kid very much, and since I can't, it hurts too much to be around any."

The cat grunted and settled down into the covers. Merry lay back next to him, staring up at the ceiling. There was a pattern in the plaster, almost like waves, one following the other, endlessly on toward the wall. She rolled over onto her side.

"Promise not to tell if I show you my secret?" She reached for her purse and took the tattered newspaper picture of the Calhoun County spelling-bee finalists from her wallet, spreading it out on the bed. "There he is, the fourth kid from the right in the back row. My son."

She squinted at the photo as she had a million times since the newspaper had come in the mail, but she couldn't really get an idea of what Jason looked like. She couldn't get even the slightest hint of what kind of a person he was. Was he wearing a sports team T-shirt? Was he a shirt-and-tie guy? Did he wear braces?

"What do you think?" she asked Zachary. "Does he look like a neat kid? He must be smart, right? I mean, he made it to the spelling-bee finals, which is something I couldn't have done in a million years."

She gently rubbed the top of the cat's head as she continued to stare at the photo. "One of these days I'm going to meet him, though," she said. "When I've got my degree and I'm a famous actress, I'm going to march right down there to Calhoun County and introduce myself. He's going to be so excited, so proud that his mother's really somebody special, that he's going to take me around to meet all his friends."

The cat just yawned.

"Okay, okay. I get the hint. That point's years away and you're tired." She folded the picture back up and put it into her wallet. "You know, I was just thinking. Maybe I should practice being around kids when I'm with Sean. Instead of thinking that I'm not with Jason, I could pretend that I was. Think it would work?"

Zachary just grumbled slightly and curled up, his tail flicking over his face.

Merry reached for the light, but before she could turn the switch, there was a light rap on the door. "Yes?"

The door opened slightly and Peter's mother looked in. "I'm sorry to bother you, but Zachary usually needs a little help to get settled for the night."

Merry searched Mrs. MacAllister's eyes as fear clutched at her stomach. Had she heard any of Merry's conversation with the old cat? Merry relaxed when she saw that the woman's smile seemed open. She thought she was safe and turned to the cat.

"He had himself a long drink of water just a few minutes ago."

"Oh." Mrs. MacAllister stepped into the room. "That's very kind of you to take care of him. Are you sure he won't be a bother?"

"No," Merry replied, shaking her head. "I just hope he won't be bothered by my big feet and all the space they'll take up."

"He'll enjoy something warm to lean against."

Merry smiled and scratched the cat on the top of his head. He grunted quietly. Mrs. MacAllister seemed ready to leave but didn't. She probably had something to say. Merry's stomach twisted slightly.

"I'm glad you could find time to visit us," Mrs. MacAllister said.

"It's kind of you to have me. Like I said, I enjoy a little vacation away from the big city."

There was another long pause as Peter's mother gathered up her robe around her neck. "Peter doesn't exactly share things of a personal nature with others."

Merry blinked, wondering what was coming.

"So I've had to learn to read him," Mrs. MacAllister said. "You know, check the nonverbal signals he gives off."

Merry nodded as the woman looked down and studied the floor for a long moment. "You're the first woman he's brought home since Kelly," she said, looking up at Merry.

"Oh?"

"I'm very glad my son has found you. I can tell you're going to make him and Sean very happy."

She was gone before Merry could say a word.

Chapter Three

Peter checked the back door and made sure it was locked. Growing up here, no one had to lock their doors, day or night. He doubted that crime had become a real problem in Mentone in the last few years, but he wasn't all that trusting anymore.

After turning off the kitchen light, he paused in the hall and gazed into the dining room. He'd always think of it as their holiday room. The big country kitchen had more than enough room for the three of them to eat regular meals when he was a boy, but the dining room was for holidays.

There'd been times when they'd had as many as fifty people over for a holiday meal. Peter had loved those times, sitting back, quiet as a mouse, and listening to the stories the adults told about the youthful escapades of the elders.

As a boy, Peter had been pleased to find out that his father didn't spring to life as Dr. Charles MacAllister. That stern, disciplined, hardworking town doctor had had another life as Chuckie MacAllister.

Chuckie MacAllister had been smack dab in the middle of Pete and Bertha MacAllister's brood of five children. He'd been an ordinary kid, who was kept after school often, got into mischief and spent a lot of time trying to ditch Sunday school. His academics improved once he reached high school but, according to the stories, his mischievous ways stayed with him well into adulthood.

Peter had always been in awe of his father. As a young child, he'd always gone to his mother with his problems, but when he reached puberty, there were things that he thought a boy just couldn't discuss with his mother.

It was then that the memories of dining room stories of a boy named Chuckie turned the stern man into a regular guy. One who'd torn his brand-new Sunday pants on Mr. Yoder's fence as he tried to escape with a "borrowed" watermelon. A boy who'd been caught kissing his girlfriend behind her garage and had to run for his life as her mother chased him with a broom. The type of person who would understand a teenage boy's fears and concerns.

The stories had not lied. Peter had spent many a late night talking things over with his dad, finding wisdom and guidance as well as friendship.

A twinge of pain pulled at Peter's heart as he wondered what Sean thought of him. Did he even think of him at all? Peter's father had worked a lot, but he'd still been a part of Peter's daily life. He didn't live and work in a distant city, keeping in touch by telephone and periodic visits.

Clenching his teeth, Peter punched the light switch. This was the best place in the world for Sean Charles MacAllister to grow into a man. And it wasn't as if Peter didn't spend any time with his son. And he planned to spend a lot more with him as the boy grew older.

Peter went quietly up the stairs, stepping carefully, trying to find the quiet spot on one tread before he advanced to the next. The house was as still as an empty church until he reached the top of the stairs, where he was greeted by a rather substantial woof.

"Quiet, Belle," he whispered.

The old dog woofed again, although a bit quieter.

"Damn it," he whispered. "It's me."

She growled.

That wasn't the reaction he wanted. Peter glared at her a moment. "Go to bed," he whispered hoarsely. "Go on. Go to Sean."

Belle glared back at him.

"Get moving," he said, waving his hand toward his son's room. "Go on now. Get in there."

Grumbling, the dog slowly made her way down the hall. Peter waited until she had slipped in through the partially open door. Then, shaking his head slightly, he made his way carefully toward his room.

"Ssst."

Peter paused, his hand on the doorknob, and looked toward the sound. Merry was peeking around the edge of her door, beckoning to him. He looked quizzically at her as he slowly approached her door.

"What's wrong?" he whispered, stopping a couple lengths outside Merry's door.

She beckoned again, more vigorously this time.

As he took a step, Merry opened her door wider. She was wearing a short robe that barely threw a shadow over her knees. The sight of her two very shapely legs caused him to pause and smile.

Suddenly his mouth opened wide as he gasped in pain. Merry had stepped out into the hall, grabbed him by the shirt front, along with a few chest hairs, and yanked him into her bedroom. In simultaneous motions, she shut the door while slamming Peter up against the wall.

"What did you tell your mother?" she demanded.

Peter stared at Merry, the bewilderment in his mind feuding with the excitement growing in his body. What in the world was she talking about? He had never seen Merry in anything except street clothes or her waitress uniform, and there was a certain feminine muscularity to her frame that, along with her boldness, he found very arousing.

"I asked you a question," she pointed out.

"Ouch," Peter yelped. She was pulling his chest hairs again. "About what?"

"About us."

"Us?"

"Your mother was in here just a minute ago," Merry said. "She left me with the distinct impression that she thought we were on the verge of getting engaged."

"Engaged?" Peter tried to move Merry's hand. He needed space to think, but she held on tight.

"Yes," Merry hissed through her teeth. "You know, as in engaged to be married."

"Oh."

"Yeah, oh," she snapped. "That's an interesting place for us to be, considering that we barely know each other. I'd be hard put to call us acquaintances."

"Could you let go of me?"

Merry blinked once, then looked down at her hand. "I guess," she replied.

"I'd really appreciate it."

"Shucks," she said with a grin. "I was just starting to enjoy myself."

Peter swallowed hard to still the excitement that wanted to dance in his loins. So was he, but he pushed that thought away. "What did my mother say?"

"I don't remember exactly," Merry said. "But she did say that I was the first woman you'd brought here since Kelly."

He stepped away and rubbed his hand down over his face. His physical excitement had almost completely died. "Well, you are."

"And that I was going to make you and Sean very happy."

Peter had to fight to keep his eyes from dancing along the sweet curve of her legs. "She's got a lot of things mixed up," Peter said. "I'll talk to her tomorrow."

"I think it would be best if you did."

Peter nodded. "Good night," he murmured before he opened the door.

"Good night," she whispered.

He shut Merry's door quietly behind him and was about to walk to his own room when he heard another door, further down the hall, shut quietly.

Oh, great. His mother was awake, no doubt jumping to her own conclusions. He briefly considered talking to her then, but decided against it. Eleven at night was not a good time to get into a discussion with Mom. The morning would be better. Probably not much better, but every little bit would help.

He hurried into his room and softly closed his own door behind him. He'd been bothered by dreams for the past few months now. But he had a feeling that tonight's dream would be different. It would star a barefoot, red-haired beauty.

Merry bounced down the stairs and followed the trail of delicious smells pulling her toward the back of the house Thanksgiving morning. The turkey was already in the oven.

"Good morning, Mrs. MacAllister," she said as she stopped at the kitchen door. Pie tins were scattered about the countertop, and Peter's mother was rolling out a circle of dough. It sure enough looked like the woman was going to bake a mess of pies.

"Good morning, Merry," Mrs. MacAllister said. "How did you sleep?"

"Just fine."

It didn't look as if Peter or Sean were anywhere about. Merry wondered if Peter had had that little chat with his mother yet.

"You don't have to call me Mrs. MacAllister, dear."

The tone of voice indicated that Peter hadn't. At least not about the true nature of their relationship, or even the semitrue nature.

"I just wouldn't feel right about calling you by your first name, ma'am."

The smile stayed in place, but Merry couldn't really read the gleam in the old woman's eyes. "I see," Mrs. MacAllister finally said after a long moment. Then she turned her attention back to rolling the dough.

"Can I help you?" Merry asked.

"Only after you've had breakfast. The boys had blueberry waffles this morning and there's some batter and berries left."

Merry moved quickly to the waffle iron. "Where are Peter and Sean?"

"Peter took Sean to the playground."

Merry nodded as she turned the hot plate on.

"It's good for them to do things together." Mrs. MacAllister slapped the dough for emphasis. "They should do more of it."

"It's hard with Sean living here and Peter working in Chicago."

His mother snorted. "It doesn't have to be that way. Sean could live with him in Chicago."

"Peter knows that." Merry opened the hot plate and poured the batter over it. "But he'd like his son to grow up in a small town, just like he did."

"Then Pete can stay here," his mother said. "I heard him talking to his cousin Gene once. Peter said that with what he does and with computers being what they are, he could live most anyplace in the world, and it would be just as if he were in his office in downtown Chicago. So he could spend a lot more time in Mentone."

Merry nodded as she watched the signal light on the waffle iron. Her granny said that the truth always stayed out of family arguments, so Merry preferred not to take sides. Her waffle was cooked and a great deal of it eaten in the silence that followed. Mrs. MacAllister left her pie crust and went to pour a cup of coffee for each of them.

"What he really needs," Mrs. MacAllister said, as she brought the cups over and sat down, "is a wife."

Swallowing the last piece of waffle, Merry grabbed the coffee cup. It was a good-size cup—big enough to hold a lot of coffee and big enough to hide behind.

"Folks say a maid is cheaper, even at today's prices."

Oh, boy. The pinched look Mrs. MacAllister gave her had the friendly all squeezed out of it. If Merry concentrated real hard, she might be able to drink her coffee around the foot in her mouth.

"Kelly's been dead and buried more than a year now. It's time for Peter to be getting on with his life."

Merry forced a smile. Maybe she should suggest getting on with the pies.

"I'm a widow myself," Mrs. MacAllister said. "I know all that a body has to go through. Saying goodbye takes time, usually about a year." The woman gulped at her own coffee. "You have to shed your tears and bid your farewells a step at a time. There's so many anniversaries to go through."

A silence descended on the kitchen as his mother took time to stare at the gray scene outside the kitchen windows. "It isn't just the major ones like birthdays. There's things like your first snowfall together, the first time you got caught in the rain, the first time you both woke up at four and watched the new day creep up over the horizon. In a lot of ways, it's worse if you had a good marriage.

Then you usually had something special every day of the year."

Her eyes turned inward, but they didn't seem to be seeing anything. Merry wondered if Mrs. MacAllister had finished saying goodbye to Peter's father. If she was still doing it after fifteen years, why should Peter be done after only one?

"Some folks need more time than others," Merry said softly.

Mrs. MacAllister snorted and shook her head. "Men do. They're such fragile, romantic creatures. You sometimes wonder if they live in the real world."

Merry went back to her coffee.

The older woman just sighed. "But it's hard to say goodbye when you're carrying a heart full of hurt," she said. "Things weren't going well for Peter and Kelly before she died. Neither of them said anything about it, but I knew."

Merry looked around the kitchen. She had a strong feeling that it was time to get to those pies. There were already more secrets spilled than she had a need to know.

"Kelly had a really difficult time when Sean was born and couldn't have more children," Mrs. MacAllister went on. "It didn't bother Peter too much, he was just glad that Kelly and Sean were all right. Kelly was really devastated, though. She didn't want Sean to grow up an only child, but wouldn't consider adoption."

"I'm not sure you ought to be telling me all this," Merry said, trying to get her to change the subject.

"Peter needs somebody who understands," the other woman said. "You need to know who he is."

"I'm sure he'll tell me when he feels I should know."

"Kelly seemed to grow more frantic the older Sean got, though she learned to hide it from Peter," Mrs. MacAllister went on as if Merry hadn't spoken. "She just kept searching for something to fill the void she felt was in her life. Finally she decided a big house in the country was what they needed. Peter had no real interest in moving. All he knew was that with the commute, he'd have even less time with her and Sean."

Merry clutched her cup. She didn't need to know all this, didn't *want* to know all this. But how could she tell Mrs. MacAllister that without explaining that her and Peter's relationship was just a farce? The woman hurt so much for her son. It wasn't fair to let her think Peter was farther along the road of healing than he really was. But telling her the truth would subject Peter to his mother's matchmaking, and he didn't need that in his fragile emotional state right now.

"The morning Kelly died, they had a terrible fight," Mrs. MacAllister said. "They were all supposed to go look at houses, but it was a miserable rainy day and Peter thought they should postpone it. She didn't want to, but he went to work, thinking she had agreed. Except once he'd gone, she left Sean with a sitter and went alone. Peter blamed himself for the accident. I think he still does."

"If they had all gone, they all might have died."

"If he'd been driving, they might not have had the accident."

There were no answers; they both knew that and sat in shared silence as the pain of love weighed down around them.

"Poor Peter," Merry said finally as she stared into the remains of her coffee. "Guilt always makes for a heavy load."

Mrs. MacAllister nodded with a grim smile and pushed herself upright. "We'd better be getting to those pies before we need that oven for the sweet potatoes. You're just too nice, letting an old woman rattle on so. Next time you just reach over and give me a shake. You don't, and I'll just talk your ear off."

* * *

"Catch me, Daddy!" Sean squealed as he slid down the slide into Peter's arms.

Peter barely had time to hold him before the boy had freed himself and was running back around to climb the ladder again. The playground seemed to have shrunk since Peter had played there as a child. The slide that had seemed so sleek and so high looked scratched and tame now.

"Here I come, Daddy!" Sean shouted and flew down the slide again. He hit the bottom about the same time as the first few drops of rain spattered about on the gravel around them.

"Uh-oh," Peter said as he steadied the boy. "Looks like we're going to have to hit the trail. It's starting to rain."

"Do we have to?" Sean's cry was a pleading whine, but he slipped his hand into Peter's and walked along with him away from the playground equipment.

Sean's hand felt so small and defenseless as Peter held it. He tightened his hold automatically. Was he really doing what was best for the boy, letting him grow up here? Peter'd lost Kelly and given up Sean. Was his self-imposed isolation making life better or worse for the boy?

"I wish you lived here," Sean said suddenly.

"Me, too."

"Grandma says I'm too little to go on that slide," he volunteered.

Peter smiled at him. "Don't go on it by yourself."

"I don't." Sean kicked at the stones, shuffling his feet as they walked. "Is Merry going to be my new mommy?"

Peter's feet stopped moving, surprise stunning him. "Your new mother?" he repeated, then shook his head. "No. Where did you get that idea?"

Sean just shrugged. "Grandma said I might get a new mommy someday."

The raindrops were coming down a little faster, and Peter started walking again. Good, old Mom. "No, Merry's just a friend of mine," he said. The image of her in her robe last night flashed into his heart, making it race, but he kept his voice steady. "She didn't have anyplace to go for Thanksgiving, so I invited her here."

"Oh."

"That okay with you?"

"Sure."

They reached the house a few minutes later and hurried up the stairs. The warm aromas of apple pie and turkey welcomed them.

"'Bout time you two got back." Peter's mother came to the kitchen door to greet them.

Merry was just behind her, the young woman's cheek decorated with a smear of flour that Peter suddenly had a desperate urge to wipe off. He squatted down, concentrating on taking Sean's jacket off.

"Did you need our help?" Peter asked.

"The boards need putting in the big table, and the card tables need to be set up in the living room."

"Think we can handle that, champ?" he asked Sean.

"If you carry the stuff."

Peter mussed Sean's hair as he stood up to find Merry smiling at him. He remembered the taste of her lips, could feel their softness beneath his once more.

"You guys get wet?" she asked.

"Nah," Sean said, scrambling for the basement door. "Come on, Daddy. The stuff's down here."

Peter just smiled at Merry. "I gotta get the stuff," he said.

And he had to talk to his mother, he reminded himself. Get her straight on the relationship. Then Merry wouldn't have to smile at him that way, wouldn't have to pretend that they had some torrid affair going. The cool air of the basement only partially cooled his thoughts.

Between setting up the tables, finding chairs and starting a fire in the fireplace, there wasn't a moment to spare for his talk. If he had a minute to breathe, his mother was rushing around. When she had a free moment, she took Sean off to get dressed, then changed clothes herself. By that time, family had started arriving and there was no chance to really talk to anybody.

What was he actually supposed to say to her anyway? Peter asked himself as they sat down to Thanksgiving dinner. *We're just friends, Mom.* He'd already said that on the phone, but he supposed he could repeat it.

Peter looked across the table at Merry, who was seated next to his mother. Working in the kitchen had brought a flush to Merry's cheeks and a sparkle to her eye that hinted at a fire smoldering deep inside. Would his mother believe that any man could just be friends with someone as beautiful as Merry?

"And, man, he came down like a rock." Cheryl slapped her hands together, one on top of the other. "*Splat!* Actually, it was more like a wet dishrag. A wet dishrag that was as heavy as a rock."

Peter awoke from his thoughts to find his cousin Cheryl telling the story of a ten-year-old Peter who, using a blanket for his Superman cape, had jumped off the highest point of the garage. The whole room joined in laughter, especially Sean.

"I tell you," Cheryl went on, "Aunt Claire about killed us all."

Tears were flowing down Peter's mother's cheeks as she laughed. Merry, sitting next to her, seemed even more alive as her laughter wrapped around them all. He felt drawn to her smile, to the warmth in her eyes.

"She kept saying, 'You're older, you should know better,'" Cheryl went on.

Merry briefly glanced Peter's way, then bent down to murmur to his mother, who just shook her head and kept on laughing. Peter felt a strange sensation of being left out.

He wanted those lips to laugh for him, to whisper words for him to hear.

"And all I could say was, 'But Auntie Claire, how was I to know your boy was so stupid?'" Cheryl concluded her story to a roar of laughter, which subsided into a gentle hum of chuckles as people returned to their meal.

Merry turned to his mother, and the two of them chatted as they ate. He was too far away to hear the words, but he could see the genuine friendship building between them. He felt a shadow fall across his heart. He didn't like deceiving his mother this way. Maybe when they had their little talk, he should tell her the truth.

"I'm so glad to see you're dating again," Aunt Martha said, leaning across Uncle Paul to tell Peter. "It's about time."

"Told you the boy'd start when he was ready to," Paul grumbled.

Peter went back to his turkey. He guessed his mother wasn't the only one watching him and his social life.

"And she's such a nice girl," Martha went on. "Where did you meet her?"

"Where do you think you meet such a pretty girl?" Paul said. "In your dreams. You ask the boy too many questions."

Suddenly everyone's happiness for Peter seemed too much. "Looks like we're low on potatoes." He grabbed the bowl and hurried into the kitchen.

The silence was welcome and wonderful. He put the bowl down on the counter and walked to the back window. The yard looked dreary in the steady drizzle. Fallen leaves that had escaped the rake were a weary brown, the grass was lifeless. The garden held only occasional brown stalks.

Peter felt a nudge at his leg and looked down to see Belle. He patted the old dog on the head. Her eyes were tired, but filled with love.

"I know, old girl," he said softly. "Spring'll come again and everything will be filled with life once more."

But would it? Spring wouldn't bring youth to the dog's old body or sunshine to his own heart.

"My goodness, there you are."

He looked up to see his mother had come into the room. She took the bowl and began to put in more potatoes. "Thought you got lost."

"No, just visiting with Belle." He rose to his feet and took the now empty potato pot from her. Putting it into the sink, he let it fill with water. "Sure is dreary outside."

"Good reason not to look there then," his mother said.

As if it were that easy.

"You know, Peter—" she slipped her arm into his and leaned against his body "—I really like your Merry."

"She's not my Merry," he said. "We're just friends."

His mother patted his hand as she pulled away, much the same as he had patted Belle. "I've seen the way you look at her," she said with a laugh. "You can't fool me."

"Look, Mom, I'm not ready for a relationship. Merry and I are just friends." He remembered back to his walk with Sean. "She didn't have anyplace to spend Thanksgiving, so I invited her along."

"Sure."

"I mean it."

She shook her head as she picked up the potato bowl. "For a very smart man, you are very slow," she said.

"What's that supposed to mean?"

"Your eyes and your heart tell you when you're ready to risk love again, not your head. Listen to your head, and you'll always be alone." She backed into the swinging door, pushing it open and stepping through. Belle hurried after her.

Peter stayed in the kitchen a moment, watching the door swing shut and the stillness return. No, not quite. He could hear chatter from the other side and laughter. Merry's laughter.

Suddenly he felt very left out.

"You just tell me where things go, and I'll put them away."

"No, no." Mrs. MacAllister grabbed Merry's arm and led her toward the living room. "You just sit down and relax. Peter will be down in a minute."

Merry looked for a long moment into the eyes shining up at her. She wondered what Peter had told his mother about them. Judging from the twinkle in the old woman's eyes, Merry would guess nothing. Looked like she was going to have to talk to that man again. And this time she would pull more than a few chest hairs.

"I don't mind helping," Merry insisted.

"You've done more than three people put together," Mrs. MacAllister said.

"Well, I ate enough for five people."

"Nonsense," the old woman replied as she pulled at Merry again. "Just sit down and relax. I'll put the dishes away in the morning. Does them good to air dry overnight."

There was no doubt in Merry's mind that Mrs. MacAllister had been a strong woman in her younger days. The spirit was still there, but physically the old woman was growing frail. It wouldn't take anything to set her down on her butt, march into the kitchen and put the dishes away. But it wasn't what the woman wanted, and it was her house. Merry smiled and let herself be set down in a large, comfortable old sofa.

"Peter's reading a story to Sean. He'll be down momentarily. It's just a short story."

The words had no sooner escaped Mrs. MacAllister's lips when there was a soft creak on the stairs, followed by Peter himself stepping into the living room. He smiled and nodded at them both.

"Your turn, Mom."

He was a nice-looking guy. Tall, with a soft smile and lively eyes. He'd replaced his shirt with a sweatshirt and now had moccasins on his feet instead of dress shoes.

"What story did you read?" his mother asked.

His brow wrinkled. "Something really depressing about a baby elephant. Sean loved it."

Peter seemed nicer and more relaxed here than he'd been back in Chicago. Must be the atmosphere. He was home among family and friends. No back-stabbing competitors here. He didn't have to wear his armor.

His mother nodded. "Babar. I'll read him something else." Mrs. MacAllister walked toward the door and was about to step out of the room, when she stopped. A soft grin covered her face. "I've had a hard day. I'm going to bed myself right after I read Sean his story. You children behave yourselves."

Merry sighed as Mrs. MacAllister disappeared into the foyer. There had definitely been no talk. The slow advance of creaks indicated Mrs. MacAllister was going upstairs.

"Have a nice chat with your mother?" Merry asked.

Peter sat down next to her, a look of surprise on his face. "I tried, I really did, but she just wouldn't listen."

Merry glared at him, but it did no good. Peter just went right on looking alone and vulnerable. Merry hated that combination. It was guaranteed to do her in if she let it.

He leaned against the sofa back, closing his eyes with a sigh. He seemed tired, and she fought the urge to rub his shoulders. This whole situation couldn't be easy on him. These were people he cared about, people it probably hurt to fool.

He opened his eyes to look at her. "Care for a nightcap? Mom has some very good sherry."

His gaze was soft, vulnerable. She could see a lost little boy in those eyes, someone needing help, needing a hand to hold.

"No, thank you," she replied, picking up a magazine and flipping through it. Too many things were getting to her. This old house. Peter's family. Not to mention Peter himself. It was all too much. The last thing she needed was a nip of sherry.

Guys like Peter, with money, background and education, had always been the downfall of girls like her. Joe O'Connell had made her feel special, too, being her boss and all at the hardware store, and look how long that lasted. Just until she got pregnant; then she found out what he really thought of her.

She suddenly sprang to her feet. "It's been a long day all around," she said. "I'm going upstairs."

"You can relax here," Peter said, patting the sofa by his side.

"What I really want to do is get these shoes off," Merry said. "My toes want to be free and my feet want to breathe."

"Take off anything you like," Peter replied. "Whatever makes you comfortable."

A sweet, boyish smile came to his face. He looked so soft, his stiffness seemed to have melted away. Her heart twisted. It had been so long since someone had held her, since someone had made her feel special. And it would have to be even longer, since she wasn't giving in and jeopardizing her goals this time.

With a sigh, she bent down and kissed him lightly on the lips. A tiny flame inside her begged to be allowed to come to life, but she refused. "Good night, Peter."

He took her hand before she could escape. "The night's still young."

"But I'm not," she replied as she fled up the stairs.

Chapter Four

Peter sipped his coffee as he glared out at the gloomy overcast pressing down on the backyard. Winter had followed them in from Chicago, and only the warmth of the lake had turned the flurries into a cold, drizzly kind of a rain.

Now what were he and Sean going to do? They certainly couldn't play outside, and he didn't really like the kind of board games a five-year-old kid could play. While he was pondering their day, Sean was slurping the last drop of chocolate milk from his glass.

"Good morning, all."

Peter's gloom suddenly dissipated. "Good morning."

"Good morning, dear," his mother said.

Sean continued sucking on his straw.

"Sean," Peter's mother said gently.

"Hi," Sean said.

"Would you like to borrow some slippers, dear?"

His mother's question caused Peter to look at Merry's feet, clad in thick white socks.

"No, ma'am," Merry replied. "These socks are just fine. Besides I doubt you've got slippers that would fit me."

"Land sakes, child. Your feet aren't that big."

Merry just shook her head, a soft smile looking into the past. "My granny always said that I was supposed to be twins, but by the time the Lord finished making my feet, there wasn't enough material left over for another body."

Peter's mother laughed. "You're stuffed fuller than a Christmas turkey."

"You're truly right."

She had a lovely accent, Peter thought, soft with fingers that soothed the frazzled endings of his nerves. He could listen to her voice for hours.

"What's her name?"

All eyes turned toward Sean. Outside of the forced greetings Wednesday night and this morning, this was the first time he'd spoken directly to Merry.

"Your twin sister," Sean said. "What's her name?"

"Oh," Merry replied. "You mean the one that wasn't born?"

Sean nodded.

Merry paused for just the slightest moment, enough time for a shadow to fall across her sparkling eyes. Peter felt his breathing grow a bit strained.

"Louise."

"Do you talk to her?" Sean asked.

"Sometimes."

Peter was uncomfortable, although he couldn't say why.

"Especially when I have something secret to talk about," Merry said. "Then I always tell Louise first, because I know she won't tell anybody else."

Sean slowly nodded his head in solemn agreement, pumping tension into the silence that hung over them.

"I have a twin brother," he said.

Peter felt his stomach tighten as the memories of Kelly' longing for another child swept over him. *Sean can't grow up an only child. He's alone too much. He needs a brother or sister.* Had Sean heard Kelly's worries and taken them as his own?

"His name's Barney," Sean said. "And no one else can see him or talk to him but me."

Everyone stared at Sean. From the corner of his eye Peter saw Merry's lips smile, a smile tinged by the gray of the overcast day outside. He'd been hoping that Sean and Merry would warm up to each other, but he hadn't wanted this unique affinity for the melancholy.

"Well, what should we do today, sport?" Peter put an extra measure of hearty into his voice.

Sean shrugged.

"It looks pretty yucky out there," Peter said. "I don't really want to play outside, do you?"

Sean shrugged.

"Want to play a game?"

He shrugged again.

"Want me to run out and get a movie?"

He shrugged still again, and Peter felt his nerves approaching the edge. Damn it, why did the kid have to be so difficult?

"Why don't you all go out to the Bell Museum?" his mother suggested. "He just loves that place. Don't you, Sean?"

Sean nodded. It was a slow, reluctant response, but at least it wasn't a shrug.

"Great, great!" Peter exclaimed. "We'll have ourselves a look-see. Then we can skip out to Warsaw and grab a burger and fries. How about it, big guy?"

His son had returned to shrugging, sending Peter back to gritting his teeth.

"Would you like to come along?" Sean asked Merry.

"Why, sure."

"We gotta wear shoes," Sean said, raising one stock-inged foot up to the table.

Merry made a face. "Oh, well. If we gotta, we gotta."

"Is Louise coming?" Sean asked.

That discomfort washed over Peter again and he searched for a way to change the subject.

"She sure is," Merry replied. "She goes everyplace with me."

Sean nodded, his face so solemn that it almost hurt Peter to look at him. "Barney's coming, too."

"Good," Merry said. "I'll go with you and Louise will go with Barney. It'll be a double date."

"I never been on a date before."

"That's okay. I've been on a lot of them. You just watch what I do. Hey, what's this?" Merry stopped and reached over by Sean's ear. "It's a quarter!"

Sean, mouth open in astonishment, took it from her. "Wow!" he breathed and slipped his other hand into hers as he continued to stare at the quarter. "How'd you do that?"

Peter watched them until they were out in the hall, and then the creaking sounds told him they were upstairs. It was amazing how completely Merry had turned things around. One day she looked to be scared to death of the kid, and the next they're old pals going on a date.

"Where'd she ever learn magic tricks?" his mother asked.

"At some café she used to work at." He was unable to get Sean's words out of his mind. "How long has Sean had this imaginary pal?"

"All children have imaginary friends," she assured him, getting up to rinse out her coffee cup. "Especially only children."

He stared at her.

"For heaven's sake, don't look so solemn. You had a number of them yourself."

He let his eyes drift toward the window. The mood of the weather was unchanged. Gloomy and wet. "Sean has quite an imagination," Peter said.

"He's a normal, intelligent little boy. You'd have cause to worry if he didn't have one."

But a longing for someone who didn't exist? Or was the real longing for someone who had existed but was gone? Maybe a five-year-old couldn't express his grief and acted it out in other ways.

Sean's laughter came into the room just ahead of him as he raced away from Merry. His face was more alight and childlike than Peter had seen for ages.

"Help! Help!" Sean darted behind Peter.

"He's not gonna be able to save you." Merry laughed as she grabbed at the squealing boy.

Peter wanted to be part of their laughter. He wanted to feel that glow of pure happiness on his face, too. "Hey," he cried. "Grandma doesn't like people fooling around in her kitchen."

They paused in their roughhousing and stared at him. Sean's look was filled with disgust.

"Well, I got her to stop," Peter told his son. "I saved you. Just like you asked."

Sean was not impressed by his father's creativity and didn't let him into his sunshine. "Let's go get our coats," Sean told Merry, taking her by the hand.

Peter trailed along after them, feeling as awkward and gawky as a twelve-year-old.

That feeling went away somewhat as the weekend progressed. Merry was aptly named, as her cheerful, sunny attitude warmed all of them. Peter couldn't remember a time in the past year when laughter had rung out as much as it had in the past few days.

By the time Saturday evening came around, Peter was congratulating himself on his wisdom in bringing Merry home with him. She was even willing to go to his cousin's high school basketball game.

"This is a little beyond the call of duty," Peter said as he pulled into the Tippecanoe Valley High School parking lot. "I may have to give you a hardship bonus."

"I like high school basketball."

Peter found a spot and parked his car. "I'm not fooling. The noise in that gym is going to be deafening."

"No problem. My eardrums can use the exercise."

They got out of the car, and Peter hurried around to take Merry's hand. She was dressed in what she'd called her city slushing outfit—hiking boots, jeans and a down jacket. She fit in as if she'd been born and raised right here.

"A daughter of one of my dad's brother's kids—I guess that makes her a second cousin—plays for Valley and she's starting tonight. Mom said I had to go as a representative of our branch of the family."

"Good," Merry replied. "I wasn't in the mood for chamber music."

"I wouldn't have done anything that dull."

"I never said chamber music was dull. I just said I wasn't in the mood for it tonight."

Peter gave her a quick frowning look, but Merry's expression was as innocent as an angel's. He decided not to press his luck. Merry seemed to be able to more than hold her own in verbal sparring matches. Though they did hold a certain appeal, he chose to keep the conversation on the upcoming game.

"These events can get a little rowdy at times," he warned.

"That's okay," Merry said, patting his arm. "Don't you worry yourself none. I'm here to protect you."

"Thank you," Peter said. "I feel so safe now."

"You should."

Peter growled deep in his throat. It was obvious that this was a woman who always had the last word. He took her arm again and led her into the high school gym. She felt good at his side. He liked the feeling of being part of a pair again. It would definitely be a good idea to date her when he got back to Chicago. Then his attitude would stay on the corner of Bright Avenue and Chipper Street.

The old gym was filling rapidly, and the low murmur of the crowd was making the rafters hum. Once the game started, the roof would be set to flapping. Valley was playing Rochester. They were bitter rivals back when he went to school and it looked as if they would forever remain such.

Peter bent close to Merry's ear. "Where would you like to sit?"

"Right smack dab in the center of things."

"That's where a lot of the students and young folks sit," he warned her.

She gave him an ornery grin. "Don't you fret none. I told you I'd take care of you."

"Right," he said. "I keep forgetting you're my bodyguard."

Peter hesitated as he looked over the gym. *Ladies first* wasn't a good concept when it came to plowing through this crowd. Before he could take a first step, though, Merry was already well ahead of him. She gave him a wink over her shoulder and started up the bleachers.

She didn't exactly shove or push anybody, but the crowd parted before them like the Red Sea. He followed her, trying not to stare at the shapely legs just ahead of him, but it was impossible not to. She moved with such strength and grace. She could be a figure skater or ballerina. Or maybe a diver. Lord, but he'd love to see her in a swimsuit, getting ready to do a double flip.

"How is this?" Merry asked.

He cleared his throat and his thoughts. "Very good."

"I told you I'd take care of you," she replied.

"Yeah, I can see that now." They both sat down. "You take care of me like I was a rock star or something."

"No problem."

Pretending to look elsewhere, Peter watched Merry from the corner of his eye. Her eyes were sparkling and a broad smile lit her face as she watched the girls in their green-and-gold uniforms warming up on the court below.

A brief question bubbled in the back of his mind. Merry had said that she'd grown up in the suburbs, yet she didn't quite fit the image he had of middle-class suburban women. He turned his full attention back to the playing floor. She seemed more like...

Country. That was the only word that came to mind. The type of girl who could milk the cows, put a splint on a broken arm and drive the tractor as well as any man. Sighing, Peter forced himself to concentrate on the girls going through their pregame rituals.

"Hey, Pete." A heavy hand slapped him on the back. A tall man with black hair, brown eyes and a long jaw stood at Peter's side. "How the hell are you?"

Peter stood up and took the man's hand as he began scanning his memory bank, searching for a name. "Just fine. And yourself?"

"Not bad. Get three squares a day, the roof don't leak and my wife lets me sleep with her."

The man's name was on the tip of Peter's consciousness, but it wouldn't step out to the forefront. He wanted to take another few seconds and see what his memory came up with, but the man was standing there, grinning at Merry.

"This is a friend of mine," Peter said, taking Merry by her hand as she stood up.

The man's grin grew broader. "Yeah, I heard about that." He thrust his hand out toward her. "Hi, Merry. Welcome to Indiana. I'm Matt Browder."

Browder. Relief and irritation met head on. Peter remembered Matt now. The man had been a senior in high school when Peter had been a freshman.

The irritation came as he wondered how the hell Mat
knew Merry's name, but then they'd been here two day
now. A small town like Mentone didn't need much time
Most folks probably knew her shoe size and color of un
derwear by now. He had a uneasy flash of curiosity as t
just what color she did wear, but he pushed it aside.

"Matt was three years ahead of me," Peter said. "W
were on the baseball team together. I was his backup. W
both played second base."

"I got out while the gettin' was good," Matt said with
hearty laugh. "If I'd stayed around any longer, I woul
have been riding the bench backing this guy up. Old Pet
here was a helluva player."

"I get better as the years go by," Peter told Merry.

"Hey, he made all-state in his junior and senior years."

Peter shrugged. "That was all ages ago. So, what are yo
doing here? I didn't know you cared about basketball."

"Baseball is still my first love, but my oldest daughte
lives for basketball."

"So you brought her to the game?"

Matt laughed. "She's on the team." He pointed dow
toward the Lady Vikings. "She's the tall, thin blonde un
derneath the basket. Made varsity even though she's just
freshman."

"That's very good," Merry said, as Peter just stared a
Matt.

Matt noticed Peter's stunned silence and just laughe
more. "Time moves on, old buddy. We're all getting
older."

"You have a daughter in high school?"

"Ain't no mystery to that. All you gotta do is get mar
ried right after you finish college." Matt paused a momen
to broaden his already wide smile. "Janie is our first one
Got five more at home."

"Must keep you busy," Peter said.

"Keeps me out of bars and from chasing wild women," Matt said before he turned to Merry. "Where're you from? You're not from these parts, are you?"

"Atlanta," Merry replied.

"Oh, yeah?" Matt said. "My wife's got a cousin in Atlanta."

"I actually lived in the suburbs of Atlanta."

"So does her cousin. He lives in Stone Mountain."

Merry nodded. "I've heard of it." She turned to Peter. "You want any popcorn or a candy bar?"

"I don't," Peter replied. "Which do you want? I'll get it for you."

"Don't you fuss," she said with a laugh. "I need to go to the little girls' room anyway."

"You're going to leave me all alone?" Peter asked.

"I'll hurry back, sugar." She kissed him on the cheek. "Besides, Matt will look after you, won't you?"

"Sure thing, ma'am. And I'll see that no wild women come by and snatch him away."

Merry left them with a quick wave and a smile before being swallowed up in the crowd. Peter watched her cap of dark red hair bob and weave through the people in the stands. It was absurd, but he missed her. He felt alone and lost.

"That's a mighty fine young lady you got there, old buddy."

Peter had been savoring the warm spot on his cheek where Merry had kissed him. "Yeah," he said, finding it almost hard to speak. "She is nice."

A whistle sounded on the floor and the two teams collected their balls and gathered around their respective coaches.

"Folks are all glad to see that things are working out for you again. Man wasn't made to live alone, Pete. Especially when you have kids."

His old teammate's obvious joy and concern brought such pain to his heart that Peter had to look away.

"Well, I gotta run, old buddy." Matt reached out and seized Peter's hand, shaking it vigorously. "I'm sure you've got enough to do this weekend, but if you find yourself with some time and nothing to do, drop in on us. We're always home."

Peter nodded.

"Dad's retired and I run the old family place now. Grow corn and raise pigs. Regular pigs for hams, and then I raise some of them Vietnamese pot-bellied critters. Folks buy 'em for pets. Can you beat that?"

Peter shook his head.

"Well, don't be no stranger," Matt said. "And bring your boy with you when you come visit. He'll have a ball."

Then, with a last slap on the back, Matt was gone to join his family, leaving Peter alone to stare at everything and nothing before him. He sank down into his seat, letting the crowd and its noise fade away into the oblivion on the edge of his consciousness.

What a joke he was. What an absolute fraud. Merry was right. She was his bodyguard. He'd thought it was a joke, but now he knew how true it was. He, Peter Blair Mac-Allister had hired a pretty, bright-smiling, redheaded woman to protect him from the real world.

"Boy, are you looking solemn!" Merry laughed as she fell into her seat next to him. "Somebody steal your scooter?"

His world was suddenly light and happy. Her thigh pressed against his and it became more than happy; it held the promise of all sorts of joys. "And where was my bodyguard when it was happening?" he teased.

She leaned over to brush his lips with hers. "Poor baby. Want to share my popcorn?"

"Maybe."

She offered him the box, and he reached in for a handful. God, her eyes were so bright. It was as if she were so full of sunshine and cheer that it had to spill out her gaze and her grin. Could her life have held only good things? Whatever, he wanted to stay close to her, stay where that sunshine would spill out over him.

Merry snuggled up close all of a sudden, slipping her arm through his. "I hear we're playing our arch rival," she whispered, her words tickling his ear. "Does this mean we get to be rowdy?"

He looked at her. She was so close, so alluring, her lips were just too tempting. Heaven danced between them, pulling them together. He leaned in just a bit and found her lips meeting his.

She tasted slightly like popcorn and somehow it seemed right. She was Saturday night at the movies and curling up before a roaring fire. She was football games and parties. Warmth and joy and laughter all tumbled into his heart. He felt young and alive, ready to do battle, ready to slay dragons.

Cheering erupted around them, and the teams parted. The starting lineups were about to be introduced. A silly reason for their kiss to be interrupted. Maybe Merry felt the same, for she snuggled up close, taking his hand in hers. He was sorry all of a sudden that they were going back to Chicago tomorrow.

"Well, Zach, it's just about over," Merry told the old cat as she folded her robe and put it into her suitcase. "Peter's picking up his mother's prescription at the pharmacy, and once he gets back we're on our way. I'd say it went really well, wouldn't you?"

The old cat just sat up and stretched.

"I must be a reasonable actress. No one doubted a thing." Merry took a last look around the room, then closed her suitcase. "Best of all, I earned some pretty easy money toward next semester's tuition."

Zachary yawned.

Merry put her suitcase on the floor and bent over to brush the top of the cat's head with her lips. "Thanks for sharing your room, pal."

Zachary made no stirring farewell speeches. In fact, he just turned around and began to wash his face. Merry took her case downstairs where Mrs. MacAllister was cleaning up the lunch dishes.

"You sure you don't want me to help you clean up?" Merry asked her.

"Don't be silly. You're our guest."

"But—"

"No buts, young lady." The older woman turned from the sink and gave Merry a quick smile over her shoulder. "You aren't a hired girl, you know."

Merry felt as if she'd taken a punch to her stomach. All right, so that aspect of the weekend hadn't been easy. Once she'd gotten to know Mrs. MacAllister, it had been downright hard to deceive her, but it was Peter's business to tell his mother the truth, not hers.

Still, it would be good to get back to Chicago. Back to the big city and back to her own life.

"I just don't feel right doing nothing," Merry said.

Before Mrs. MacAllister could reply, Sean walked into the kitchen, swinging over to the counter to pick up an oatmeal-raisin cookie.

"Sean, would you please take Merry and keep her busy until she and your father are ready to leave?"

The boy looked at Merry solemnly as he completely chewed the cookie he had in his mouth. "Wanna go outside?"

"Sure," Merry replied. "I don't want to get any of us in trouble."

Sean blinked at her; then he reached for another handful of cookies. "Want some?" he asked, turning to look at her over his shoulder.

"No, thank you," Merry answered.

They moved toward the back door, Merry holding his cookies while Sean slipped into his jacket. After returning his goodies, Merry put on her own coat. They stepped out into the backyard and stood there until Sean finished the last of his snack.

"What do you wanna do now?" he asked, his eyes solemn as they stared at her.

"Why don't you show me around town?" Merry suggested.

Sean shrugged. "It's just a bunch of houses and stuff like that."

"Show me where your friends live."

He looked at her doubtfully, but then, shrugging again, he said, "Okay," and led her out to the street.

They walked quickly and purposefully down the narrow streets just north of Mentone's small business section. Sean pointed out where his best friend, Roger, lived, and his good friends, Ronny and Susie, as well as where Meg, Johnny and Rachel resided. Although the latter were not really good friends, he played with all of them. After the tour, they found themselves standing across the street from the egg.

"I got other friends," he said. "But we gotta have a car if you want to see their houses. Can you drive?"

"Yes, but I don't have a car."

"We can ask Grandma for hers," he replied.

"That's okay," Merry said. "Let's save something for next time."

"You coming back?"

His solemn child's eyes stared at her, and Merry found herself growing uncomfortable. All right, so this part of the weekend wasn't a snap, either. It wasn't as if she and Sean had become such great buddies that he was going to miss her.

Merry glanced across the street at the egg. "I think this is the only town in the world with a giant egg on Main Street."

"It ain't really an egg," Sean replied. "It's just a big rock that they painted."

The boy stood there and stared, almost glared, at the rock masquerading as an egg. He was such a solemn little guy.

"Well, I think it really is an egg," Merry said. "And I think one of these days the giant chicken that laid it will come back. And when it does, it's going to bring so much magic back to town that nobody'll ever be unhappy here."

Sean just stared at her, skepticism and hope warring on his earnest little face. He wanted to believe her, she could see that, but giant chickens probably seemed a bit much for even a five-year-old.

"Want to go back home?" Sean asked.

"Okay," she replied.

They walked quietly back to the big yellow house on First Street. Merry would have held the boy's hand, but there really wasn't a chance to. Not even at the crosswalks. There wasn't any traffic in this town.

Sean stopped at the driveway of his grandmother's house. "Wanna see the backyard?"

"Sure thing, sport," she said heartily.

Her voice sounded false even to herself, but Sean seemed not to notice. He led her up the driveway, past Peter's car and around to the back of the house. There was a broad expanse of backyard lined with evergreens and a big, old oak in the center.

"Daddy says when I get bigger, he's gonna build me a tree house in that tree there," he said, pointing at the oak.

"That'll be fun."

He shrugged.

"Hey, you can have your friends sleep over in it."

Sean blinked but, from the momentary brightness in his face, it was obvious that he hadn't thought of that.

"We got a lot of grass. And Grandma's got a whole bunch of flowers, but they're all dead now."

"Not all of them are dead," Merry said. "Some of them are just dormant. That means they're asleep until spring."

He made a face.

Merry looked around the yard. She wanted to find a perennial so she could scratch the bark and show Sean the living green skin underneath. Her eyes fell on a plant by the back door still clinging to its summer mantle of green.

"That one's still alive. And it isn't even dormant yet."

"That's a dumb plant," Sean replied.

"How do you know it's dumb? Did you give it a test?"

Sean ignored her attempt at humor. "Grandma said it sometimes blooms on Christmas."

Merry looked closer at the formation of the leaves. "Oh, it's a Christmas rose."

"I never seen it bloom."

His young eyes were hard, as they had been when they looked at the rock that adults called an egg.

"Maybe the winters have been too cold," Merry said. "Maybe the magic's not here yet."

"I bet it don't never bloom."

A wind whipped around the corner of the garage, and Sean's small shoulders shivered in their jacket. Merry felt a prickling at her eyes, but blinked it away. These weren't her kin; these weren't her problems. She had her own woes awaiting her, practically more than she could handle. She didn't need any more.

"We'd best get in the house," Merry said. "Your daddy will be wanting to leave soon."

Without a word, he turned and made his way up to the back porch, with Merry following. She forced herself to think of the homework waiting for her, of all the time lost to finish her research for her sociology paper.

"Did Sean show you my Christmas rose?" Mrs. Mac-Allister asked as they stepped into the kitchen.

Peter was sitting at the table with a cup of coffee. He put his arms around his son as the boy came near him. Sean didn't pull away, but he didn't fold into his father's grasp, either. It hurt to look at them, but Merry couldn't take her eyes away.

"I do believe that rose is going to bloom this year," Mrs. MacAllister said. "I just have this feeling."

Merry forced a smile. "I hope it does." Neither Sean nor Peter seemed even slightly moved by her cheerfulness. Each hurting, and each locked away in himself. Damnation, not one thing about this weekend had been easy.

"And I hope you'll be here to see it," Mrs. MacAllister said.

"I surely will, ma'am."

Judging from Peter's expression, he was shocked at the words that had come out of her mouth. Well, the hell with him. He'd paid her a lot of money and the job wasn't done yet.

Chapter Five

"You don't have to come back over Christmas," Peter said once they were on Route 30 heading west.

"It's okay."

"No, it's not okay." His voice sounded snappish even to him and he tried to force the annoyance away. It was just that a part of him wouldn't mind her coming back. Not at all. "I didn't expect Mom to put you on the spot like that."

"It's still three weeks away," she said as she stared out the window. "Why don't we wait and see?"

Wait for what? He thought of how his mother had warmed to her and how Sean's face had been so alive when Merry had been chasing him. How the kid had clung to her hand as they wandered through the tiny Bell Museum, telling her all about native Mentonian Lawrence Bell and the jet-propelled airplane he designed, the first plane to fly faster than the speed of sound. How even Zachary had gravitated to her warmth.

Hell, why not be honest? He had been no exception. Every touch, no matter how slight, had driven all rational thought from his mind. He felt as if he were waking up after a long sleep, feeling alive again. But those same feelings also brought along a measure of fear. And fear made him want to drive her away.

"I only agreed to pay you for Thanksgiving," he said suddenly.

She turned at that, her eyes burning. "That was a cruddy thing to say. I don't remember asking you for money. For all I care, you can keep what you already offered."

He bit at his lip, staring at the road ahead of him. The heavy gray sky was unforgiving. The wind whipping across the empty fields was brutal. The angry beast inside him deflated.

"I'm sorry," he said. There was so much more he ought to say, but no words would come out. He couldn't explain his fears, not even to himself.

She glanced his way. Though she said nothing, he sensed he'd been forgiven. He'd make it up to her, he promised himself. He'd show her that he wasn't the churl he acted.

They drove on in silence for some time, until they were nearing the Indiana-Illinois border. A restaurant sign popped over the far edge of the land, and Peter considered stopping. A cup of coffee and maybe a piece of pie would be nice. Give the two of them a chance to talk.

"Care to stop for a bite to eat or some coffee?" Peter asked.

"I'm not hungry," Merry replied. "But if you want to, that's fine with me."

"You're easy to get along with."

A soft smile lit on her lips, like a small bird on a tree branch. "Sometimes," she said softly. "I can guarantee, though, with hundred percent certainty, that that's not an absolutely permanent condition."

He laughed, chasing the last of his dark mood away. "All right," he said. "What're the Christmas holidays going to cost me?"

She looked at him for a long moment, and Peter began feeling uneasy. Maybe she hadn't forgiven him.

But the storm in her eyes seemed to pass just as quickly as it came on. She turned to look out the window. "I didn't hardly earn my fee," she said. "Figure you already paid for Christmas and New Year's."

"No, fair's fair. Name your price."

She stared at him as he drove, her eyes narrow and thoughtful. When she finally turned away, he felt relieved. "Tell your mother the truth," she said. "I'll come over Christmas if you tell her we're just friends."

"I did tell her that," he said. "She didn't believe me."

He wasn't going to repeat everything else his mother had said, her implications that he was more interested in Merry than he knew or that if he'd stop thinking, his heart would tell him where to go.

He was interested in Merry, just not in the way his mother thought. She'd be a fun companion, but he wasn't looking at her as a substitute wife or mother. He wasn't looking at anyone that way.

"Don't you miss him?"

Peter felt grabbed by the back of the neck and yanked back into the real world. "Huh?"

"Sean," Merry said. "I just wondered if you missed him."

He blinked at the overcast sky that was darkening before them. A storm was blowing in from the west, coming in over Iowa and southern Minnesota and bringing cold, wet misery for all.

"I mean, you don't see him all that often, do you?"

"Two, three times a month." Peter shrugged. "Sometimes just two when I've gotten tied up at work."

His cheeks grew warm and Peter felt angry all of a sudden. Angry at Merry, angry at the situation, but most of all angry at himself. He didn't have to submit to this third degree. Hell, he was doing the best he could. He knew that some men living in the same house with their kids saw them less.

"You miss so much when you're not there every day." Dark clouds inhabited her voice, and she was back to staring out the window. "You're not there to welcome them home from school. You don't hear their latest news firsthand. Yours isn't the first smile they see every morning. You're not there to tuck them in at night."

The pain in her voice opened up the scars in his own heart. Peter concentrated on the steering wheel, on the road, on his driving.

"Someone else raises them for you," Merry said softly. "You don't do any of the work, but you don't get to share any of the joy."

Merry's cloud of gloom spread and reached out to wrap itself around Peter like a suffocating mantle of despair. He felt himself getting angrier.

Here she was, twenty-five, single, with no one dependent on her. Where did she get off with this crap about not being there for the important parts of his son's life? He was doing the best he could for Sean. Sean was growing up in a house full of love and stability, just as Peter had.

Maybe Merry was watching too many soap operas. Or more than likely, she was planning to audition for one.

"Hey, Captain," Merry suddenly shouted. "Restaurant up ahead."

He flicked her a glare.

"Well, this land is so flat that it feels like we're sailing the ocean."

Peter glared hard at the horizon. Now she was cheerful and happy. And all he had to do was fall in.

"You said we could stop for coffee, didn't you? Well, I decided I want to."

Still silent, Peter slowed down and pulled into the parking lot. He turned off the ignition, set the hand brake, undid his seat belt, stepped out of the car and walked around to open the door for Merry.

But she was already scrambling out the door by the time he got there. It was obvious that she didn't know how to act around a gentleman. Maybe he shouldn't even bother. He turned on his heel and stalked toward the restaurant.

"Hey, wait up." Merry ran up, putting her arm through his. "You're mad at me, aren't you?"

"Of course not."

"You don't look like a happy camper."

"I didn't know we were camping."

She didn't reply, and they continued walking toward the restaurant. His body leaned into hers without any thought on his part. It was a nice, compact body. Soft where it was supposed to be soft and hard where it was supposed to be hard. Every muscle and bone was in the right place, honed to the right tension.

A smile pushed itself through his anger. Peter MacAllister, he told himself, you're just plain horny. It was time he stopped being a monk.

She let him open the door for her and once they were seated, she put her hand over his. "I'm sorry."

"Don't worry about it."

"No," she said. "It's none of my business. And everybody is doing the best they can for Sean."

He nodded.

"His grandma loves him dearly."

"We should do more things together," Peter said.

Suddenly her smile faded; her eyes turned serious. "It doesn't matter any if you do things together," she said, her voice almost hoarse. "All that matters is how much love you carry in your heart for him."

She had a rare understanding of things. He turned his hand under hers so that he had hold of her. He wasn't sure he wanted to let go.

"No, really, this is fine," Merry said. "This is closer than any parking place."

"But your bag—"

She just laughed as she hopped out of the car. "I've carried heavier. Pop open the trunk, will you?"

They were double-parked just outside her apartment. Peter'd wanted to park and carry her bag up to her apartment for her, but Merry knew from experience that the nearest parking spot could be blocks away, and that the sooner she said goodbye to him, the better. Too much had happened over the past few days, and she needed some time alone to sort it out.

Rather than use the trunk control inside the car, Peter got out and opened the trunk for her. She grabbed her bag out and slammed the lid down before facing him.

"Thanks for everything," she said, ignoring the annoyed look on his face. She was forcing him to violate every rule in his Gentleman's Handbook. "I imagine I'll see you at the restaurant."

He started to say something, but a truck was waiting behind and loudly protesting the wait. He glared its way, then took a step closer.

"Thank you for everything," he said.

Before she could escape, she was in his arms. He must have thrown away his Gentleman's Handbook for his touch was anything but soft and polite. His lips were hungry and as impatient as the truck driver honking behind them. She felt equal hungers awakening in her soul, fires that wanted to flare up and consume.

The trucker honked again, punctuating his impatience with a few choice words. Merry pulled away. She felt shaky and uncertain.

"Guess I'd better let you go," she said and hurried up to the sidewalk. From that position of safety, she waved as Peter got into his car and with a look of extreme annoyance at the truck driver finally pulled away.

"So long, buddy boy," Merry whispered and took a deep breath that ended in a shiver. A cold, damp wind was blowing off the lake, suggesting the need for a blazing fire and a body to cuddle up to. Well, she didn't have to have either, not with a good, thick blanket on her bed and an extra pair of socks in her drawer.

She went into the tiny lobby between the drugstore and the dry cleaner's. Their mailbox was fair to middling full, which meant she was the first one back. Just as well, that meant no explanations needed to be made.

Tucking the mail under one arm, she climbed the flight of stairs to the apartment and unlocked the door. The apartment seemed drearier than usual, so she turned on all the lights before she took her suitcase into her room. After about two minutes spent unpacking, she went back into the kitchen to make herself a cup of tea while she sorted through the mail. A few bills for Sandi, a few letters for ZeeZee and a newspaper for her. The tea was forgotten as she opened up the previous week's edition of the *Calhoun County Courier.*

The front page held the usual news—a holdup at the gas station, a tax referendum that was voted down and the annual Thanksgiving dinner for the poor and elderly at the social center. Some of the names were familiar, bringing to mind a few friendly memories and a few not so friendly ones, but she'd learned to deal with those emotions ages ago.

She waded through church news and school-luncheon menus before she hit pay dirt. There it was on page eight, right below the accident report, the schedule for the local schools' Christmas pageants.

Washington Elementary's "Home for the Holidays" would be performed two weeks from Tuesday.

She closed her eyes and saw herself there. Dressed to kill, surrounded by friends as she watched Jason sing Christmas carols with his class. Afterward, he'd rush over to her side where she'd hug and hug and hug him as if she'd never let him go.

"Hello there," Sandi called from the living room. The bumping and thumping of luggage being dropped to the floor accompanied her call.

Merry got to her feet and went into the other room. "Hi, have a good trip?"

"Great. Just the best." Sandi shoved one suitcase into the living room with her foot and shut the door. "I love getting away."

Merry just smiled and suddenly awoke to the whistling of the teakettle. "I've got some hot water on, if you'd like some tea."

"Sounds divine. I feel halfway to warm at just the mention of it."

While Sandi took her bags to her room, Merry went back to the kitchen and poured the boiling water over tea bags. As she waited for the tea to steep, she glanced out the window. An icy rain had started to fall, coating the glass and distorting the world outside. The neighbor's porch across the way became a tree house, the stop light at the corner her very own star.

Halfway to warm. She could be halfway to meeting Jason. She could go to his show. She couldn't meet him yet, she wasn't ready. But that was all right. She didn't have to meet him, didn't have to talk to anybody. There'd be a big crowd there, enough to lose herself in. And she could actually see him, maybe even hear his voice.

Dare she try? Dare she go back, after all the threats Joe had made? Hell, she wasn't a scared kid anymore, with no one to turn to. She was an adult and knew that all those things he'd said were just to keep her quiet and to convince her to give Jason up.

She'd held all the trump cards back then, if only she'd known how to play them. Joe'd been her boss at the hardware store and had begun wooing her as soon as she'd started working there. She'd been so stupidly flattered. He was older, wiser, had money and a pinky ring. What could he see in little, old her, she often wondered, but she loved the rush of fire his looks brought to her face and the little trinkets he used to surprise her with. A set of fluorescent bangle bracelets. A little book of poems. The red satin bikini underwear that should have shouted a warning to her. But no one'd ever made her feel so special before. She could still remember racing to her part-time job after the school day was finally over.

Living as he did way over in Highland, she had no idea he had a wife. She didn't find that out until she got pregnant and he wanted the child. His wife had been barren through the seven years they'd been married, and Joe would have done anything to keep his child. With a little luck and someone to turn to, Merry could have fought him and won.

The rain came down harder, blurring the magic outside into a swarm of colors, muted and miserable. No, she wouldn't have won, not really. No matter why Joe had said the things he did, he had been right. She was a nobody. She had nothing to offer their child, just a life of poverty and hopelessness like she'd had. Would she want him working in the mines, assuming they were still open by the time he was old enough? Or would she want him to run a chain of hardware stores across the county? Did she want him to be respected and educated, or in trouble with the law for underage drinking and vandalism like her younger brother?

The only thing she'd been able to give him was away.

Her eyes watered and she blinked at the wetness. Things were different now. She could go back and see him. She could get a camera and have a real picture to carry in her wallet, not an old newspaper photo.

Excitement grew in her heart until it was fit to burst. She wanted to tell someone, wanted someone to tell her that it was possible, that she should do it. She closed her eyes, and the first one who came to mind was Peter. She wanted to talk it over with him.

She opened her eyes. And how could she do that? How could she explain that this middle-class girl from the Atlanta suburbs had had a child out of wedlock while a teenager in Tennessee?

Nope, she was still alone and she'd better not let her heart forget it. She went into the bedroom and got her copy of *The Brothers Karamazov*. Number 27 on the list. Only twenty-three more classics to go.

Peter stepped into the restaurant, shivered from the chill wind and let his eyes search the room for Merry. It was two days since they'd gotten back, but this was the first time he'd made it to the restaurant. Not that he was avoiding her. No, he'd just been really busy. He had customers in yesterday, and they'd wanted to go to the Blackhawk for lunch. Then today, he'd had so much work that he had planned to eat at his desk, but his computer crashed just after noon and the system didn't want to come back up. He had no excuses to stay away.

He found himself holding his breath as his eyes swept the room, then holding it even more when Merry didn't seem to be anywhere about. Damn. Was Tuesday her day off?

No, most of these lunch places closed on Saturday and Sunday, so Merry would have the weekend off. She just had to be here. His regular table in back was empty, so he started walking toward it.

"Hey, stranger."

The air seemed lighter and a smile popped in place even before he saw her. "Hi," he said.

"I was afraid you didn't like us anymore." She came toward him with bright eyes and an easy smile.

"I got all tied up yesterday," Peter said.

"Whoo." She raised her eyebrows. "Was it fun?"

He tried to frown at her but failed miserably. "It was all business."

"Don't mean it can't be fun."

Peter gave his smile free rein. He grew more relaxed as he felt its glow fill his face. "Are you going to let me eat or are you planning on starving me to death?"

"I heard there were better ways to kill a man," she replied. "Ways that are more fun for all involved."

"Is that so?"

"Must be," she said with a shrug. "I read it in a book."

His heart wanted him to throw his head back and laugh, but his mind would only let him chuckle. There was no controlling the joy that spread through his being, though.

"Your table is available," Merry said, looking toward the back of the dining room.

"I don't own a table here, so I can sit anywhere I want." He looked around the restaurant, somehow feeling the need to prove that he wasn't stodgy and bound by tradition. "I'll sit here," he said, pointing to a small table near the window.

"Okay." Merry followed him to the table. "Our soup of the day is chicken noodle."

"I'll have the chef's salad." She was already writing in her order pad even before he spoke, so he hurried on with the rest of his order. "With blue-cheese dressing on the side and—" he hesitated for just a moment "—coffee to drink."

She stared at him for a long time, but Peter wouldn't let his returning gaze waver.

"Boy," she said, looking down to finish writing on her order pad. "You're just a wild, crazy kind of guy."

"Just call me unpredictable. You know, like hard to pigeonhole."

Merry didn't say anything as she turned to go to the kitchen with his order, but she did leave the golden glow of her smile behind.

He glanced out the window, surprised to see that the sun was shining through the clouds overhead. Probably all caused by Merry's smile. He should tell her to go easy on spreading all that joy around. Another few days and she'd melt the polar ice cap and they'd lose California.

"There you go."

A bowl of salad dropped gently before him, pulling Peter back to the present. She placed the salad dressing by the bowl along with a cup of coffee.

"Are you busy?" he asked.

"Not really," she said, shaking her head. "Most of the lunch crowd has come and gone by now."

"Would you mind sitting down a minute?" he asked, indicating the seat across from him.

"Who do I have to protect you from now?"

Peter forced a frown onto his face. "You know why donkeys don't go to college?"

Her grin spread wider as she sat down. "Because nobody likes a smart ass."

"Where did you learn all your punch lines?"

"Here and there."

Peter thought he saw a momentary flicker to her smile. Just like a light bulb when the power would fade for an instant. He pushed aside the hard-boiled egg and tomatoes and spread dressing over the rest.

"Don't you like eggs?" she asked.

"Nor tomatoes," he replied. "Would you like them?"

"Sure."

He speared the hard-boiled egg and stretched toward her generous mouth.

"I'll get you another fork," she said.

"Don't worry about it. I like to live dangerously." After giving her the other egg, Peter started on the tomatoes. "You haven't had lunch yet, have you?"

She shook her head.

"Hope I'm not spoiling your appetite."

Merry laughed. "It would take a lot to do that. I eat like a horse."

"You don't look like a horse."

"I walk a lot," she replied. "Walk and climb stairs."

Peter openly admired her form. "Seems to be working. You ought to bottle it."

"Ain't no secret to hard work."

He started nibbling at his salad. Ask her, stupid, he berated himself. If you don't ask her, she'll think you just want to hire her as a bodyguard, or what she called a bodyguard.

"Let's go out to dinner," he blurted out.

Merry didn't reply immediately, so Peter plunged on.

"I mean, if you want to." He sighed. "Would you like to go out to dinner with me tonight?"

"I'm sorry, I can't. I have class tonight."

"Tomorrow?"

She shook her head. "I have this big research paper I have to do, and the only time the computers at school are free is around dinnertime."

"We can go afterward."

Merry didn't say anything, but her face looked as though she wished he'd stop asking her.

"We need to get to know each other better," he said.

Merry frowned.

"I mean, we did okay for a few days, but if we don't sound like we go out on a regular basis, my mother is going to get suspicious."

"We'll do okay."

"No," Peter insisted. "Mothers know about these things. It's like radar."

She laughed, but didn't say she would go out with him.

"I have a computer at home. You can use it any time you want."

"You have word-processing software?" Merry asked.

"But of course." She just needed a nudge, a little one. "There are no lines at my computer."

She blinked once.

"You can use it as long as you like. Come early, stay late."

She looked off in the distance before turning to him again. "I really do have a lot of work. I can't afford to take time off to go out to dinner."

"We can order in."

"I pay," she said.

"Sure," he replied. Anything to get her to agree.

"We could have taken the stairs," Peter said as he pushed the button in the elevator.

Merry just nodded. And miss this? The elevator wasn't very large, but it was about a hundred times ritzier than anything she'd ever seen. The whole back wall was mirrors and they reflected the polished wood and gold trim of the other walls. Even the carpeting on the floor was special— it was about a foot thick, so that a body sank into it.

The elevator glided to a stop, and the doors parted silently. Peter led her into a hallway that seemed an extension of the elevator—mirrors and ritzy trim. There were also tables here and there, and not cheap pressed-wood ones, either. Dark carved wood with gold lines painted on them and marble tops that held flowers. She felt lucky when her hallway didn't have somebody's garbage dumped in it.

They came to a door marked 23 A and not saying anything, Peter unlocked it. Then he stood back, waving her in.

Merry stepped into an entry foyer with white walls and a highly polished parquet floor. Brightly colored modern paintings covered the walls and a small metal sculpture that didn't look like anything in particular stood in one corner.

It all looked rather simple, but Merry had been in the big city long enough to know that simplicity meant really expensive. Geez, was she out of her league. How had anybody in Mentone believed that Peter was dating her? She considered turning tail and running, but a body could never go back, just forward.

"Nice place," she said, trying hard for nonchalant.

"Can I take your bag?" he asked.

"No, that's okay." She slung her backpack down off her shoulder. "Just show me where I can work."

"Right down here."

Peter started down a hallway and Merry followed, trying not to stare at his broad shoulders. His smile could make this place seem like home. His laughter could take all the scariness out of it all. They crossed the living room, and her eyes wandered away from Peter. Her feet stopped moving altogether.

The other side of the room was all windows and they looked out over the lake, dark and brooding in the lingering light of the late afternoon. Nothing but sky and water unless, Merry suspected, one tiptoed right over to the edge and looked down at the street. She inched forward slightly. But even that looked magical as the streetlights wove a glittering chain into the distance.

Back home in Tennessee, Old Baldy had been the highest point in the whole county. A body could see all the way over to White Pigeon. Merry didn't know whether Old Baldy was higher or lower than Peter's twenty-three stories, but the view out his wall of windows was enough to take a person's breath clean away.

"It's a beautiful sight," she whispered to Peter, who had stopped to wait for her.

He nodded as if the beauty failed to move him anymore. "Come on, I'll give you a quick tour."

She watched him go down the hall. How could this beauty not move him? she wondered. Was it just natural grief over his wife's death or, as his mother thought, lingering guilt? She wanted to rush after him and drag him back to the living room. She wanted to make him see the magic and beauty. She wanted him to feel the potency of nature as she had felt it. But he was too far away, and not just in feet.

He opened the double doors at the end of the hallway. "This is the master bedroom," he said.

She hurried to catch up. The bedroom was large with a king-size bed in the middle. The furniture was big and heavy, a white rug covered the floor, and like the living room, there was a wonderful wall of windows all along one side. She had a moment's vision of the sun waking her up as she slept in Peter's arms, but pushed that thought quickly out of her mind. The last time she'd let thoughts like that take control of her body, she'd landed in a heap of trouble.

"I imagine your wife loved this view," Merry said.

"She was looking for a place in the suburbs."

There was an undertone to Peter's voice. It sounded like anger, but Merry wasn't sure. She was sure that the message was, let's not talk about my wife. Maybe he still pined for her. For some reason, the idea hurt.

Peter went on and opened another door. "This is Sean's room."

She looked through the door into a little boy's room. The bed was a race car, and posters of Chicago Bulls and Chicago Bears players decorated the wall.

"Nice," Merry said.

"It's for when he visits me."

Merry nodded as Peter went on to the last door.

"And this is my home office," he said.

This was the smallest room she'd seen in the apartment so far, but it was still bigger than the living room of her apartment. The stainless-steel-and-leather furniture was very male and somehow almost like being in Peter's arms. She forced herself to stare at the pure white area rug on the floor.

"I'd better take my shoes off," she said.

"You don't have to."

"I couldn't work with my shoes on. I'd be scared to death that I was spreading dirt all over that beautiful white rug."

He shrugged. "Make yourself comfortable."

Comfort, now there was an interesting concept. There were all sorts of ways she could be comfortable. In Peter's arms, leaning against his shoulder, lying at his side. She shut down those thoughts and walked over to the computer.

"This it?"

"Yeah," he said as he came over to turn it on. "Need any help?"

"Nope." She shook her head and took off her coat. "Everything looks like it should." She took her diskette out and sat down at the desk. "If I run into any problems, I'll holler."

"We're here to help."

Merry smiled at him and felt a little ripple run down her spine. This place was intoxicating all by itself. Throw in Peter with those sad eyes and lost-little-boy air, and she'd be beyond recall. She forced herself to concentrate on the computer.

"You need any technical assistance, a tall, cool drink, a back rub, anything. All you have to do is call."

She doubted her need for any technical assistance, but those other two things were sure tempting. Squinting her eyes up, she stared hard at the screen. "Goodbye, Peter."

"You sure you don't need anything?"

Her body was getting downright needful, but she had to finish her paper and, even more important, she needed to stay out of trouble. "Out," she growled.

"Boy," he muttered.

His footsteps were muted by the thick rug, and Merry held her breath until the door closed behind her. Then she breathed a deep sigh of relief. She didn't know if there was a lock on the door, but knew that keeping Peter out wasn't the problem. What she needed was a bolt on the other side to keep herself in. Sighing, she sorted through her notes, hoping that her mind would follow.

Her mind did follow, although it took Merry a while to accustom herself to the quiet of Peter's office. The library at school was quiet, but it was different. It was muffled coughs, shuffling footsteps and whispers generated by crowds of people. Here she had only herself, and out beyond the closed door, Peter.

She forced her fingers to move across the keyboard. Between work and school, she'd met her share of men and had had her share of come-ons. She'd had no trouble turning them down, one and all, and staying focused on her goal of a degree and success. Yet there was something much more appealing about Peter, and much more dangerous. He was drowning and didn't seem to know it. Locked within himself, he was going down for the third time, and she seemed to be the only one around to pull him back.

That was crazy, she told herself. He had a family, friends, people he worked with. He didn't need her, except as a temporary pretend girlfriend, not as a real-life savior.

Her scoldings lost steam about the same time her stomach became active. Luckily, she'd actually gotten a fair amount done on her paper, too. She leaned back and wiggled her toes in the thick rug, letting her mind savor the pizza that Peter was going to order in. Had he ordered it yet or was he waiting for her to finish?

She got up and walked to the door, savoring every soft tickle on the soles of her feet. Merry frowned. She'd better be careful or she'd go completely soft. She had a long way to go before she could relax.

As she was about to open the door, there was a light tap on the other side. She opened the door.

"Ready to eat?"

Peter had changed into a beige sweater, dark slacks and moccasins, and his face had lost some of the tightness he'd brought home with him. He looked as if he might actually enjoy the evening.

"Sure am," she replied.

"Then," he said, stepping aside, "dinner is served."

"Okay." She stepped back into the room to rummage in her backpack. "How much do I owe you?"

He blinked.

"Come on now. We agreed I was paying for the pizza."

"I didn't exactly get pizza."

She started to glare at him, but he reached out and took her hand. It was either wrestle him or follow him. Merry chose to follow. For now. "What did you get?"

"I had some old fish lying around," he said offhandedly. "So I took that and threw some odds and ends together."

Some old fish and odds and ends? He made it sound like something he found while jogging along the lake that he just tossed together with some old socks and an empty pop can, but she wasn't fooled. The smells from the kitchen were heavenly. There were spices, many of which she couldn't identify, cheeses and fish. Peter led her to the dining room and pulled out a chair for her.

"I don't need anybody waiting on me," Merry said, trying not to be awed by the wall of windows in front of her.

"Let me do it," Peter insisted. "I want to make sure that I haven't lost my touch. There haven't been guests here for a long time."

There was a poignancy in his voice. A sad-little-boy tone of a lad who'd been denied the pleasures of life. Who was she to deny a man simple pleasures? She sat down and let Peter serve the meal.

He filled her plate with fish, potatoes and vegetables. Then he took warm bread out of the oven, pouring each of them a glass of white wine before he sat down. They touched glasses, sipped and began eating.

The food was as wonderful as the scents had promised. The view was magnificent. But the company...

Well, she couldn't get Peter to maintain a conversation to save her life.

"Food's great," she began.

"Thanks." Silence again.

She nodded toward the windows. "Guess you must not be bothered by heights."

"Nope."

After some French vanilla ice cream covered with sinfully delicious cherry sauce and a glass of Japanese plum wine, Merry leaned back and gazed at her host.

He looked so alone, with the vast night beyond him. That bleakness that had been in the clouds over the lake seemed reflected in his eyes, making her want to lead him away from the dark storms. She could help him back into the warmth of sunshine, if he would let her. She would make him feel he wasn't alone.

The room swam before her eyes as ideas and desires danced in her mind. She ought to go home before she got into trouble. But there was a world of difference between being a kid and being an adult. As a kid, trouble could be overwhelming. As an adult, trouble could even be fun.

"What do I owe you?" she asked.

Peter's brow wrinkled.

"I'm supposed to be paying for the meal. So what do I owe you?" She could feel a lazy smile slowly roll across her face. "In cash money, that is."

He looked down at his now empty wineglass for a moment. "That's hard to say." He looked up. "I don't remember what the fish cost. And the stuff like the potatoes, spices and cheeses, I only used a part of what I already had on hand. I don't think I can come up with a dollar amount."

"Well, there are other ways of repaying a debt."

For just the smallest moment Merry was shocked at the words that fell from her mouth. But what the hell? The food was good, the wine was great, Peter was so handsome. And there were times when a girl just couldn't take any more lonely. A pleasant warmth radiated through her body.

He got up and began to clear the table. She followed him into the kitchen with the wineglasses.

She came in closer, taking her time but moving with purpose as she took the dishes from his hands and placed them on the counter. Then she went into his arms ever so smoothly. They closed around her surely and possessively as if she were coming home.

Her lips came up to meet his and they touched softly at first, like the gentle drizzle of rain on the petals of a rose. Their dance was hesitant and restrained, but then something happened. Like a storm suddenly bursting into life, the gentleness fled. He was the thunder; she was the lightning. He was the wind; she was the rain. Their hunger, their needs grew more intense.

His arms tightened around her, pulling her into his heart, and she strained to be even closer. The sweet tenderness of the first touch was gone as his lips devoured hers, taking her raging hungers and blending them into a tempest of passion. The room spun, disappearing into a misty haze of unimportance. They clung together, then suddenly they were apart. He had let go.

Peter just stood there, barely a foot away, but miles distant from her in some way. His gaze was on some far-off place or time. The cold from the floor seeped into her bare feet and doused the flame within her body. Didn't he want her?

"Maybe you can return the favor," he said, looking at her then. "Dinner can be on you one night."

Wasn't he attracted to her or was he just a decent man? "Okay," she said simply.

"You got much more to do on your paper?"

Merry cleared her throat. "I'm about as far as I can get today. I need to be getting on home."

"You can use my computer any time you want."

"Thanks."

"I'll take you home," he said.

"That's okay." She walked back into the dining room for the rest of the dishes. "I only live a few blocks from here."

"I don't care if you live a few doors from here," Peter said. "I'm not letting you walk the streets alone at this time of the night."

Merry smiled. He was a decent man, just not particularly attracted to her, she thought.

Chapter Six

"There you go, sport," Merry said, handing the man some bills. "Keep the change."

The cabdriver's sharp features and dark visage were merged into a scowl as he looked at the money in his hand. Merry just nodded to Peter as they got out of the cab.

Peter suspected that Merry's unhappiness with the man's driving had been reflected in her tip, but the guy had been driving like a demented ambulance chaser racing to an accident scene, weaving in and out of traffic, driving into the oncoming flow to pass and totally ignoring traffic signals.

"Sure was a cheerful little feller," Merry said. "Especially for a man with suicidal tendencies."

Peter laughed and put an arm around her shoulder, brushing her hair with his lips. "Don't worry about it. You're safe now." He liked the feel of her. Not just the way her softness brushed against him as they walked, awakening a slow heat in his blood, but also the way she made him feel deep down in his soul. As if he mattered, as if he were needed.

Not that he was always sure what he wanted to do about those feelings. Like the other night when she'd been at his apartment. She would have stayed if he'd asked her, but as much as his body longed for hers, just the thought of holding—loving—someone made all the shadows come rushing back. Even now, they hovered not too far in the distance.

"I don't know how long that cabdriver's been in this country," Merry said. "But he sure doesn't have the hang of traffic lights. Green was go, yellow was speed up and red was go like the devil was after you."

Her smile warmed him. "I offered to drive, you know."

She shrugged. "I didn't want your car to get ripped off. This isn't the greatest of neighborhoods."

Peter looked around at the dim city streets. The small businesses were now dark, windows protected by steel grates. Litter filled all the stray corners and gathered along the curb, while old beaters lined both sides of the street. The neighborhood didn't have the boarded-up despair of a slum, but it was hanging on to respectability by its fingernails.

"I doubt if there would have been a problem," he said. "All the professional car thieves are working the expensive neighborhoods. They like a wider selection of new cars."

"Well, it doesn't matter," she said. "This is my treat."

He let his hand slip off her shoulder and took her hand, letting her lead them down the street. Funny how he didn't want to let go of her. They'd only really known each other a couple of weeks, but she had become important to him, to his sense of peace.

"It's not much farther," she said. "It's a little Mexican place back here. The food is great."

She stopped them in front of a narrow store. The sign in the window, if Peter remembered his college Spanish correctly, advertised the Little Rooster. A menu, all in Spanish, was taped to the inside of the door.

"Smells good," Peter said, as he opened the door for Merry.

"It better be." Her voice was grim, but there was a twinkle in her eye. "Or José's gonna be singing soprano in the church choir."

The door nudged him in the back and Peter stepped in to let it close. The dining room was long and narrow. Rough-hewn booths lined one side of the wall. The lights were dim and a narrow path led to a brightly lit kitchen in back.

"Hey, José," Merry shouted, and a tall, thin man turned toward them. A bright smile split his face as he saw Merry.

"Merry, so good to see you." He bowed slightly and kissed both her hands before he turned toward the kitchen. "Mama," he called. "Tía."

Peter frowned. José still had hold of Merry's hands, as if he was renting them for the evening. A knot formed in the pit of Peter's stomach.

"José's in some of my classes," Merry said over her shoulder to Peter as two older women, gray streaking their black hair, hurried toward them. "He shared some enchiladas with me one day. I thought I'd died and gone to heaven."

Peter just grunted an acknowledgment and tried not to glare. She hadn't raved this much about his food.

José spoke in Spanish to the women, who then hugged and kissed Merry, forcing José to let go of her hands.

"I told my mother and my aunt that your name means happy," José said. "My mother said that your smile says that more beautifully than any words."

"Tell her she's too kind," Merry replied.

Her smile brought sunshine to all the dark corners of the room, but its warmth wasn't aimed at Peter, and his heart kept a slight chill. He could have told her that about her smile, but he hadn't thought he should be so personal.

José's mother pulled at his sleeve and murmured something to him. "My mother wishes to make the acquaintance of your friend," he said.

"Oh, sorry." It was hard to tell in the dim light, but it looked as though Merry was blushing. "This is Peter MacAllister."

Peter shook hands with José and bowed his head to the women, before putting his arm around Merry's shoulders. He wasn't sure why he did it, it just felt right. Felt necessary.

"A special friend?" José asked, arching one eyebrow.

Merry's face was still flushed, and the women stood smiling at them. "Sort of," Merry replied.

José shot a few words of Spanish toward his mother and aunt. Their smiles broadened. Peter found himself smiling back. They were special friends. There was something exceptional in their relationship.

"Actually, he's more like an employer."

Peter's smile fell slightly. Didn't she feel it, too?

"He hires me as a bodyguard when he goes to Indiana."

Peter frowned as José translated that. The smiles dimmed for both women, his mother spoke to José.

"My mother says that parts of Indiana can be very dangerous. We have cousins that live in Gary. She says she wishes we had a bodyguard when we go visit them."

Peter frowned even more at Merry, but her grin stayed in place. "The really dangerous place is Mentone," she said.

"Mentone?" José said.

"Oh, yeah," Merry replied. "They got this egg in the center of town that's bigger than I am. The chicken that laid it has gotta weigh at least three hundred pounds."

José blinked once, then turned to speak to his mother and aunt. The women laughed, hugged Merry and shook Peter's hand before hurrying off to the kitchen in back.

"I told them that you two were very hungry," José said. 'Maybe later, when there is more time, I will tell them about those three-hundred-pound killer chickens."

He led them to a booth in the center of the dining room, much to Peter's relief. He didn't like sharing Merry, he realized. He was never sure of where he stood with her when others were around. Her laughter seemed more mocking, ike quicksilver, and he couldn't get ahold of what it meant.

José started to hand them menus, but Merry stopped him. "I want you to take care of everything, José. You know, from *A* to *Z*, soup to nuts. Everything."

José smiled and bowed, before going back to the kitchen. Peter watched him go, then turned back to Merry. Now that he had her alone, he wasn't sure just what to say to her.

"I hope the Mentone chamber of commerce never hears about you," he said. "They wouldn't take too kindly to your rumors about three-hundred-pound killer chickens."

She giggled. "Hey, that might bring in the tourists in droves. You could have giant chicken roasts, organize killer-chicken hunts, all kinds of exciting stuff."

José returned with a bottle of wine in an ice bucket and glasses, as well as a basket of tortilla chips and salsa. "I have spoken with my mother and aunt," he said. "We will start with a chicken soup. Then we will prepare a combination plate. Enchiladas, tostadas, tortillas."

"Sounds great to me, José," Merry said.

Once José returned to the kitchen, Peter picked up his glass. *Here's to your beautiful blue eyes. Here's to the way your laughter sets me afire.* "Here's to three-hundred-pound killer chickens," he said.

Merry lifted her glass and touched his. "And giant eggs."

"And giant eggs," he agreed.

He sipped his wine. It was a smooth, pleasant California blend and went down easily. He took another sip. It might be the wine or maybe the lights, but Merry's eyes seemed to have a special glow to them. Their cool blue depths had always been inviting, but tonight they seemed to hold something more. He reached over and took her hand in his.

"This is a great place," he said. It was quiet and dimly lit. The high walls of their booth created a cocoon around them and held them safe.

"Yeah, it is nice." She squeezed his hand and her smile grew. "The city is full of neat little places like this. I love trying to find them."

She would. She was the type who would love trying something new and different, and he would love tagging along, being her bodyguard and companion. Suddenly his life seemed so tame and ordinary.

Just as suddenly, guilt churned his stomach into a seething cauldron. Just because Kelly would never have come to a place like this didn't mean that their life together hadn't been good. So she'd never been one for unknown, ethnic little places like this. She had been filled with love. Maybe too much love, since her inability to have more kids seemed to have eaten away at her. A melancholy Spanish love song was playing in the restaurant, and his depression grew.

"A dime for your thoughts." Merry's smiling face tried to lure him from his thoughts.

It was a hard job, but he shook some of his moodiness free. "A dime?"

"Yeah, a dime." She sipped a bit of her wine. "I didn't think a penny would do. There's inflation, and then you have so many degrees to you that I figured your thoughts ought to cost more than most."

With the help of those eyes, he managed to find a smile somewhere inside of him and put it on. "Not really."

"Still worried about those three-hundred-pound killer chickens?"

He shook his head and reached for her hands again. Maybe her touch could keep his thoughts at bay. Maybe he sunshine could chase away the storm clouds, if not for good then at least for the evening.

"Excuse me." José put hot, steaming bowls of soup in front of them.

"Boy, I'm glad you finally got here, José," Merry said. "I was almost ready to start chewing on the table."

José laughed. "How about you, *Señor?* Were you also going to attack the table?"

"Yeah," he agreed with a halfhearted laugh. Merry frowned at him, as if sensing his deeper mood, but he just smiled at her. It was easier this time, not nearly so hard to find or force to his lips. There was something in her presence, just knowing she was there, that gave him strength.

Sandi and ZeeZee were both there when Merry got home from school the next night. Sitting in the living room, they looked up at her entrance with such anticipation that Merry felt uneasy.

"Boy." She laughed as she hung up her coat. "You guys are a pair to draw to."

"We want to have a party this weekend," Sandi said. "You know, like before all the rest of the Christmas parties start."

"Fine by me." They all pitched in with the apartment, so Merry had no problem with her roommates having a party. She'd just go to the library or a movie. Maybe both.

"We want you to help us," ZeeZee said.

"Sure," Merry said. "I'll help clean Saturday morn—" Sandi butted in. "We want you to come to the party." Merry shook her head. "Nah."

"Come on, you're always working. If it's not your job, it's school. You gotta take some time off for fun."

"We can find you a date."

"Yeah, Brad knows this real cool guy."

"And he's just been dying to meet you."

Oh, Lordy. They were on their Let's-fix-Merry-up-with-a-date kick. "Look, roomies, I—"

They were staring at her, determination in their eyes. Suddenly she was tired of being the odd man out. "I have to check with...with my gentleman friend and see what he has going."

Surprise filled their faces, but only for a moment. "What's his name?"

"What does he do?"

"Where did you meet him?"

"How long have you guys been going together?"

"Hey, hey." Merry dropped her book and raised her arms in a protective gesture. "Back off, will ya?"

They did, but their eyes still burned with fervent eagerness, like that of a scientist about to discover the cure for frizzy hair. Merry took a deep breath. Their excitement was contagious, but still she didn't want to say too much.

"His name is Peter," Merry said slowly. "And he works downtown. We met at the restaurant."

"Was it like sparks across the room?" Sandi asked. "Have you known him long?"

Merry shook her head. "We met just before Thanksgiving."

"Ah-ha," ZeeZee said. "That's why you didn't want to go with me to Minneapolis."

"What did you guys do over the holidays?" Sandi asked.

"We went to Indiana," Merry said. "To Mentone."

"Huh?"

"It's the Egg Basket to the Midwest."

That little bit of information was obviously overwhelming, as neither of her roommates could reply.

"It's a three-hour drive," Merry said. "We went down Wednesday afternoon, right after I got off work, and spent the long weekend with his mother and son."

"Oh."

The word was said knowingly, and though she had no reason to, Merry blushed. "Look, we just took a little trip. Had plenty of home cooking, fresh air, quiet and friendly folks. It was real nice."

"I imagine it was," Sandi said.

"Was that it?" ZeeZee asked.

Merry shrugged. "He had me over to his place a few days later."

Their grins returned.

"I had to work on my sociology paper," Merry said hotly. "And I was having trouble finding computer time. He has a computer at home."

"What does he do?" ZeeZee asked.

"He's got a bunch of degrees," Merry replied. "He does statistical and actuarial stuff for a bunch of big companies."

"Whew," Sandi said. "He's big-bucks kind of people."

Merry frowned at her. She guessed he must be, considering his apartment, but she hadn't really thought about it. Why would a "big bucks" person want to be friends with her?

"Seriously," her roommate assured her. "My dad uses people like that. I mean, we're talking six-figure income. Easy."

Six figures? Lordy, was she that good an actress that she could fool someone with a million degrees and more money than she could ever imagine?

"Actually, we're just friends," she said slowly.

"A good place to start," ZeeZee said.

"Yeah," Sandi said. "Some of your better relationships start that way."

"We don't have a relationship. We're just friends."

"But isn't friendship a—" Sandi stopped and waved her hand. "Ah, forget it. Just call him. This Saturday. Have him come early, maybe he can help."

Merry just nodded and wandered down to her room. How could she have been so blind? Everything about his life here in Chicago said money, yet she was treating him like one of her fellow students.

What was she going to do about the party? She couldn't really go calling on him again. It was his turn to decide things. If she called now, he would think she was chasing him.

Hell, this whole thing was all his fault. If he had ordered a pizza like she'd asked him to, she would have paid for it. Then they would have been even and there would have been no need to take him out to dinner last night.

Sighing, Merry stood staring out her window at the night. Damn, damn, damn! Suddenly she was afraid to ask him.

Why?

The sinking sensation in the pit of her stomach told her why. Because he might say no. Because he might be tired of her.

Hell. She closed her eyes and leaned her forehead against the cool glass of the window. She was tired of this modern-woman stuff. She was ready to go back to when the guys did all the asking.

"Mrs. Hanson took my turkey down today," Sean said.

His son's voice seemed especially faint this evening. It was probably just a bad connection, but Peter felt it was symbolic. His son was drifting farther and farther away from him.

"She probably took everyone's turkey down," Peter said, trying to stay upbeat.

"Uh-huh."

"I'm sorry I didn't get to see it."

"That's okay," Sean replied.

Peter restrained his urge to sigh. His mother had been right. He should have gone down earlier. Then he would have had time to go to Sean's school and see all the decorations his son's kindergarten class had put up on the walls. Hell. This remote parenting was turning out to be a flop. Although it was probably single parenting that was the culprit.

"You brought your turkey home, didn't you?"

"Yeah."

"That's good. I'll get to see it the next time I'm home. Or maybe you can bring it up when you come in next weekend."

"Grandma says I can't come. I got a cold."

Peter felt like a balloon whose air had swooshed all out. Damn! He'd had all these plans. Shopping at Water Tower Place, a trip to the Sears Tower and then lunch at that place in Lincolnwood where the waitresses were all on skates.

"Grandma's saving all my school stuff," Sean said.

"That's good," he replied, fighting a valiant but losing battle to keep the cheer in his voice. "Then I can get to see it all."

"Yeah."

He was indeed lucky that his mother was helping. Peter wasn't sure that he'd keep up with things, saving all Sean's drawings and schoolwork the way his mother was. He'd read someplace that women were the keepers of the bonds, the connectors of the generations. Now he knew what that meant.

"I gotta go," Sean said, interrupting his thoughts.

"Oh. Okay."

"He's going to feed Zachary." His mother was on the phone now. "He does it every night. He enjoys taking care of that blind old cat."

Obviously he enjoys it more than talking to his father, Peter thought.

"Actually, he's very good at taking care of anybody who needs it. He might be a doctor someday, like his grandfather."

His mother paused, and Peter rubbed his eyes. He should go take a walk or something. His depression was building. It looked like dump-city time again.

"I think he'd be a good doctor, don't you?"

"I have no idea," he said. "I hardly know him."

"Of course you do. You're just feeling sorry for yourself again."

He wasn't feeling sorry for himself. He was just being realistic. "He hardly talks to me. He tells one thing that happened that day, gives me thirty seconds of monosyllabic responses and he's gone."

"Very few five-year-olds have acquired the fine art of sipping sherry and carrying on long conversations." His mother was in one of her sarcastic moods. "Five-year-old boys are like little bumblebees. They spend their days zipping about and nibbling on a wide variety of life's experiences."

Peter grunted.

"You call almost every day. That's good. It gives Sean a chance to tell you something that's important at the moment. It gives him a chance to stay in touch. Two minutes every day is better for him than two hours once a week."

"I guess."

"There's no 'I guess' to it. I know what I'm talking about." She sighed. "Well, that's enough trying to cheer you up. You're too old to be needing my help anymore. At my age, you should be cheering me up. Tell me something happy about yourself. How are things with Merry?"

"Okay," he replied. She was like a bright star in his sky. She brought cheer and warmth to his heart, but he couldn't let himself get too close.

"Just okay? Is something wrong?"

"No, Mom. Nothing's wrong. Things are fine. Just like I told you."

"You're spending too much time with numbers, Peter. Words are much better. They give richer and better explanations." Suddenly there was a murmur in the background. Then his mother was back on the phone. "Sean's ready for bed. We have to go."

"Okay, Mom. See you. Take care." He waited, holding the phone to his ear.

"Good night, Daddy," Sean said.

"Good night, Sean. Sleep tight."

"Yeah. And I won't let the bedbugs bite."

The phone went dead, the dial tone replacing the string of childish giggles. Peter set the receiver down and walked over to the wall of windows.

It was night. An overcast, dark night, so that the only thing he could see was a large black abyss. He felt as if he were staring at his life.

He should call Merry. Ask her out, even if it was just for a walk along the lake. The dismal emptiness of his life was getting to him.

Before he could gather the strength to lift up the phone, though, it rang. It was Merry. Some mischievous god must have been eavesdropping on his thoughts.

"Hey, me and my roommates are having a party Saturday night," she said. "Want to come?"

"A party?"

"Yeah. You know, food, drinks, fun and games." She paused. "It's okay if you can't, though. I'll understand."

She sounded ready to to sign him off, to leave him to that black abyss. Fear dried his mouth and he had to swallow fast. "No, I'll come. I'd like to." He was suddenly afraid of being alone.

"Great. Eight, okay?"

"Sure. Fine."

"See ya." She was gone, and without her smile in the air, the shadows came rushing back.

He hadn't gone to a party for eons, not as Peter Mac-Allister, anyway. His most recent forays into partying had

been as half of the unit known as Mr. and Mrs. Mac-
Allister. He didn't have that identity anymore.

What would he say to a roomful of strangers? He wasn't
up on the latest movies or singers or sports news. Managing his work and staying in touch with Sean had seemed all
he could handle. Now it seemed he was woefully out of it.
There was no way that he could become a social being in
two days. It was like having to cram for a final when you
haven't attended class all semester.

He should call Merry back. Give her an excuse. Make up
an illness. Anything. Just get out of it. He knew it was going to be a disaster.

It started off badly. He arrived promptly at eight with a
box of Godiva chocolates—hazelnut rum balls to be exact.

"Ooh, groovy," ZeeZee purred. "Merry hates hazel-
nuts. That means we get to eat them all."

"Great choice," Sandi echoed.

"It's the thought that counts," Merry assured him, kissing him for his thoughtfulness, but not nearly long enough
or hard enough to make him forget he'd goofed. He made
do with a drink while Merry and her roommates did their
last-minute prepping.

The evening moved into catastrophe mode when the
guests started arriving. He was the only one wearing a suit.

"I think you look handsome," Merry told him, but he
knew he looked stiff and foolish. Taking the jacket off and
loosening his tie only made him look worse, pretending to
be casual. Another drink made him feel less stiff, no matter how he looked.

Merry went off to greet some of her friends from school
and that's when the evening went cataclysmic. Left to his
own devices, he wandered about the living room, sipping
at still another drink and trying not to look lost.

He hated being on his own at these things. He needed
somebody to laugh with, somebody to remind him who

everybody was when he forgot. He needed somebody to talk to, because he was no good at ten-way conversations. All he saw were happy groups of people with no need for another participant, certainly not one who was a stranger in a suit. He should have stayed home.

Peter glanced around the room, seeking refuge. The Christmas tree in the corner had an odd appearance, and he sauntered over. He frowned. It looked as though someone had tossed garbage into it. Crushed beer cans were stuck on branches, the plastic rings from the top of a six-pack was tangled into a knot and tossed onto the top. He reached in for one of the beer cans.

"Hey, buddy, don't mess with the ornaments," Merry said with mock brusqueness.

Peter jumped and let the can in his hand fall to the floor. "Sorry," he said. Ornament? He hung the can back up on the tree. "I was just fixing it...."

Merry took his hand and led him away from the tree. "ZeeZee's our resident artist. The Christmas tree is her baby. She feels it makes a environmental statement."

"Oh. Sorry." Just went to show how bad he was at partying. Everybody else looked at the other guests, he looked at trees. He started to smile, but then noticed the drink in his hand. He gulped at that instead.

"Merry," someone called from over near the door. "Paging Miss Merry."

Merry glanced toward the voice, then back at Peter. "There's a group about to play a game of Trivial Pursuit. Why don't you join them?"

He made a face. "I'm not very good at games."

"Merry," the call was repeated. She glanced up, then back at Peter. "Come on, you'd probably be good at it. Put all those degrees to work."

He wasn't enthused, but followed along behind her. Why was she always mentioning his degrees? Did she think he was some super-educated nerd who knew nothing about life? He wished he had never come. He stopped to refill his drink, then caught up with her in the dining room.

"Hey, guys," Merry said. "Got room for Peter on one of your teams?"

"Sure. He can be on our team," Sandi said. She scooted her chair over to make room for his. "Merry says you're one smart cookie."

He just smiled and tried not to feel panic as Merry wove toward the door. He'd been stupid to think she'd be spending her whole evening with him. A hostess had responsibilities.

"Get ready, Peter," Sandi said. She nudged him as she rolled the die. "Here we go. Oh, great. Science."

A member of the other team pulled a card from the box. "Who first measured the distance from the earth to the sun?"

Sandi groaned. "You know?" she whispered to her boyfriend, Bill.

He just frowned. "Galileo?"

Peter shook his head. "Foucault."

"What's your answer?" the question reader asked.

Sandi looked from Bill to Peter. "Foucault," she said.

"Right."

Sandi cheered while Bill just rolled the dice again and moved their token. "History," he said, his voice a bit surly.

"What canal opened in 1869 that enabled sailors to bypass an entire continent and speed up world trade?"

"Panama," Bill said.

"Suez," Peter said.

"Panama," Bill repeated, just little louder.

Sandi swallowed hard, then with an apologetic smile at Peter, said, "Panama."

"Wrong. Suez." The other team was gleeful and went about taking their turn.

"Looks like you know everything," Bill muttered.

"Not by a long shot," Peter said. "I'm really lousy at stuff like literature." He gazed anxiously toward the door, but Merry was nowhere in sight. He finished the rest of his drink as it became their turn again.

"Literature," Sandi said after moving their token.

Bill sneered, or at least Peter could have sworn he did. Peter ignored it, pretending to listen carefully to the question. It wouldn't do to get into a fight with Sandi's boyfriend.

"What's the name of the baby elephant made popular in a series of children's books?"

"Dumbo," Bill decreed.

Sandi turned to look at Peter when he said nothing.

"Babar."

Sandi bit her lip in indecision, so Bill jumped in to answer. "Dumbo."

"Wrong. Babar." The other team roared with laughter.

Bill flung himself back in his chair, his face red and his angry gaze on Peter. "I thought you didn't know literature," he snapped.

"So I got lucky." Peter didn't need this. He got to his feet. "I think I'll go find Merry."

"Guess we're not smart enough for you, huh?"

Bill was rapidly becoming a jerk, but Peter did his best to ignore him. "If you'll all excuse me..." he said to the group as a whole, as he skirted around the table.

"I won't, fella."

"Bill." Sandi sounded like she was trying to calm him down. Everyone else in the room seemed to have gone mute.

"You can't come here and make a fool of me, then just waltz off."

Bill's voice echoed around him, and Peter had had enough. "I don't think you need anyone to make of fool of you," he said smoothly. "You're doing that quite well on your own."

"Hey," Sandi cried. The mother hen in her rose up in protection of her own, but Peter managed to escape into the crowd in the living room. It swallowed him up, and like the sun coming out from behind a cloud, the murmur of conversation came slowly back.

"What's going on?" Merry was suddenly at his side.

A frown rested between her eyes, and he had a real longing to kiss it away. And while he was there, kiss a number of other things, too. Those deep blue eyes that promised peace and rest. That nose that curled up so intriguingly when she laughed. Those ears that were almost hidden behind the curtain of dusky red hair. And that hair—how he'd love to bury his face in it, to lose himself in its softness.

"What's Sandi so upset about?"

Peter shook his daydreams from his mind and forced it back to more trivial matters. He shrugged. "I guess she just found out that her boyfriend is a jerk."

Merry glanced back into the dining room, then frowned up at Peter. "Did something happen?"

Her scent was intoxicating. It set his blood to boiling. "Not yet, but if we left this dumb party, something probably could."

She scowled at him. "How much have you had to drink?"

"Not enough," he said, peering into his empty glass. "I'm not having any fun yet."

She gave him a look that he knew wasn't good, then grabbed hold of his arm, dragging him out of the apartment and down the stairs to the front stoop. He stood there a long moment, staring at the street and its passing stream of traffic. What in the world were they doing out here? He'd much rather they retired to the privacy of his place.

"It's cold out here," he said, moving a little closer to her.

"It looks like you still have some normal feelings left."

Showed how little she knew. "I've got nothing but normal feelings left." He wrapped his arms around her. "Want to see?"

The look in her eyes didn't match the fire in his body. "You're going to be suffering feelings of extreme pain if you don't let go of me."

He didn't have the slightest idea why she was so upset, but he let go of her. The steel in her voice told him to.

"Want to go back in?" she asked.

For more torture? Reality poked its ugly head up through the fog of all those drinks he'd had. He hadn't belonged here earlier and he sure didn't belong here now. He shook his head. "I should be getting home." He looked down the street. "It's not far from here. And a walk would do me good."

"The walk might be good for you," she said. "But I don't think a mugging would help any."

Peter glared at her.

"Hey," she said. "You're a first-class kind of pigeon. Had a little too much to drink and are obviously wealthy."

"I can take care of myself." Hadn't he been having to do that for the past year? He didn't need or want her help.

"Here comes a cab," she said and dashed to the curb to flag it down. Once it stopped, she helped him into the backseat. "Thirty-four hundred Lake Shore Drive."

The driver pulled away in a squeal of tires. Well, all evening he'd been longing to go home. Why didn't he feel excited now that the wish was becoming reality?

Chapter Seven

Peter dragged himself down to the restaurant. Saturday night replayed itself in his mind like a greasy meal sending up bubbles of heartburn. Both left him with a bad taste in his mouth, feeling sick and disgusted with himself.

He knew that Merry could never forgive him for being such a jerk, but he couldn't part on that kind of a note. Certainly, she'd never want to see him again, and she shouldn't have to. But he just had to let her know that although he was an adult and responsible for his actions, what he'd done could only be explained by stupidity.

"Good afternoon, Mr. MacAllister." The hostess's greeting was friendly, her lips were smiling, and her gaze was open and pleasant. "Would you like your usual table? Or would you like to sit up closer to the front?"

Peter looked at the booth, far in the back. It was private even when the restaurant was at its most crowded. Now it was almost like an island in the middle of the ocean.

"I'll take my usual."

"Very good, sir." The hostess led him toward the back. "I'll send a server right over," she said, as she seated him and handed him a menu.

"Ah." Peter swallowed hard. "Is Merry around?"

"Yes, she's back in the kitchen. I'll tell her you're here."

Suddenly he was alone, awaiting his doom. He tried to read the menu, but the letters swam before his eyes. Merry could do two things. She could refuse to wait on him or she could grab a cleaver and storm into the dining room after him. Either way things weren't going to turn out well.

"What can I get you, sir?"

His eyes slowly left the menu and climbed up Merry's soft curves. Unlike the words outlining his meal choices, reading Merry's body language was no trouble at all. Her smile was still broad, but it had a newfound rigidity to it and her eyes had no sparkle.

"Could you sit down?"

"We always stand when we take customer orders, sir. That way we can get to the kitchen quicker and you'll get your food that much sooner."

"I'm not really hungry."

"Would you just like something to drink, sir?"

Peter looked outside for a moment. The sunshine was gone and snow was falling. Coming down sideways, the flakes were pushed along by a cold, biting, chill-you-down-to-the-bone northwest wind that he could feel even inside.

"Actually, all I want is a piece of pie."

"Apple, custard, banana cream—"

"Humble," he said. "And make it an extra large piece."

Her smile sagged and she blinked, obviously confused.

"I want to apologize for being an utter, absolute, total ass."

Merry took a deep breath. She dropped her order pad into her pocket, crossed her arms and jacked up her smile a couple of feet. "That's okay," she said. "I shouldn't have asked you to come."

His mouth just dropped open and hung there. "You shouldn't have asked me? Why? Is something the matter with me?"

"Oh, no," she hastened to explain. "It's just that—" she looked away a long moment, appearing to gather her thoughts "—you're who you are and my friends are who they are."

Peter flashed back to the party. There were many things he didn't remember, but the people were easy to recall. They were an eclectic mixture of rich and poor, multiethnic, multicultural. Interesting and exciting in their attitudes and ideas. His feelings of self-worth fell even further.

"I'd also like to apologize for acting like a snob," he said. "I haven't been out socially like that for a long time, and I screwed up royally."

Merry looked away and time stood still. He'd been a jerk, he knew that, and he didn't deserve to be forgiven, but if only she would . . .

She slowly turned back to face him, reaching into her pocket for her order pad. "Can I get you anything?" she asked softly.

"Get us both some coffee and sit down and talk with me."

"Peter, I—"

"If you don't, I will throw a tantrum."

Her look was disbelieving.

"I mean it," Peter said. "I'll roll around on the floor, kicking and screaming."

She hesitated, and he pressed his advantage.

"Look, just sit across from me and pretend you're listening. I'll say my piece, then I'll get out of your life."

She kept her silence.

"Please. If the hostess says anything about it, I'll pay for fifty meals, a hundred. I just want to try to explain things."

Merry turned on her heels and went into the kitchen. There was a chance that she wasn't coming back, but he was sure that she would. She didn't look like the type who ran away from anything.

He rubbed his face with both hands. And he didn't want her to. Oh, Lord, how he didn't want her to.

Within moments, Merry burst through the double doors out of the kitchen and strode toward him, carrying two large, steaming mugs. She set them on the table and sat down across from him. He clutched his cup, sucking its warmth, hoping to drive away the cold fear that filled his heart.

"I don't know where to start," he said. "Except to apologize again."

"Peter—"

He held up his hand. "I was in poor shape when I arrived at your place."

Her brow wrinkled. "You seemed fine to me."

"Physically, I was fine. But I was a wreck inside. I know I'm single again, but I'm not used to partying alone. When I had too much to drink, the controls just gave way."

"I see," she said, looking into her cup.

He knew that she didn't really, so he hastened to explain. "I was absolutely terrified of going to your party."

For the first time since he'd stepped in today, her smile stretched out to near its natural limits. "There wasn't any reason for you to worry," she said. "I'm your bodyguard. I protected you in Mentone and I'd have protected you in Chicago."

The laugh they shared felt so good, like ice-cold lemonade after a day of tasseling corn in the hot July sun. He wanted to reach out and touch her, but he was afraid that, like a nervous young doe, she would just take off and run.

"I appreciate that." He took a moment to get control of his hungry hands. After taking a big swallow of hot coffee, he went on. "I've been a widower for a little over a year. I should have the hang of it by now. But I'm obviously not coping as well as I should be."

"I thought you were doing fine," she said.

"I'm getting through the day-to-day things. And, according to my mother, I'm even doing okay by Sean."

"That's the most important thing."

He paused and nodded. "Anyway, I was scared to death about going to your party. I almost turned and ran a million times."

"But why?" Merry asked. "My friends are a little different, but they aren't all that bad."

"It has nothing to do with your friends and everything to do with me. Since Kelly passed away, I've had nothing but social disasters. Women are pushed at me, I push myself at women. If I didn't have Sean, I'd go become a hermit."

"Then it's a good thing you have Sean. Not everyone is so lucky."

Peter paused for a moment. He thought there was a catch to her voice, but she said nothing else. "Anyway, I wanted you to know that I'm very sorry."

Merry said nothing as she stared out the window. Suddenly, as if she'd just noticed he'd quit talking, she started. "Don't worry about it," she said. "We all do dumb things at times."

Peter felt it was safe to take her hands. "Am I forgiven?"

"Sure." The smile was still there, but it seemed somewhat subdued. "But it's more important that you forgive yourself."

He nodded. "I just want to make it up to you."

She laughed and pulled her hands away. "Let's not do a party for a while."

"Can I take you out to dinner?"

She shrugged.

"Please."

She nodded. "When we're both ready again."

"When will that be?" he asked.

"I would guess soon." She stood up from the table, collecting both mugs. "After all, we have to keep practicing for our return visit to Mentone."

Turning on her heels, she walked quickly toward the back of the restaurant. Peter had never ordered lunch, but he didn't really feel hungry. Damn. He'd hurt Merry and now he'd have to give her time to heal.

Peter stamped his feet on the sidewalk and pulled his coat collar up closer. The bitter wind just seemed to blow right through him, but he wasn't budging. According to Sandi, Merry'd be getting off this train on her way to school.

He looked at his watch. She'd have to come by here. Unless she took a bus or a cab. Peter clenched his teeth. This was stupid. So what that he had been out of town for a few days; he should have just waited until lunchtime tomorrow.

The screech of metal wheels on metal rails told him that an elevated train had arrived at the station above. He looked at his watch again. Merry would have to be on this train or she would be late for class.

Within moments, the aging structure rumbled and rattled as the train left. He scanned the faces streaming down the steps and onto the streets. There seemed to be either young students coming to their night classes or middle-aged women who cleaned offices at night.

Suddenly he saw Merry's face, smiling like the sun breaking through a bank of dark clouds. He took a step forward. Then, just as suddenly, Peter stopped. Merry was walking with a small group of men. Young men. Handsome men, in a sloppy, studentish sort of way.

But why shouldn't she be walking with men? They certainly weren't going to run away from her. Not to mention that it wasn't a good idea to wander around alone here at night.

How would she greet him, if she even did? Maybe she didn't want to see him here. Sure, she'd forgiven him, but she didn't appear all that enthusiastic about going out with him again. That little crack about their need to keep up appearances for his mother hadn't exactly been encouraging.

"Peter?" She stopped. "What are you doing here?"

"Waiting for you."

Merry turned to her companions. "Why don't you guys go ahead? I'll catch up with you."

The young men voiced their agreement and nodded at Peter before they went on ahead. Peter waited a moment, savoring the warmth in her eyes and the safety of her smile.

"I tried to call you," he said finally.

"I got your messages on the answering machine, but I couldn't get ahold of you. I called your office, but all they'd say was that you were out of town."

"I could have told them to give you a number to reach me, but I didn't want you to be making any long-distance calls. Besides, I was hard to reach."

"That's okay. It's cool."

Her smile seemed to echo her words, and he began to believe that maybe she wasn't still angry at him. They began to walk toward the college. Slowly, though, as if to treasure every second.

"I was hoping that it was soon enough to take you to dinner," he said.

"Tonight?"

Something in her voice made his heart sink. "Got a date?"

"Yep. A date with Professor Crawford. I've got a big sociology test."

Relief swept over him. "Maybe you'll be hungry afterward."

"It'll be late."

"That's okay. This is the night I get to stay up late."

"The test period is two hours long, and I'm going to need very minute of the time."

Two hours. Hell, that was nothing, not with the prospect of seeing Merry's smile at the end of it.

"I have a lot of reading with me." He held up his slender briefcase. "Why don't I wait in the library for you?"

By the time they stepped out of the college a few hours later, the few clouds had dissipated. The night was clear and the stars so bright that Peter almost felt he could reach up and touch them. Suddenly he felt so very much alive.

A cab came into view, and Peter started to raise his hand, but Merry caught it. "Let's walk."

"Walk where?"

"I don't know," she replied. "Let's just walk north."

"It's late."

"Don't worry," she said. "I'm a fully certified bodyguard and I'll take care of you."

Would she? He was more than willing to let her. He didn't feel he needed protection especially, but he could use some taking care of. Someone to chase away the nightmares, to bring the sun back into his life. She had done all that to some extent already. Would she do more? He took her hand in his, and they started walking north up Michigan Avenue.

Lights illuminated the tops of the Prudential Building, the Standard Oil Tower and the other skyscrapers on the lake side of the Loop. Down closer to the ground, there were lights playing on the two stone lions guarding the entrance to the Art Institute.

There was a sense of magic in the air that he hadn't felt before. He squeezed her hand and smiled down at her. The cold air was invigorating, stimulating, not a reason to run away and hide.

"So am I finally forgiven?" he asked.

"I guess."

Her voice sounded thoughtful and for a moment his heart stopped.

"Let's go this way." She tugged at him, turning him first onto a side street, then back north onto the State Street mall. "Now, this is the real Christmas."

Lights were strung from every tree. Giant candy canes protruded from light poles. Store after store had carols blasting forth from loud speakers.

"This is the real Christmas?" he repeated, wondering how she could be impressed by any of it. "It's all commercial."

"Nah, it's lights and sounds and magic." She pointed toward a vendor along the mall. "Roasted chestnuts. Want some?"

"Do I have to sing the carol?"

She just hurried him over to the cart and ordered a small bag of them. He was surprised as he munched on his first. There was something special about the warm, crunchy nut and the cold starry night. Best of all was the sparkling laughter of the woman with him.

"Okay. I agree these are good."

She cuddled up close to his side, hugging his arm to her. "It's all good, if you just let it be."

"Hmm."

With her looking at him that way, he could almost believe she was right. That the world could hold happiness and the stars held a magic that could make him smile.

She stopped at a store window. A mammoth animated display of an Alpine town lay before them. A train ran continuously on a serpentine track while villagers came in and out of houses.

"You see that little guy over there?" Merry said, pointing to an old man far off in one corner, sweeping his front step. "That's you."

He frowned. "I'm short, pudgy and wear a red hat?"

She punched him playfully. "You're all by yourself."

"I am not," he protested. "I'm with you."

He'd meant for her to laugh. He wanted to see her smile light her eyes, but she just shook her head.

"It may be your turn to get mad," she said. "But there are some things I think you should hear."

He didn't like the sound of that and concentrated on the train weaving its way through the village, on Santa in his sleigh up amid the clouds.

"You have to stop comparing the way you do things now to the way you used to do them."

"I don't."

She ignored him. "You have to believe that even if things are different, they can still be good."

"I do." His eyes were somehow on the little old man in the red hat. No matter what happened around him, he just kept on sweeping.

"You have to let yourself have a good time without asking if you deserve to."

He didn't bother to answer her. Just as the man in the red hat didn't bother to look up when the carolers came by. Sweep, sweep, sweep, that's all the man did. A heaviness seemed to come over Peter, weighing him down suddenly.

Merry pulled at his arm and started walking again. People and sounds surrounded them. The Alpine scene was lost, except in memory.

"We all lose loved ones," she said softly. "And if we all shut down, it would be a pretty miserable place. We'd be sad and grumpy and never want to be anyplace but by ourselves."

"I'm not grumpy."

She laughed, and the sound of magic seemed to echo around them. The stars shone brighter, the carols were sweeter. A bell ringer was up ahead, and Merry stopped to dig in her pockets.

"I've got it," he said and pulled out his wallet.

She still pulled a wad of change and bills from her pocket and stuffed it into the bucket.

"Bless you," the woman said, never losing the rhythm of her bell.

Peter put his own money in, then frowned down at Merry. "Why didn't you let me put in something for both of us?" he asked. "I can afford it a lot more than you can."

Merry just shook her head. "Because the giving says I'm doing great compared to some others, and my recognition of that makes me alive. It puts all my little problems in perspective."

"Some problems are harder to put aside," he pointed out.

"And those are the ones that just have to be accepted. Look, you can't bring Kelly back, no matter what you do or don't do."

"I know that." He was starting to lose patience. He had been looking for some lighthearted fun this evening, not a lecture.

"Suppose you had died in the accident, not her. Would you want her moping around, being only half alive?"

"For god's sake, I just screwed up one party."

"Would you want her moping around?"

He sighed. "No, of course not."

"So why are you? Are you saying you're a better person than she was, that you loved her more than she loved you?"

He suddenly stuck his hands into his jacket pockets. "Love is such a huge commitment. It's opening yourself up totally to someone else. It's letting them see everything about you, the good parts and the bad parts. Letting them see the polish on your shoes as well as the holes in your underwear. I will never let myself get that close again." He paused. "It would have to snow in Death Valley. Pigs would have to fly. And the three-hundred-pound chickens would have to come back to Mentone."

She shook her head. "Love is seeing the holes in some-one else's underwear and not caring about those holes. But I wasn't talking about loving again. I was talking about living. Oh, look," she exclaimed as she pulled him to a sudden stop before a window filled with stuffed toys. "Isn't that great?"

Peter stared at the collection. It was like Noah's ark, with every animal imaginable crammed into the window.

"Look at the snake," Merry said, pointing to a huge stuffed snake, curled like a cobra. "Sean would love that!"

It would be fifteen feet long when stretched out. "He would?"

"Little boys love snakes. They sit in them, sleep in them, wrap them around themselves and pretend they're being squeezed to death. Stuffed snakes are very versatile."

"I was thinking of getting him a computer for Christmas."

Merry just looked at him. "He's five years old!"

"That's not too young."

She just shook her head and pulled Peter along. "Buy him both. There are just some things the soul needs that can't be explained."

He felt her hand tighten on his and she was suddenly his lifeline, his link with the rest of the world. He knew exactly what she meant. He couldn't explain it, but he needed her with him.

"Since you're such an expert on parties, want to come to one with me on Saturday?" Peter asked. "You can make sure I behave and have a good time."

Merry stepped out of Peter's car. The houses here were huge, mansions even. Bigger than the school in Four Corners. Bigger than the mayor's house in White Pigeon. And the Christmas decorations—well, they were like something out of a movie. Tiny white lights all over the trees, houses and the street-side mailboxes. Even the snow here was fresher and prettier than in the city.

Merry's heart sank into her stomach. What was she doing here? These people would have about as much to say to her as a bird did to a worm.

Peter took her hand and smiled at her, making her almost believe certain things were possible. With her hand in his, she felt strong. And when he smiled at her that way, she was sure that nothing bad could touch her.

She glanced up at the sky and its canopy of stars as they walked up the long, curving drive lined with luminaries. They were the same stars she used to wish upon back home. She bet if she were sitting on one of those stars, everyplace down here would look the same.

She tightened her hold on Peter's arm. "I like the city and all," she said, "but I like it out here where you can see the stars."

He looked up at the sky, but said nothing.

She continued to stare upward, knowing he didn't find the peace and strength in the stars that she did. She wished she could open his eyes to the joy around him. Not just the stars, but friendships and Sean, too. But the stars were a place to start.

"Sometimes stars are the only thing you can share with somebody you love," she said. Her eyes closed and she saw the shadowy figure of Jason.

She felt Peter stir and opened her eyes to find his gaze on her. "Sean could be looking at these same stars right now."

He looked back at the sky a moment, as if searching for something he couldn't see. "It's late. He said he was going to bed right after I talked to him."

Merry shook her head. "There you go again, refusing to believe. Come on, you've got to let a little magic in sometimes."

He just laughed softly. "Someday I will, I promise."

"Sure."

They walked the rest of the way up the driveway, the night's stillness closing in on them. In the safety of the flickering darkness, all sorts of warring emotions were colliding within her. She was so thrilled about her trip to see Jason; she didn't know how not to share her excitement. But she was also scared. Not really of Joe's threats, but of the whole idea of going back. Afraid somehow that the poverty and despair would capture her.

"Nice neighborhood, isn't it?" Peter said.

"Very." She shook off her preoccupations and forced her mind back to the task at hand. She knew all about this place. Although the architecture was different from the Pill Hill area back home, Winnetka smelled the same. The scent of power and money hung heavy in the air, telling the world that folks here didn't have to play by the same rules as regular folks. They could make their own rules as they went along. Nobody or nothing was gonna stop them. Merry shivered in spite of her resolve.

"I told you that you should have worn boots," Peter scolded.

"Wasn't worth it." She nodded at the brushing of snow barely covering the driveway. "I could walk barefoot in this."

"Sure."

That would have made some impression on his managing partner, she thought, even more so than Peter had made on her friends. She had a strong feeling, though, that her friends were more tolerant than his.

Tonight she was going to have to be careful. More than careful. She was going to have to do the acting job of her life.

"Why do you always have to sound so tough?" he asked. "Maybe you should pamper yourself the way others would like to pamper you."

His words surprised her, as did the sudden softness of his voice. She turned to look at him and he reached out, brushing a stray curl away with a gentle touch.

"It'll never stay put," she warned. "My hair's got a mind of it's own."

"And why do you always have to joke?"

His voice came on a breath, like the stirring of angel wings, as his lips came down to hers. The night was so silent and still that the touch seemed almost like a blessing. Her wishes would be granted, favors bestowed, all from the magic of his kiss.

Her heart churned, wanting to fire up with hungers and needs. But it wasn't the time for that. Her spirit found peace and certainty in the touch of Peter's lips. Strength flowed from his mouth, his soul, and she knew that the stars were smiling on her.

"We're kind of late," Peter said as he slowly pulled away and rang the doorbell. "Most of the people are going to be well on their way to loose."

Merry smiled, reveling in the lingering scent of his embrace.

The door flew open, and a young woman stood there. "Peter," she squealed and gave him a big hug while holding firmly onto her drink glass.

"Hi, Liz," he replied, rolling his eyes at Merry. It was obvious that Liz was past her first glass. Peter freed himself and stepped back, taking Merry's arm. "This is a friend of mine, Merry Roberts. Merry, this is Liz Terrell."

They exchanged greetings. Liz's smile stayed in place but uncertainty flickered in her eyes. She was probably wondering where she'd seen Merry before.

"Merry is a drama student at Columbia College," Peter said.

The uncertainty in Liz's eyes dimmed, and Merry smiled. That was good. Liz would probably think she'd seen Merry on a TV ad. A lot of kids at school took background jobs.

"Come on in," Liz said, stepping back. "Bart will probably tell us that he has no intention of heating the whole outdoors."

Both Merry and Peter laughed as they walked through the door. Liz indicated they should put their coats in the den, then disappeared in the crowd.

"Care for anything to drink?" Peter asked as he helped Merry with her coat.

"I'm not much of a drinker," Merry said.

"I'll get you a glass that you can carry around then," Peter said. "That way no one will bother you."

Peter went over to the bar, leaving Merry to smile at those around her, acting as if she couldn't be more relaxed. ZeeZee had lent her this black velvet dress with assurances that it would be perfect for the occasion, but Merry wasn't so sure. It didn't have any of the glitter and sparkle of those around her. She should have made some wishes on those stars she was admiring outside. She should have made Peter stay with her.

"Oh, what a lovely dress," an older woman said, pausing at Merry's side to finger the dress's full skirt. "Armani's?"

Merry shook her head. "ZeeZee's."

The woman's eyes widened slightly. "A new designer? Oh, don't you just adore finding these new people before the crowd does?"

"Definitely."

Peter arrived just as the woman left. He handed Merry a glass of ginger ale. "You don't waste time, do you?"

"What?"

He nodded at the woman who was almost lost in the crowd. "Mrs. Kripner. Bart's wife. A notorious snob, and she was smiling at you."

"Was she?" Merry sipped at her ginger ale, a smile of satisfaction deep in her heart. She gazed into his eyes and relaxed. Suddenly this whole evening was unimportant. She could get through it in a snap because the only one she had to please was Peter, and she could see by the look in his eyes that she was already succeeding.

The only stars she needed to wish on were the ones Peter made spin around her.

Chapter Eight

Peter watched Merry wolf down the salad they'd picked up after she'd finished her research at the library. The impatient honk from behind pointed out that the light was green. He turned his attention back to driving.

"You're going to give yourself an ulcer," he warned. "The way you stuff that junk down your gullet."

"What do you mean 'junk?' This is healthy stuff here," she said, nodding at the plastic container sitting on her lap. "It's all rabbit food and low-cal dressing."

His eyes weren't really interested in the container of salad, though. No, they preferred to wander over her jeans, which showed off her waist-down curves and a short jacket that emphasized her waist-up curves. That impish smile on her face was enough to drive a sane man over the edge. And those riotous curls, they had to reflect the fire in her heart. In fact, everything about her shouted passionate energy.

Peter shook his head, forcing himself to watch the traffic before him. Next time he gave her a ride home, she'd have to ride in the trunk. Otherwise his own dam of re- straint would break. Then what would control him? They'd probably get arrested for blocking traffic or something.

"I'm not talking about what you're eating," he pointed out. "I'm talking about how fast you eat."

"When my body says it's hungry, I feed it."

He glanced at her face, shining in the light of the street- lights, then quickly looked away as he swallowed hard. God, she was so beautiful, so alive.

"I don't believe in teasing it."

"Does that apply to everything?" he asked.

"You betcha."

The window before him appeared to be steaming up. Pe- ter wiped it with the back of his glove, then gripped the steering wheel hard and rolled his head to relax his neck muscles. Given the way his body was reacting to Merry, you'd think he'd had a bucket of oysters for lunch, instead of an egg-salad sandwich and soup. The sound of paper rustling told him that Merry had completed her dinner.

"I'm thirsty," she announced.

"I told you to get something to drink when you bought the salad."

"I didn't want anything then. Besides, I have some fresh squeezed orange juice at home. Want some?"

"Sure."

As they neared Merry's building, a minivan pulled out, leaving a parking space free in the same block as her apart- ment. "The gods are smiling on me tonight," he said, ma- neuvering his car. "I've never found a space this close to your door before."

"Actually, it's me they like."

Peter finished parking, killed the ignition and took a moment to look at Merry. Her mouth, generous like ev- erything about her, was stretched in a coast-to-coast grin. He wanted to wrap her in his arms and turn that grin into a soft smile of ecstasy. God, how he wanted her.

"I can't argue with you there," he said gruffly before getting out of the car.

She was already out and waiting for him by the time he'd come around the car.

"You're supposed to let the gentleman help you out of the car," he said.

"What for? I'm no cripple."

"It gives a young gentleman something to do," he replied. "Makes him feel useful."

"You'd best be able to do more than just open a car door if you want to feel useful." She turned and gave him a full blast of her impish smile. "I mean, if you're really all that young."

Unable to resist her any longer, Peter reached out and crushed her to his chest. His lips met hers in a blinding rush of passion. Soft and moist, her mouth opened like a flower beneath his touch, and he could barely contain his hunger for her.

It was like holding fire in his arms. She filled his embrace so completely, her softness threatening to consume him. He knew to go deeper, to hold her tighter was to risk being burned, but his heart was about to explode with needs and longings. He pressed her closer, his hands denying that they would ever part while his mouth took strength from her. The city night sounds suddenly intruded, and he let her go.

"What was that for?" she asked, her voice more than just a little breathless.

"That's for nothing." His voice was husky, as if speech were a new skill. "So you better watch your step."

Merry said nothing as they walked to her apartment. "Hi, guys," she said to her roommates, who were lounging in the living room.

"Hi, yourself," they replied, staring at the two of them. Their voices sounded just a bit tentative. They were probably worried about what he was going to do.

"I brought Peter in for a drink," Merry said.

"Just orange juice," he explained before they spooked and called the police.

Merry took her coat off and threw it onto the chair; then she kicked her boots off into a corner. She was wearing a Bulls sweatshirt that did nothing to hide her curves.

"We were just going to our room," Sandi said, standing up.

"Yeah," ZeeZee echoed. "We were going to watch that National Wildlife special on tigers in Africa."

"I thought tigers lived in Asia," Peter said.

"Most of them do," ZeeZee replied. "That's why these are so special."

Sandi just nodded as the women quickly left.

"I guess that could have been an interesting conversation," Peter said. "But I wasn't sure that I wanted to get involved."

Merry laughed. "Just sit down. I'll be right back."

He watched her walk into the kitchen with mixed emotions. He was glad to get a moment to pull himself back together, yet he didn't want her out of his sight.

Calm down, boy, he told himself as he leaned his head against the back of the sofa, closing his eyes. Merry was so vibrant, so full of passion and life that it was only natural for him to be attracted to her. But it was best to go slow. Think things through.

"Here you go."

He opened his eyes as she sat down next to him, holding out his glass of orange juice. She'd also removed her socks.

"That's the one bad thing about winter," she said, putting her feet up on the low table in front of the sofa. "My feet come near to dying, being cooped up all day."

"How about the rest of your body?" Peter asked. Lord, what a question. Slow and easy, that's what he had decided just moments ago.

Merry looked at him with her sparkling blue eyes. They were so cool and inviting, like a pristine pond in the wilderness on a hot summer's day.

How he wanted to dive into those eyes. He wanted their coolness to soothe the fevered heat of his body. He wanted to wrap his arms around her curves, wanted those strong legs to wrap themselves around him.

He set his glass down, and Merry did the same. An unseen hand reached down, pushing them together. Peter could feel his heart stop and his mouth go dry. She was in his arms again, his hunger feeding off hers. His lips dying for a taste of her sweetness.

"Excuse me."

They both jumped back, like children found with their hands in the cookie jar.

"I gotta go to the bathroom," Sandi said, a lopsided grin on her face. "Sorry."

They sat back. Peter didn't know about Merry, but it took an effort on his part to resume normal breathing. They'd have to wait for Sandi to come out. Then what if ZeeZee needed to use the bathroom?

This was insane. He was insane. Just the slightest, merest touch and his body was on fire. There was no way he could sit here on her couch, necking like a pair of teenagers. He'd better get out of here before her roommates had real reason to call the police.

"I have to get going." He stood up. "I have to call Sean, then I have to pack. I'm leaving for a couple of days in Omaha tomorrow morning."

Merry also stood up. "Take care of yourself."

Her voice sounded almost normal, while his seemed thready and weak. Wasn't she affected by his touch?

He grabbed up his coat, fighting the need to grab her back into his arms instead. "You, too. I'll call you."

"Okay."

"Oh." He stopped at the door. "I have a couple of cli ents and their wives coming in Friday. I promised to take them to dinner at Ambrosia. Could you go with me?"

"Will I have to protect you from them?"

"No," he said frowning. "Why do you ask?"

"Just wanted to know whether I should charge my reg ular bodyguard rate or what."

"You'll just be a dinner companion."

"Well." She moved up close, put her hand behind hi head and pulled him down to her lips. "Then I guess you'l get the regular dinner-companion rate."

"You planning on putting your brand on this little girl Pete?"

Merry almost laughed out loud at the expression of shock and disbelief that sat for the briefest of moments on Pe ter's face. Old Mr. Wright had called him Pete, called Merry a little girl and talked about Peter owning her all in one sentence. In a few short words, the old feller got him self an *F-* in political correctness.

Peter seized his glass of water, obviously taking the time to compose himself. "No, Mr. Wright," Peter replied. "Merry and I are just friends."

"I sure don't understand being just friends with such a beautiful woman," the old man snorted.

Mr. Wright was in his early sixties, the CEO of a large computer company in Minneapolis and about to retire. Tall, with longish white hair and a face like old shoe leather, he was an old-fashioned Texan with a native shrewdness behind his bluff, hearty manner and country ways.

"Aren't you friends with your wife?" Merry asked.

"Hell's fire, young lady," he replied with a laugh. "At my age, there ain't nothin' else we can be but friends."

"Yeah," Mrs. Wright, a short, pleasingly plump grand mother type, said. "He's fading fast. I'm looking around for a replacement. A young fella that's still got a lot of juice left in his battery.''

They all laughed, then settled into a long moment of silence. The dinner had been delicious and everyone was sitting back, relaxed.

''I'm certainly glad you could come with us,'' Mr. Roegiers said.

Peter had filled her in on both men before dinner. Mr. Roegiers had been recently appointed to succeed Mr. Wright as CEO upon the latter's retirement. Although completely different personalities—Mr. Roegiers was a sophisticated man who'd graduated from Harvard—the two men and their wives got along quite well.

''I'm glad you could join us also,'' Mrs. Roegiers said softly. ''I've always been fascinated with the theater. Although, what I really appreciated was your wine selection for dinner. The chardonnay was out of this world.''

''Thank you,'' Merry murmured.

She settled back to bask in an aura of satisfaction. She hated to brag but, like the folks said, she had done quite well. The food and drink recommendations she'd made were good, and she had no trouble at all in holding up her end of the conversation.

The Roegiers were interested in her theater classes and experience, while the Wrights enjoyed her waitress stories. Merry smiled. She'd learned way back that as long as a woman labeled herself an actress, she could work at anything from waitress to call girl and be quite acceptable.

''Would the ladies and gentlemen like anything else? Some chocolate mints perhaps?''

Their waiter had returned to check on them. Merry noticed that his French accent had been getting a little heavy as the evening had progressed. Peter scanned the group as everyone indicated they'd had enough. Good. She'd enjoyed herself, but the evening had been long and it was time for Cinderella to head back to her hearth, kick off her shoes and flop down in bed. Although as long as she was in bed, there was one other little thing she wouldn't mind doing.

Merry could feel her cheeks warm slightly. Like Peter said, they were just friends. But the vibes she'd gotten the other night said that he'd be interested in being *really* good friends. And her body was screaming out its own agreement.

"That'll be all, Charles," Peter said. "Just the check, please."

The waiter bowed slightly and walked away.

Mr. Wright stood up. "I'm going to visit the little boys' room before we leave."

"I want to freshen up myself," Mrs. Wright said.

The Roegiers got up and followed the Wrights, leaving Merry and Peter alone at the table.

"Thanks for helping me out," he said softly.

"No problem," Merry replied. "Hope they'll still be your customers after tonight."

"Are you kidding?"

He smiled at her, a broad smile that spread its heat from the top of her her head down to the tips of her toes. She could live in that smile, take it to the bank as collateral for a million-dollar loan. Or use it to heat the house in the dead of winter and still have enough left over to steam up her soul.

Peter took her hand, his touch sending shivers up and down her spine. "I think they're going to demand that I bring you along whenever I go to Minneapolis on business."

"I hear Minneapolis is a nice town," she said, trying to sound cool and unaffected.

"I have a feeling that any town would be nice with you in it."

"Better be careful." She tried to sound stern, but her voice came out all soft and wavery. "Flattery is liable to get you everything."

The silence surrounded them and filled their ears. Peter had those big brown eyes, the kind that could go from puppy soft to rock hard in a split second. Right now they seemed to burn with a hidden fire that invited her to come closer.

"Here's your check, sir. I'll take it whenever you're ready."

The spell was broken and they parted. Peter's eyes flicked up to the waiter, then he did a double take as the lack of French accent dawned on him. Merry and the waiter began to laugh.

"Sorry, Merry," the waiter said. "It's been a long day."

Peter was sitting back, faint question lines furrowing his brow. "You two know each other?"

"Yep," Merry replied. "This is Bobby Wisnewski. He's a student at Columbia. Works here nights as a waiter. Bobby, this is my friend, Peter MacAllister."

The two men shook hands, then Peter pulled a credit card from his wallet and gave it to Bobby Wisnewski, aka Charles, the French waiter.

"I guess it's all show biz," Peter said once Bobby had left.

Merry nodded. "Sure is. Didn't old Willie Shakespeare say something about life being nothing but a stage?"

"Something like that."

Voices floated over from the front of the dining room, announcing the return of the Wrights and the Roegierses. Peter put on his pleasant business face, and Merry turned up her smile a notch.

Just because it was show biz didn't mean it was easy. Sure, this little restaurant gig had turned out well for her, but it hadn't just happened. She'd spent almost an hour here after work, talking to the waiters and chefs. Seeing what was going to be served that evening and getting wine recommendations. Checking ingredients so she could talk knowledgeably about the food. She also talked to the piano player and found out which tunes he could do best.

Peter had been depending on her, and she wasn't about to let him down.

"Yahoo!" Merry shouted as she stepped into Peter's living room.

He was lying back in his recliner, watching television. He rolled his head toward her. "What are you yahooing about?"

"I finished my paper. I'm done! *Finis.*"

She walked over to the back of the recliner and glanced at the TV set. The Bulls were playing the New York Knicks and they were only ahead by one point. She bent down and hugged Peter around his neck.

"Hey, down in front." He squirmed around to keep his eye on the screen. "This is a good game."

Merry dropped down in his lap. "I know another good game."

"Oh?"

She let her hands roam over his shoulders until her arms encircled him; then she leaned forward to ever so gently brush his lips with hers. He leaned into her, but she backed away, climbing back off his lap.

"Oops, I forgot. You want to watch the game."

"Get back here," he said with laugh and pulled her back into his lap.

"Are you sure?" she asked. Her fingers ran through his hair. She felt so good. She wanted to celebrate.

He picked up the TV's remote control, aimed it at the set and turned it off. "Positive." He tossed the remote onto the table as he slipped his arms around her.

"Now, about this game of yours. What's it called?"

She just laughed and snuggled into his arms. "It's called Your-Sociology-Paper's-Done Celebration."

"I see. Is it a hard game to learn?"

"Not really." She ran a finger along his jaw. It was so strong, so rigid. It seemed to say he was unbending, but she had seen softer, gentler sides to him.

He grabbed her hand suddenly and brought it to his lips. The look in his eyes said her teasing caress had been too much. He held it, held her as if he'd never let her go. Which was absolutely just fine with her.

"So what are the rules to this game?" he asked.

"Well, first of all you have to choose a topic," she said as she leaned over to touch his lips with her tongue. She felt the shiver go down his spine, felt the fire leap up in him. And felt the answering hunger in her soul.

"You know," she said. "Some area you'd like to explore."

"I see."

His hands slipped under her sweatshirt. They felt cool against her suddenly feverish skin, cool and delicious as they roamed over her back. There were so many needs that came rushing forward, clamoring to be met. She closed her eyes and let her body call to his.

His lips pressed against hers, a questioning, examining kiss that asked things of her heart. Things that her mind couldn't answer, that her ears couldn't hear. That only the very depth of her understood and responded to. Then he gently pulled away his mouth, and she lay against him, her heart racing and her breath hard to catch.

"So," she said after a few moments. "Did you see an area you'd like to explore?"

"Several."

His voice was as thready and weak as hers. Maybe together they could find strength. She covered his mouth with hers, a union of their souls, a blending of their voices. They moved and danced against each other until time stood still. It was wonder, it was magic.

There was no yesterday, no tomorrow. There was only now and here. Only this moment in Peter's arms and the deepening desire to find fulfillment in his embrace. Dark shadows of the past held no terror, for they were forgotten.

"So what is this now?" Peter whispered into her hair. "Are we doing research?"

"Definitely," she said. She kissed the corner of his mouth, then blazed a tiny trail down to his neck. "The more we do, the better the end result."

"We could be at this a while," he said.

"I hope so."

His hands were under her sweatshirt again, loosening her bra so her breasts were free. He touched them, cupped them, ran his fingers over their surface. Her breath came faster, her hunger for more of his touch came on stronger.

"Might be very late when we're done," he warned.

"That's okay. This is my night to stay up."

His hands stopped their caress, and she felt lonely, abandoned. She frowned at him. What was wrong? Had she done something? Not done something?

"What do you say we adjourn to someplace with a little more room?" he said.

She had dreamed of that bedroom, of lying there beneath a blanket of stars, but she couldn't. Not yet. That was Kelly's room. Kelly's bed. She looked into Peter's eyes. He wasn't Kelly's husband anymore, at least not tonight, not with that hunger for her in his eyes.

She looked at the floor. "Looks like lots of room right here."

He frowned at her, confusion and concern colliding in his eyes. "Why? Are you worried that I—"

She covered his mouth with the tips of her fingers. "Because I love this room," she said. "There's only one thing I'd change."

He just stared at her, so she got up and turned off the light by his chair, then the light in the entryway. In the semi darkness of the night, she found her way back across the living room and pulled open the drapes. The night spilled into the room. Stars danced across the sky and into her heart.

"Now it's perfect," she whispered and, taking him by the hand, she pulled him to the floor.

Under the blessing of the stars, she slowly pulled off her sweatshirt, then her bra. Peter lay her back onto the thick white rug and kissed her. First her lips until she couldn't breath, then her neck, creating a necklace of feather-light kisses until she thought her heart would stop. Then his lips caressed her breasts, tugging, holding, teasing her nipples until she felt the stars rising up to meet her.

"You're so beautiful," he whispered.

She couldn't speak, her voice was lost amid the night somewhere. She'd never felt so cherished, so wanted. Her hands tugged at the buttons on his shirt, then pushed it off his shoulders. She wanted to run her fingers over his chest, to feel his heart beating beneath her touch. She wanted to belong, to be possessed.

Suddenly Peter's touch was fevered. An urgency had crept into the darkness and swallowed them. Their needs took over, their hearts cried out for fulfillment. Hands stroked heatedly, with purpose and insistence.

It was suddenly so right and necessary. It was what life was all about. They came together in the darkness. She took his passion inside her and together they exploded into wonder and joy and contentment. The stars came down to meet them and carried them up to the heavens. Then ever so slowly, wrapped in each other's arms, they floated back to earth.

Peter stopped at the closed bedroom door, his hand on the knob. Sure, Merry was in there and he didn't know if she was dressed yet, but why should that matter? It wasn't as if they didn't know each other. After all, people who make love, sleep together and then make love again-in the morning can hardly classify themselves as strangers.

"Oh, hell," he muttered, knocking lightly on the door. "I'm about to put the omelets on. Are you almost ready?"

"Ready when you are, Freddy."

Suddenly the door opened and he started back. Merry leaned against the doorjamb, dressed only in his black Bulls championship T-shirt. The sight caused everything to tighten up on him. With her white skin and red hair, she looked like no other woman he'd ever seen.

"Hello, sailor. Looking for anything special?"

Peter cleared his throat. "Cheese-and-bacon omelet okay?"

"Sure."

A tightness appeared around Merry's mouth. Maybe she'd wanted him to say something else, but he didn't know what. He wasn't sure how to act or what to think. This was all new territory for him, and he definitely didn't feel at ease.

"I could run out and get a green pepper if you want," he said.

She shook her head. "Whatever you have is fine. I'm flexible."

She certainly was, but then she was many things. As well as flexible, Merry was strong, Merry was...

Merry was hungry. His face warmed. Merry was hungry for an omelet and so was he. Peter turned on his heel and hurried toward the kitchen. Soft footsteps behind him told him that Merry was following.

"Need any help?"

"No."

"Are you sure?"

"Quite sure," he snapped. "I normally live alone, you know."

She looked uncertain for a moment, then sat down at the small table in the kitchenette. He went about making the omelets and pouring the orange juice and coffee.

All right, so he hadn't meant to snap at her. It was just that he didn't know how he was supposed to handle all this. Did it change things between them? Would she think it did?

Neither spoke as they ate breakfast. Merry didn't seem as hungry as usual. Maybe she wasn't a morning person or maybe he wasn't reacting right. Sighing internally, he sipped at his coffee. Damn.

"This is cold," he said. "Want a warm-up?"

She shook her head.

Boy, he certainly was handling this smoothly. What did she want from him? Maybe more importantly, how did *he* feel about things now? He peered deep into his soul. Damn! He didn't know.

"You still want me go to your mother's with you?"

"Huh?" That was an intelligent response. It wasn't that he hadn't heard her. His mind was just out of sync with his senses.

"I said, do you—"

"Yeah, yeah. Of course. Why not?" He forced a laugh out of his throat. "I still need a bodyguard."

She nodded and stared into her cup. "Good."

"Is it still okay with you?" he asked. "I mean, if you have something else planned...."

"I don't."

"That's good."

"I just didn't know if you'd want to change your mind."

"No," he protested. "Why would I?"

She shrugged. "You know, sometimes you do things with a guy and..." she hesitated, wagging her head from side to side "...and things change."

"Change?" Who was thinking up this dialogue for him? Wasn't change just what he was worried about?

"Yeah," she replied.

They stared at each other a long moment. He tried to read her eyes, but failed miserably. Was she saying last night had changed things for her? Did she want them to change or not want them to? He took a chance.

"It would be dumb if it did," he said.

"Yeah," she agreed.

"I mean, if we're friends, we're friends."

"Right."

"If we're not, we're not."

"Right."

So which were they? They shared another well of silence that brought him no answers.

"Want another omelet?"

"No," she said, standing up. "I'm full to overflowing. Gonna have to walk some extra miles the way it is."

He stood up and started clearing the table. "I've heard that ice-skating is even better," Peter said. "It burns more energy."

"It does?" She began rinsing the dishes in the sink.

"Yeah." He took the dishes from Merry and put them into the dishwasher. "They've opened up the ice rink downtown. Wanna go one of these days?"

"Yeah," she said shrugging. "I guess. You want to?"

He shrugged. "It might be fun."

"Stuff like that is always more fun when you do it with friends."

"Oh, absolutely."

They stood in the center of his kitchen, looking everywhere but at each other. He wanted to take her into his arms again and relive the magic they'd found last night, but he couldn't. Passion had burned away at his senses, but the fires were under control now. The bright light of reality was shining down on him, and he felt blinded by all the possible directions that lay before them. Rather than take a misstep, he didn't move at all.

"I'd better get going," she said. "I have to clean my room."

"I should do some shopping for Sean."

They nodded in unison.

"See you," he said.

"Right."

Chapter Nine

"Maybe Prince Charming is off on a business trip."

Merry spun away from the window, turning her wrath on the gray-haired bartender. "If you want to be wearing that smile on the back of your head, Willy, then keep putting your nose where it doesn't belong."

"Hey, ease up," Willy said, raising his hands in surrender. "I'm sorry."

She continued glaring at him, but the fire of her anger was already fizzling out. It was too damn bad that Willy was such a nice, old guy. Merry was just aching to mix it up with someone.

"That's all right," Merry said. "Sorry I took a bite out of you."

"No problem," he replied with a soft smile. "That's what us old guys are for."

She turned back to stare out the window. It had warmed up a bit today. That meant instead of a bitter-cold wind there were gray clouds hanging overhead, threatening to dump rain on them at any minute.

"I'm probably right," Willy said. "You know how it is with these big-business hotshots. There ain't a minute they can call their own. They got phone calls, meetings, trips out of town, what have you."

"Yeah," she agreed.

Except that she wasn't watching out the window, fretting because Peter hadn't come to lunch yet. No, she was worrying that he would. She just wasn't ready to face him yet. What had she been thinking of Saturday night? Actually, thinking hadn't entered the picture at all.

Hell, she'd practically jumped on his bones. A pleasurable warmth returned to the far points of her body, but she refused to let it sway her. She had goals to reach, goals that were still years away. She couldn't afford to have someone distracting her from them.

Yet here she was, staring out the window for a glimpse of him like some love-struck teenager. Afraid he wasn't coming and afraid that he was.

It was obvious that they couldn't be friends anymore. She should have known better than to hook up with a smooth-talking moneybag. He'd wined and dined and romanced her, whispered sweet nothings in her ear and put her under his spell better than any hypnotist.

Well, she was going to have to send out some signals, strong and clear. Bye, bye. Adios. Farewell. Goodbye.

There'd be no skating date. No nothing date anymore. If she had to go to Mentone with him, she would, for Sean's sake. But it would be all business. She'd let her feelings for a man run her life once and was still trying to recover from it. It definitely was not going to happen again.

Suddenly her trip to White Pigeon tomorrow morning loomed importantly. It would refocus her, set her feet on the right path again. Jason was the center of her life, not Peter.

"Guess he was just running late today."

Willy's voice cleared enough of the fog from her eyes to see Peter standing outside the restaurant talking to someone. Her heart quivered at the sight of him; her resolution wobbled. She wanted to smile and dance, to run over and greet him, to bask in his smile forever.

She had to go. She couldn't stay here and see him. It was obvious that her heart wasn't strong enough, not yet.

"Willy, I'm gonna duck out a little early. Remind Denise that I won't be in for two days, will you?"

"You gotta go now?"

"I surely do," she replied.

"What about your gentleman friend?"

"I'm not the only waitress in this place," she said. "Someone else can wait on him."

She had to get out while she could. Maybe she was being a coward, but there were some things that were more important than childish name-calling. Like her sanity.

"Merry!"

Damn. She'd been too slow.

She turned, pasting a bright smile on her lips. "Hi, Peter. How you doing?"

"Starving to death."

His eyes were laughing, inviting her to join in. Oh, how she wanted to! She would have liked nothing better than to dive into his arms and let him hold her until forever was over. She had an overwhelming need to belong, to put an end to the parade of lonely nights.

But that was just being weak. The very reason she'd wanted to leave before he'd seen her. Whatever silliness her heart wanted to indulge in, her mind knew better.

"Want your regular table?" she asked.

"Any'll do." He nodded toward the nearest one. "This is your station?"

Her heart wavered. Those brown eyes could make her smile, make her feel alive. Why was she being so silly?

What harm would it do to serve him lunch? They were friends, after all.

They'd been lovers, her mind contradicted. And now she was acting like a lovesick schoolgirl.

"Actually, it doesn't matter," she said before she lost her nerve. "I was just on my way out."

"You were?" His voice echoed his disappointment, his eyes were shadowed with regret. He looked like a little kid who'd come too late to see Santa.

Merry stiffened her resolve. "I was taking off a little early today."

Those eyes were on her, bringing back memories of passion and tenderness, of longing and fulfillment. For a few minutes the other night, he had been everything to her, but those moments had passed. She had to cling to her own life, her own path. She would make no explanations.

Merry smiled at him. "I'll get Lona to take care of you. She won't let you starve." She glanced around and spotted the waitress coming out of the kitchen. "Lona, can you take care of this customer?"

"Sure thing, Merry. Be right there." She sent a smile their way as she went to deliver a bowl of soup.

"The chicken noodle was great today," Merry told Peter. "But I'd stay away from the patty melt. I had a number of complaints."

"Can't you—"

"Oops, look at the time," Merry cried, glancing toward the clock before she grinned at Peter. "Gotta run. See ya."

This time she did escape and didn't falter a step, even though she felt his eyes on her back and his hurt in the air. There were times when a girl had to take care of herself.

"Oh, Lordy," Merry gasped as she fought the steering wheel and attempted to bring the rental car under control. "You'd better pay attention to business, gal. Else you're going to roll this heap and let the whole three-county area know that LuEllen's little girl is back.''

Those dark clouds that had been hanging over the mountaintops when she'd landed in Charleston were fulfilling their promise now that evening had fallen. Huge snowflakes, just dripping with water, were covering the ground and making the roads slick and treacherous. The snow plus the mountains made for a devilish combination, and she breathed a sigh of relief as she eased the car back into the flow of traffic.

The palms of her hands were covered with sweat, and Merry wiped first the right, then the left on her jeans. She was rapidly becoming a basket case.

This was foolhardy. Absolutely crazy. She might be an adult now and not so vulnerable to Joe's threats, but there were just so many ways this whole thing could backfire. The paper could have gotten the date of the pageant wrong. Jason might have transferred schools and no longer be at Washington. Joe might recognize her and publicly humiliate her.

Worse, Jason could be miserable or ill or a spoiled brat, and there'd be nothing she could do about it. Or what if somehow the whole story came out and Jason rejected her? What if he treated her like dirt, the way his father had ten years ago?

If only she'd been able to talk this over with Peter. But then that had been a whole other something that had backfired.

She took a deep breath. She should have known better than to get involved in Peter's life in the first place. What made her think she could dictate her emotions? She'd gotten this far because she'd been so careful to avoid involvement. Now she had to back up, reassess things and find her path again. And stay on it, no matter what.

A sign appeared on the side of the road, warning that the speed limit would drop ahead. She was almost there.

Nothing would go wrong, she reassured herself. She had a long coat to hide her body, a dark wig to hide her red hair and wraparound sunglasses to mask her face. No one would recognize her. And if the paper was wrong, or Jason wasn't at that school anymore, it would be disappointing, but not the end of the world.

She rounded a bend and was suddenly in White Pigeon. It felt so much the same, she was scared. About two streets over was where Momma had moved with the kids about a year after Merry'd left, and somewhere around here was the jail her younger brother Billy had ended up in many a night. He had died in an alley fight about six years ago, just before Cassie'd run off. Momma died not too long after, and Merry lost track of the rest of her kin. She knew Robbie'd joined the army and Beth Ann had married some boy from school, but Merry thought they'd moved out west someplace. Jackson, the baby of the family, had been following in Billy's footsteps the last she'd heard.

She turned a corner and there was the drugstore where she used to get a soda after work on Saturdays. On the next block was Minnie's, the dress store where everybody bought their prom dresses. Well, not everybody. She'd never made it to that magic time. That blue satin with the tiny rosebuds had made someone else feel like a princess.

Swallowing hard, Merry drove on. The past didn't matter, just tonight. Tonight this town would hold nothing but happiness for her. She paused at a flickering yellow warning light, then proceeded through the intersection. The school was just down the street.

She drove past the parking lot. People were still heading toward the entrance, so she took another turn around the block. Best not to join the crowd going in. Strangers stuck out like sore thumbs around here. She'd go in when she could go in alone. If the performance had started, the lights would be dimmed and everyone's attention would be focused on stage.

The parking lot was deserted when she came back around, so she pulled in, putting the car into a slot over in a far corner. For a long moment, she just sat there, still gripping the steering wheel. Now that the moment was here, she was terrified. She longed for Peter's reassurance, for that look in his eye that made her feel anything was possible.

Finally, after gritting her teeth until her jaw muscles ached, Merry undid her seat belt and got out of the car. She didn't need Peter to tell her she was competent. She wasn't some weak, simpering little miss who couldn't do a thing without a man to protect her. She moved across the deserted parking lot like a rabbit crossing a road, ready to dart at any shadow.

She had timed it well. The performance had already started, and no one was standing in the halls as she approached the auditorium. Even the collecting table was empty, so Merry just left a five-dollar bill. She picked up a program, her stomach tying itself in knots as her eyes scanned the list of students.

There he was! Jason Byron O'Connell, her son. Merry's knees felt weak, her eyes stupidly watery. Geez, it was just his name, she scolded herself. Taking a deep breath, she went into the auditorium.

The munchkins up on stage were all dressed as Christmas trees, looking absolutely adorable as they sang their hearts out. They must be kindergartners. She slumped against the back wall as the tears returned.

Jason had once been that age, probably wearing the same mixture of solemnity and terror as most of those kids. But she hadn't been there to watch his fledgling steps.

Her eyes closed and she saw another little boy, one just at this age now. Did Peter know how special all these little moments in Sean's life were? Did he realize how they'd never come again? If only she could make him see all he was missing, realize how precious every second was. But to so that she'd have to knock down that wall he'd built around his heart and she suspected that even Sean couldn't do that.

She put her hands in her coat pockets, the fingers of her right hand wrapping themselves around the small throw-away camera she'd bought.

The little critters were being herded offstage and the whole scene began swimming before Merry. She took a deep breath and gripped her lower lip with her teeth. Her plan was to be inconspicuous. Bursting into tears would sure put the kibosh to that. Just concentrate on the show and don't think, she admonished herself.

Fortunately, the first-, second- and third-grade performances went by quickly. When the principal came on to announce the fourth grade, Merry had only a slight tremor in her hands. She held the camera tightly, staring hard at the stage. The kids marched out, dressed in their Sunday best.

Her throat tightened up, her breath seemed gone as she searched each boy's face as he came onto the stage. What if she didn't recognize him? She had been so sure....

He was there. One of the last to come onto the stage, but it had to be him, with Joe's height and her red hair. He settled in his place on the riser and smiled slightly. She bit her lip. He had her brother Robbie's smile. The scene blurred before her, and she swiped impatiently at her eyes.

The class started their performance with "The Twelve Days of Christmas," but Merry barely heard the words. Her eyes scoured Jason's face, trying to read his childhood in a few moments. Was that a scar on his chin? How'd he get it? He seemed to be squinting slightly. Was it just the lights or did he need glasses?

She slid forward along the side wall, needing to be closer. The boy next to him must be a friend because they kept nudging each other. Their little grins told of unspoken

conspiracies, and she felt incredibly left out. She didn'
even know his friend's name.

Jason was so tall, getting close to her height, and s
grown up that he barely seemed a child anymore. She ha
missed his whole childhood. He would be a teenager soon
and she hadn't seen any of the pieces that had made hir
who he was.

Tears began to flow, but they were silent tears, and Merr
didn't even try to stop them. Granny had always said ther
was no sense crying over spilled milk, and she was right
But sometimes the tears just had to come out. Sometime
a body was so sad that there was no way to stop them.

The little boy she'd carried for nine months under he
heart, the one who squirmed and kicked like he was to
alive to be cooped up inside her, the tiny, squawling chil
she'd held for such a few precious moments, was suddenl
tall and confident.

And a stranger.

She'd let him go because she'd had nothing to offer him
and he hadn't missed her in the slightest. It was how i
should be. It was how she wanted it to be. But, oh, Lordy
how it hurt!

The tears started to come down even harder, and Merr
fought to blink them away. She couldn't fall apart now, no
yet.

But then the kids were marching off the stage. Her mo
ment with Jason was almost over. She pulled out her cam
era, trying to find Jason through the viewfinder and failing
miserably. She dropped it slightly, her eyes searching fran
tically, but he was already gone. His row of the risers wa
empty.

Stupid, stupid, stupid! Joe had been right. She was jus
a stupid nobody who couldn't do anything right. This wa
her one chance to have something to hold and cherish an
she blew it.

She turned and ran out of the auditorium, tripping over numerous unseen feet along the way. Hot tears poured down her face, but she didn't care. Soon she was outside and running for the car.

Damn Joe O'Connell. Damn him and all the rich guys of the world.

She managed to get into the car just as she started to sob, but she started the motor, anyway, and pulled out of the parking lot. The car somehow found the route back to Charleston.

Damn their rotten deal.

Joe's deal was that he would take the baby and give him advantages that she couldn't even dream of. All she had to do was stay away from Jason the rest of his life. No big deal, at least not in Joe's mind.

The snow was coming down harder now, and Merry turned the windshield wipers up to their top speed. She shouldn't have come. She should have kept up her end of the agreement. Occasionally missing a shadowy figure would have been a snap compared to missing the tall, red-haired boy with the wide grin. With her grin.

Suddenly the tears were flowing as if a dam had burst and along with them came painful, gut-racking sobs that shook her whole self. She finally had to pull over to the side of the road; there was no way she could continue.

She didn't know whether it was two minutes or two hours, but she cried and cried and cried until there were no more tears, then she cried some more. She cried because her son'd never get to know how much she loved him. She cried because she'd never gotten to hug him when he'd hit a home run or hold him when he scraped his knee. And she cried because Peter didn't understand what a precious thing he was letting slip through his fingers.

Eventually she was too exhausted. There were no more tears, no more pain. Just a growing anger seeking a focus.

It was too late to walk her son to school his first day, to take him trick-or-treating or to see his first baseball game, but it wasn't too late for Peter. How could he turn his back on what she'd give half her life to have?

"I called you," Peter said. "No one would tell me where you were."

He'd had a lousy couple of days—battling a cold, up to his neck in projects at work and trying to buy Christmas presents even though he didn't know what anybody wanted or the size they wore. He'd needed her smile, her teasing, her laughter, but she seemed to have fallen off the face of the earth.

Merry didn't reply, concentrating instead on lacing up her skates. When she was finished, she stood up to stretch her legs. They were very nice legs, but Peter wasn't up to admiring them.

"I wondered what happened to you." He could hear the growing tension in his voice but didn't try to control it. He didn't like needing her, and certainly didn't like admitting to himself that he did. "After all, we did have a date."

"Not really," she said as she started to skate in small circles near him. Her voice was as cold as the ice she stood on. "We said we'd go skating sometime."

"I assumed 'sometime' meant sometime soon. Like in the next day or so." He finished lacing up his own skates and got to his feet. The world felt wobbly and uncertain beneath him, not a feeling he liked. It made his voice snappish. "You were damn rude going off without saying anything."

"I didn't think I had to report in to you," she said, slowing to a stop.

"You don't. But you've never taken off like that before." He sounded angry and impatient even to himself, but he didn't care. He'd thought they'd been friends, that she was someone who understood his pain, but obviously he'd been wrong.

"I didn't just take off," she said. "I had to go out of town for a couple of days, that's all. You go off all the time. Aren't I allowed to do the same?"

What was with her? Two days ago at the restaurant she'd been rushed but fine. He'd been worrying that somehow that night of love would change their comfortable relationship, but she had seemed just fine. So what had happened in the meantime?

"Of course you're allowed to go out of town," he said. "But I would have thought you owed me the courtesy of letting me know. I always tell you."

Her eyes were chips of ice. "That sounds an awful lot like a relationship," she said. "I didn't think you wanted to be that close to anybody. Not even to Sean."

He felt like the floor had been knocked from beneath him. Anger was the nearest thing to cling to. "What the hell is that supposed to mean?"

"Exactly what I said. You've locked yourself in an ivory tower and seem to be quite proud of the way you've shut everybody else out."

"You make it sound like some choice I've made."

"Haven't you?"

"No, I haven't." Who was she to question his love for his son? She was a drifter by her own admission, someone who'd probably never made a minute's commitment to someone else. "And I happen to love Sean very much."

"I don't think you know the meaning of the word love."

Suddenly his anger made it all crystal clear and it wasn't a pleasant revelation. "Oh, I get it now," he said. "This all goes back to the other night, doesn't it? I was supposed to say some magic words and I didn't, so you punished me by refusing my calls. Was I supposed to just declare my love and propose marriage, too?"

Even as her eyes blazed, her hand swung out and slapped him on the cheek. It was a hard, stinging blow that almost knocked him off his feet. His hand automatically went up to rub his cheek, but their eyes stayed locked. Anger, betrayal, regret all mingled in their gazes.

Christmas carols blared out over the loudspeakers, but they couldn't drown out the angry words. They hung there like dark storm clouds hanging over an Indiana cornfield.

In that long moment, he saw that he'd been wrong. Whatever the reason why he hadn't been able to reach her, it had nothing to do with her expectations of him. Fear of this strangely argumentative Merry had made him act stupidly. He took a deep breath and looked away.

He knew only one thing for certain—that they were through now. His stupidity had made sure of that. Well, it was probably for the best. They'd been seeing too much of each other and that would just lead to problems that neither of them wanted, anyway.

"You don't have to come to Mentone with me over the holidays," he said.

She shrugged, her anger seemed to have dissipated also. "I don't mind going, but I won't if you don't want me."

If he didn't want her? Want didn't begin to describe the feelings raging in his heart, but he couldn't actually put a title to them. All he knew was that the intensity of his emotions scared him. They were stronger than they had any right to be, than he wanted them to be.

What happened to his isolated existence? He'd been happy alone, concentrating on existing, on staying a safe distance from smiles that warmed the chill in his soul and eyes that set fire to his heart.

Peter looked into Merry's blue eyes. Just a second ago they had been filled with the fires of anger. Now they mirrored only the clouds of despair. He wanted nothing more than to take her in his arms, but he couldn't.

"I don't want to impose on you," he said softly.

"I told your mother I'd be there."

"She'll understand."

"I told Sean I'd see him."

He felt his shoulders slump in defeat. What the heck could he tell a five-year-old kid? Daddy made an ass of himself and now Merry hated him for it?

Chapter Ten

"There's a lot more snow here than in Chicago," Peter said.

From the corner of his eye, he saw Merry look out the passenger-side window. She stared at the snow-covered expanse stretching from one end of the horizon to the other. The stubble-filled sea of brown that they'd sailed through on their last trip to Mentone was now winter white.

"That's lake-effect snow," he added.

"I see," she replied without looking at him.

"The cold air moves across Canada from west to east," he explained. "In the winter a portion of that air mass called the Alberta Clipper dips down into the Midwest. It picks up moisture as it passes over Lake Michigan, which is still relatively warm, and turns it into snow. Which, in keeping with the holiday spirit, then dumps it on Indiana and Michigan."

"Interesting," Merry said.

"That's why the average temperature is colder on the west side of the lake, while the average precipitation is greater on the east side."

"Very interesting."

"Well, at least I'm trying to keep up a conversation."

"Peter, I'm not asking you to keep up anything."

Her words had such a tone of sorrow to them. He looked her full in the face for a moment. Merry's eyes matched the sadness she carried in her voice.

"Merry, I'm sorry I said that the other day."

"I know." Her voice carried more weariness than anger. "This whole thing has been a mistake from the beginning. Nothing has gone right."

Nothing? There had been moments when he'd thought things had been pretty great.

"I think I'll take a nap," she said. "I've been up late studying for exams."

Before she barely finished her sentence, she had let her seat back down slightly and faced away from him. Peter swallowed the soft words on his tongue. Years of marriage had trained him well in reading a woman's stiff back. It clearly said that she didn't want to talk anymore. He turned his full attention to driving.

"Peter." Her voice was soft and tentative.

"Yes?" His was careful and cautious.

"If you get tired of driving, I'll be glad to take my turn."

"That's okay."

"Just let me know."

"Sure."

Peter slumped back in his seat. It was going to be a long trip to Mentone, no matter who drove. He didn't think Santa Claus himself could bring any joy to this trip.

Maybe it would have been better if they'd just called it quits a few days ago. Yet he hadn't been able to do that, not so abruptly. Once they were back in Chicago for good, they would no doubt drift apart, but there'd been too many people expecting her this time. He hadn't wanted to disappoint them all.

He stopped at Bourbon where he made his usual almost-home call. "Hi, Mom. I'm at Bourbon and everything's going along fine." Merry wasn't talking to him and he was down in the dumps, but otherwise things were just ginger peachy-keen.

"That's good," she replied. "And how is Merry?"

"Fine." As far as he could tell. "How is Sean? Is he over his cold?"

"Oh, my, yes. He's all excited about Christmas and eating cookies by the ton."

"That's good," Peter replied.

"Well, there's no need keeping you. Everybody is anxious to visit with you and Merry again. So the sooner I let you go, the sooner you'll be home."

"We'll be there in about a half hour."

Merry didn't stir as he got back into the car. Though he would have liked to get some things more settled between them, he was glad she was able to get some rest. Working from about ten o'clock to four or five each day, then having classes each evening would wear out anybody. He was surprised that she hadn't worn herself out earlier.

As he made the turn for Etna Green, Peter cleared his throat. Merry stirred and rolled over slightly. She looked so soft, so vulnerable as she awoke from sleep. Normally she was strong and tough, needing nobody, but just for a moment he could believe she needed protection and sheltering. He had either been incredibly stupid or naive in believing that they could be just friends.

"We're almost there," he said and paused a moment. "We should try and act at least semifriendly."

"I know that." She put her seat back in an upright position. "I have no intention of ruining your mother and Sean's holiday."

How about my holiday? How about your holiday? he wanted to ask, but he knew that no answers would be forthcoming. At least no answers that would bring happiness back into their relationship.

Merry spent the rest of the trip checking out her hair and face in a small mirror. Peter could have told her that everything was perfect, but he knew that she wasn't really looking at herself. She was an actress psyching herself up to play a tough role. He wished he had the training that would get him through the next two weeks.

He turned onto the street and saw his mother and Sean standing on the front porch along with Belle. By the time he parked the car, they were down the steps, waving and otherwise acting disgustingly happy.

"Merry Christmas," Sean shouted, jumping up and down and clapping his hands.

"Merry Christmas." Merry's face was bathed in what looked like genuine excitement as she hugged Sean and then Peter's mother.

Peter said his hellos and then got the bags.

"Santa's coming soon," Sean told them all. Belle barked, probably adding her orders for Santa in canine.

Peter shut the trunk and, picking up the bags, turned toward the porch. His mother intercepted him.

"Welcome home, Peter." She gave him a vigorous hug. "Smile. This won't hurt."

Oh, great, he thought. She was really in a good mood. How the hell was he going to keep up pretenses for two weeks? Maybe he'd be lucky and get hit by a truck before the day was out.

"Come in. Come in," his mother said, shooing them into the house. "Come in before you catch your death of cold."

Belle helped with the herding and they were quickly in the house, stamping snow off their shoes. His mother went around collecting coats.

"We got cookies," Sean told Merry. "Lots of 'em."

"Can I have some?" she asked.

A crafty look came over his son's face as he pondered that question for a moment. "Three," Sean replied, holding up that number of fingers.

"Sean," his grandmother protested. "That's not nice."

"But she's big," Sean said. "She'll eat 'em all."

"I surely would, ma'am," Merry assured Peter's mother. "I surely would."

The three of them laughed, but the best Peter could do was a smile. He watched as they reveled in their holiday cheer, passing it back and forth like a beach ball that they weren't going to let him play with.

"Peter, let's quit this lollygagging," his mother said briskly. "Get the bags upstairs. You two have the same rooms as before." Then she turned toward Merry and said. "Zachary was quite anxious for your return."

"Yeah," Sean agreed. "He wanted someone warm to sleep with."

"We all do, honey," his grandmother replied with a wink at Peter. "We all do."

Peter thought that he'd been carrying a heavy load of depression when he came into the house, but his load just picked up a partner. He could hardly lift their bags.

Get ahold of yourself, he scolded silently. At least pretend you're having a good time.

Peter walked toward them from the little shed on the edge of the parking lot. He carried an ax and saw in his hands and a smile on his lips.

"Okay, guys," he said. "Let's do it."

"Right," Sean agreed. "Let's do it."

They were at a cut-it-yourself Christmas-tree farm, ready to harvest their yule tree. Sean was sparkling like a Christmas star and even Peter was bright and cheerful, apparently having left his mopies behind. Although she tried to control it, Merry felt a childlike excitement growing within her own heart.

"I'm ready," Merry said.

"Daddy, can I ride on your back?"

"Aren't you getting a little big for that?"

"Nope," Sean replied, shaking his head vigorously.

"I'll carry the tools," Merry said.

She took the tools from Peter as he bent down for Sean to jump onto his back. Bundled up in a snowsuit with boots and thick mittens covering his extremities, "jumping" wasn't quite possible, but with Merry's help, he was soon aboard. Peter stood up and Sean grinned at Merry, sending a quivering warmth all through her.

"The best trees are over this way," Peter said as he hitched Sean into a more comfortable position. "On the west side of the property."

Merry nodded, and they marched up the snow-crusted path with Peter slightly to the front of her. She was doing all right. It was hard keeping her emotions in check around Peter, but she was managing. Slowly but surely, her anger over what he was missing in Sean's life was dying out and she was able to just relax.

"This has become a tradition for us," Peter told her.

"Yeah," Sean added. "And we do it every Christmas."

"That's the way to do it, sport," Merry said.

It was good to see the little guy smile. He was usually so solemn that she often wondered if Sean had the heart of a little, old man. But then his young life had taken more hits than normal.

"How about that one?" Peter asked, pointing at a tree ahead of them. It was lightly dusted with snow and looked just beautiful.

"Nope," Sean said. "Too short."

"Hey, it's taller than I am."

"Grandma says you're always getting trees that are too short. She said they look like little midgets when you bring them into the house."

"What does Grandma know?" Peter asked.

"She knows everything."

"Oh, yeah?"

"Yeah."

Merry smiled at the byplay between father and son, but refused to let it touch her. Peter was an adult; he could run his life the way he wanted. She didn't have any right to agree or disagree. And it wasn't as if Sean were being mistreated.

She looked around her at the acres of evergreen trees covering the gently rolling hills and inhaled the wonderful scent of pine needles. The air was brisk and sharp; there was the promise of more snow in the wings. She should treasure this time as an interlude of peace.

"What do you say?" Peter asked her. "Is this tree too small or not?"

She suddenly found both sets of eyes on her and turned back to the tree. If she agreed it was a good choice, the time out here would soon be over. "Let's look at a few more."

Peter made a low growling sound.

She patted his arm. It was the first time she chanced a playful gesture since they had argued, and she felt a comforting rush of familiarity. "Your mother said the tree goes in the living room," she said. "And you've got a nine- or ten-foot ceiling there."

"Ha, ha, Daddy." Sean obviously took it as his victory.

"You want to get dumped on your head?"

The boy squealed in mock fear as he squeezed his arms tighter around Peter's neck. Merry laughed as they walked along, the joy of Christmas swallowing her up. She was right to have pulled back, to have recognized that her heart was becoming just a little too attached to Peter, but she was wrong to have let her hurt over losing Jason spill out into anger.

"How about this one?" Peter asked.

"Too skinny," Sean cried, making a face.

"That one?"

"Too crooked," Merry said.

She'd never put much thought into a tree before. Back home, the boys would go out and get one a few days before Christmas; then they'd all decorate it with colored paper and pictures cut out of magazines. But now, for this Christmas, the perfect tree seemed of real importance. As if it would somehow heal all their hurts and make them whole again.

Suddenly Merry saw it. "This one. Let's take this one."

"Yeah," Sean shouted in agreement.

"You guys sure?" Peter asked. "I mean, it's shorter than the pyramids."

She and Sean just exchanged glances and secret smiles.

"Okay, okay." Peter let Sean slide to the ground. "I was just asking." He took the tools from Merry and prepared to notch the tree trunk.

"Dad, no," Sean cried. "We got to talk to it first."

Suddenly Peter's holiday joy vanished like a rabbit in the brush. Darkness seemed to hover over him. "That's okay, Sean," he said softly. "We don't have to always do everything the same."

"Yeah, we do. What if it's not ready? Then it'll be sad all Christmas."

"Sean, please."

The boy turned toward Merry, his eyes were watery, his smile gone. "My mother always talked to the tree before we cut it down. She told it all about Christmas. And she told it how it would make everyone happy by coming into our house. She said only a happy tree was a good Christmas tree."

Merry didn't know what to say. It was obvious that Sean's holiday joy rested on a very fragile foundation.

"Come on, Sean," Peter said softly. "Things change."

"My Mommy died," Sean said, still talking to Merry.

"Yes, I know," Merry murmured. She stooped down to be at his eye level. "Your dad told me."

"I bet she's already talked to this tree," Peter said.

Sean turned to him, a flicker of hope just barely visible in his eye. "How do you know? Did she tell you she did?"

Peter hesitated, obviously not comfortable with the little white lie.

"She doesn't talk to me, either," Sean said, the flicker of hope gone. His voice was lifeless as he turned toward Merry again. "Grandma says that Mommy lives on a star."

Merry just nodded and took his little hand in hers.

"She says that I can talk to her. And she says that Mommy'll talk back to me." He looked down at the ground and shivered. "She says I gotta listen real hard."

"Come on, Sean." Peter's voice was almost a whisper, pain spilling out over them all. "Let me cut the tree and we'll get on home. Grandma has cookies and hot chocolate waiting for us."

"I listen hard." Sean was either ignoring Peter or not hearing him. "Real hard but—"

"I'll talk to the tree," Merry said.

The words just burst out of her mouth, but there was no way she was going to pull them back. If talking to a tree was going to ease this pain just a tiny bit, it was an easy price to pay.

"But are you a mommy?" Sean stared at her. His eyes were two sparkling bubbles of hope floating in a sea of doubt. "Only mommies can talk to trees."

There was no other way around the task at hand. "Yeah, sport," she said softly. "I'm a mommy."

His smile was like the sun popping through a break in the clouds. Merry closed her own eyes for a moment.

"Okay, guys," she said, stepping up to the tree. "Here goes nothing."

"You don't have to talk too long," Sean warned her.

"Right, sport," Merry replied. "We don't want the cookies and hot chocolate spoiling. Do we?"

Sean just grinned, looking suddenly like a regular little boy. Maybe there was such a thing as magic. She turned to the tree, staring hard at it, but couldn't think of what to say.

"Well, Mr. Tree, the holidays are upon us and the MacAllisters here are in need of a Christmas tree. Are you willing?"

The three of them stared at the tree and waited. No answer was forthcoming.

"The cookies are all baked and most of the presents are wrapped, along with some presents for poorer folks. There's gonna be a whole passel of folks over the next week or so and we'd be mighty honored to have you visit us for a spell." Merry looked down at Sean.

He nodded. "I think the tree wants to come to our house now, Daddy."

With just a slight nod of his head, Peter notched the tree, then they each took a turn at the saw. Once the tree was down, they carried it to the car and tied it to the roof.

Nobody talked much on the way home. Sean dozed, leaning against Merry while she sat with her arm around him, staring ahead. After stopping the car at a stoplight, Peter just turned to smile at her. There was so much in his glance—gratitude, joy and even a little sadness. She reached for his hand and squeezed it. It had been a special time.

He leaned over then, kissing her with the briefest of touches. So many emotions raced through her that she couldn't begin to sort out her feelings. An exquisite kind of joy tried to drown out the confusion and pain, the loneliness and wondering. For the moment, she let her soul be wreathed in sunshine.

* * *

"This is Rudolph," Sean said, holding aloft a reindeer ornament made out of clothespins. "I made him in school."

"Hey, he's pretty super," Merry said. "Where should he go?"

"Near Santa."

Sean tried to hang the ornament's loop over a branch, but his little fingers had trouble and Merry had to help him. His eyes were so solemn, his mouth so determined that she just wanted to hug him to pieces.

"Don't put too many ornaments on yet," Peter warned. "Let me get the lights up right first."

"But Merry can't wait, Daddy," Sean said. "You gotta hurry."

"Merry can't wait?"

Peter's eyes met hers in laughter, and a wonderful, warm sensation coursed through her. All the more special because of its rarity as of late. There had been so much anger, so much misunderstanding between them; it was nice to share a smile.

She wished she could sort through the mess and find the friendship they'd had. Why couldn't things be simple? Why couldn't life be simple?

"Are they done yet?" Sean pestered.

Peter started, as if suddenly awoken, and quickly went back to stringing the lights. Merry grinned. Trust a little kid to keep things moving. She suddenly saw Jason at that age, saw his impatience and his eagerness as Joe would have put the lights on their tree. But someone else helped his little fingers with the hanging loops, not her.

She closed her eyes in sudden pain. She had a real face to put into her dreams now, and it brought a real pain along with it. Her imaginings were more substantial, and so was the hurt.

"All right. Flick the switch."

Sean raced to the corner, climbing into the chair, and turned the lights on. The room was bathed with a magical glow.

"Aw, right," the little boy said on a sigh. "It's boo-ti-ful."

There was so much wonder and awe in his eyes. What was it like to be so young and so full of dreams? To believe that anything and everything was possible? Yet he'd been touched by tragedy in his young life. Maybe you had to be young to be able to escape its shadow.

"I think we've got some ornament hanging to do," Merry said. She lifted him off the chair. "And I bet it's gonna look even more boo-ti-ful then."

"Yeah." Sean raced over to the boxes spread out on the coffee table and carefully lifted out a snowman.

"My goodness, you've all been working really hard." Mrs. MacAllister came into the room with a plate of cookies. "I brought a snack in case you were hungry, and me in case you needed some more help."

"I'm going to put Frosty on," Sean announced, holding up his ornament.

"Well, I should hope so. Can't be Christmas without him up there." The older woman joined Sean at the tree, helping him decide just where the snowman should go. "How about here?"

"I want him way, way up high."

"Oh, do you?" Peter said with a laugh. "Good thing we've got a tall tree then." He took the boy in his arms and helped him hang the ornament near the top.

Merry watched the three of them, not more than ten feet from her, but feeling a lifetime away. There was so much love here, it hurt. She could walk over to Peter's other side and he'd put his arm around her, partly out of pretense, partly out of friendship. She could pretend to be a part of their love for a time, if she wanted. She could close her memory to the deal she and Peter had struck and have a real

Christmas. But her feet wouldn't take her in that direction.

Instead, she went silently over to the sofa and sat looking at the ornaments, pretending that the colored balls and smiling elves were fascinating. In truth, she barely saw them. She was a fool to have come with Peter over Thanksgiving; she was a double fool to have come back over Christmas.

All this was was a reminder of what she had lost and what she would never have. It was so tempting to pretend to be part of it, but she wasn't and never would be. The longer she pretended, the greater the risk that she'd forget it was all pretense. The greater the risk that it would stop being pretense for her.

Jason was her goal, her life. Peter was a job.

"I really appreciate what you did earlier."

She looked up, finding Peter at her side. There was a seriousness in his eyes that bothered her. She felt vulnerable at the moment, weakened by the emotions set in play by the day, and chose to misunderstand rather than let him venture into forbidden ground.

"That's okay," she joked. "Sitting at a desk all week probably causes you to lose muscle tone real quick."

"I didn't mean your help in cutting down the tree," he said. "I meant how you helped with Sean."

Her gaze skittered away, avoiding his, but she said nothing.

"Besides, I exercise three times a week at the health club in my building."

"Glad to hear that, sport." She flicked the words out like dimes to a beggar, not even looking at him. You said your piece, now go, she silently told him. Leave me alone to repair the chinks in my wall.

"He really settled down after you talked to him," Peter said.

She glanced at him briefly. Don't say anything else, she pleaded. Just drop the whole thing.

"Especially when you told him you were a mommy so you could talk to the tree. He's too young to realize the incongruity of it all."

What? Her heart stopped. What was incongruous about her being a mother? She looked away, sudden secret tears burning in the back of her eyes. She would have been a good mother, in terms of love and caring, even if she'd had no money for bikes or fancy clothes. The suggestion she wouldn't have been a good one stung, and she wanted to strike back.

"It seemed the right direction for the script to take," she said, her voice distant and unemotional. "I hadn't planned for the role to be involved, but there's nothing I won't do to make my character more convincing."

He seemed stunned by her sudden harshness. "I'm sorry," he said. "If I'd realized the role would demand so much of you, I would have paid you more. As a matter of fact, we could still renegotiate the contract."

She'd had all she could take of his trampling all over her pain, however well-meaning it might be. "Stuff it," she said and turned on her heels, stalking off to the kitchen.

Chapter Eleven

Peter slumped against the frame of the wide double doors leading into the living room. Traditions ruled his mother's life, but the holidays were especially intense in that regard. The day before Christmas Eve she always invited the neighbors over for cookies and nonalcoholic punch.

His arm was tired from carrying a half glass of punch around all evening, but if he didn't do that, someone would be shoving food and drink in his face.

"Sure is a purty little filly," said their neighbor from across the street. Herb Janisek had gone to grade school with Peter's father, and speaking his mind was the one thing he did best these days. "Got that big smile, pert as a new puppy and sharp as a whip."

Peter didn't ask who Herb was talking about. Merry had charmed the whole county. Charmed him, too, to a certain extent, even though he knew this was all a game.

"Too many fillies today, they ain't nothin' but skin and bones. Got no grit or bottom to them. Can't carry their share of the load."

Merry sure carried her share, maybe more than her share. When she decided to settle down, some guy would be damned lucky. The thought ate at him for some reason.

"Daddy." Sean was tugging at Peter's sweater. "Daddy, can I have another cookie?"

"Sure."

Herb patted Sean on the head. "You're getting to be quite the young man," he said. "We're all gonna miss you when you go back to live with your dad."

"Oh, Sean loves it here. I don't expect him to be going for quite a while." Peter smiled at his son. "Just one cookie, kiddo. It's almost your bedtime."

Sean left as Herb's daughter came over to take his arm. "We should be getting on home, Pop."

"Here's the warden," Mr. Janisek growled. "She don't want me chasing no wild women."

"I had a chat with Merry," the woman told Peter. "She's a real nice person. And so funny. She must know a million jokes."

Funny? It seemed to him lately that Merry was having a hard time living up to her name. His eyes strayed over to the far corner and found her. A new set of neighbors surrounded her, and her smile was still stretched from coast to coast, but even at this distance Peter could sense a sadness in her eyes.

What had happened that afternoon? All he'd done was try to thank her for going above and beyond the call of duty to make Sean happy. He had replayed his words over and over in his mind and couldn't figure out what he'd said to offend her. But offend her he had, and most royally so. She'd barely said two words to him since then.

Some older woman had moved on to Merry, and Peter's conscience nipped at him. She had been alone long enough.

It was time for him to go over to her side and lend a help-ing hand, pretend that they were a couple. As Herb and his daughter left, Peter walked across the room.

"Hi," he said as he came on Merry. "How you holding up?"

"Just fine, sport. Just fine."

"What's with the 'sport' bit? Forget my name again?" His words were a gentle teasing, but she didn't respond.

At least, she didn't send him on his way. That could be because she was surrounded by their guests, though, not because of any warmer feelings on her part. He decided not to quibble over reasons, but to accept the gifts when the gods chose to bestow them. He sat on the arm of her chair, putting his arm around her shoulders.

"Can I get you anything? More punch? Some cook-ies?"

"No, I'm fine, but I think your mom might need some help. She told me she didn't, but you know how she is."

So much for not sending him on his way. He got to his feet. "I'll check on her."

Merry went right back to the conversation she'd been in the middle of, apparently not about to miss him in the slightest. But that's how it should be, he reminded himself as he went to the kitchen.

"Hi, Mom. Need any help?"

His mother didn't look up, but went on arranging some cookies on a plate. "You two been arguing? Merry was in here no more than two minutes ago, all by herself, looking to be helpful."

"We're just very helpful people," Peter said.

She made a face and looked at him sharply. "What are you two arguing about?"

"We're not arguing, Mom. Honest." How could they argue when they were barely talking to each other?

"You're a lucky man, Peter."

"Yeah, I suppose I am." He started putting sugar-coated crescents on another plate.

"Suppose nothing," his mother snapped. "You got your health, a beautiful little boy and now you have a fine lady."

"Sorry about the phrasing, Mom." He reached across her for the can of cherry-topped butter cookies. "I was just trying to be cool."

"You be careful you stay cool and don't cross over into cold."

Peter fought desperately to hold on to his smile. The only crossover problem he could see was in this conversation. It was moving into an area filled with mines. Even stepping carefully might not be enough to keep him safe.

"Sometimes people who've spent a good bit of their time swimming in a river of pain forget that." His mother's face hardened a bit. "Of course, talking to machines all day doesn't help any."

"Mom," he protested softly. "I don't talk to machines. I use computers in my work. There's a big difference, you know."

"She's been good for you, Peter."

Good for him? Why wasn't he sleeping, then? Why was he mad and irritable all the time? All he needed to top off his life at the moment was the plague. He opened the can of jam puffs.

"You've changed," his mother said. "You're gentler, more personable, more approachable. Your lady's worked her magic on you."

"Yep, that certainly describes her. Merry the Magician."

His mother took the can from his hands. "Go out and find your lady. Kiss and make up," his mother said. "That's the fun part of an argument."

"We're not arguing, Mom."

"So what? Is there a law that says you have to be mad at each other before you can kiss and make up?"

His mother grabbed him by the arm and dragged him to the door leading into the dining room. She looked over the holiday crowd filling their living and dining rooms with the air of Christmas cheer.

"Ahh, there she is," his mother exclaimed.

He saw Merry at the same time his mother did. She had moved and was now talking to one of the younger couples from the neighborhood.

"You'd better get out there and keep her entertained," his mother warned. "You don't and someone'll come along and snatch her on up. Then you'll be left with nothing."

Maybe he was happy with his nothing. "Have a heart, Mom. I spent a good part of the day tramping around the hills and cutting down a tree. All that fresh air and exercise is making me sleepy. I'm not up to entertaining. I need some shut-eye."

"Sounds to me like you need a little more excitement in your life. Get over there and give Merry a hug," his mother said. "That should set your blood to racing."

"Mom."

"That's if you don't let all those numbers get in the way of your normal male emotions."

"Thanks, Mom."

"Peter."

"I'm going," he snapped. "I'm going."

Peter moved slowly across the room toward Merry. His feet felt like lead and he was extra polite in moving around people. If he played his cards right, he shouldn't reach Merry until late tomorrow. That would keep away the pain of interacting with her. But not the pain of being away from her.

Damned if he did and damned if he didn't. Between a rock and a hard place. Right smack dab in the middle of cliché heaven.

As he got closer, Peter could see Merry was still wearing her mismatched combo of a broad smile and sad eyes. Her speech and hands appeared animated, but there were tiny lines of fatigue around her eyes and mouth.

What in the world was wrong with her tonight? She had seemed fine when they'd gotten the tree, and she'd been lively and funny as they'd decorated it. Her mood swings were totally baffling to him.

"How you doing?" Peter asked softly when he finally reached her side.

"Hey, sport." Her voice was loud and full of seasonal joviality. She threw an arm around his shoulders. "Where you been?"

Now what? Obviously, she was adding a new dimension to the part she was playing. "I've been around," he said.

"Didn't notice you." She turned, laughing to the couple in front of her. "He's such a quiet little feller," she said. "I swear, I'm going to put a string of those little bells on him. That way I'll always know where he's at."

The young couple—he thought their name was Barton—stood and grinned at him. He wondered if their smiles would stay in place if he banged their heads together.

"Yeah, that's me. Quiet Peter."

It didn't have much of a ring to it, but it was the best he could do on short notice. He wondered if Merry was a tad tipsy. His mother's punch was nonalcoholic, but he knew that some of the neighbors brought their own liquid pepper to spice up their drinks.

"Hey, Peter," Merry said. "The Bartons here and some of their friends are going to the VFW hall in Warsaw after this. Let's go with."

"Mom will need help cleaning up."

"I know that."

A slight frown creased Merry's forehead, and he wasn't sure what her eyes were saying. What he was sure of was the message her body was sending. Young, alive, vibrant.

"But we're all going to pitch in. Then us young'uns will head for Warsaw and the old folks will head for home."

That glint in her eyes was a challenge. They were asking which group he placed himself in. He thought briefly of dragging her upstairs to her room and giving her a personal demonstration. He turned his smile up a notch or two.

"We can stay here and have a private party."

Merry didn't even blink. "I want to stomp and holler," she said. "That wouldn't be fair to your Momma or Sean. There's no reason for them to stay up unless they want to."

"All right," he said. "I'll go with you. But only after the house is all cleaned up."

"Hot dog!" Merry kissed him hard on the mouth, sending shivers of excitement down his spine. "And I'll promise your momma that I'll look after you, like a good little bodyguard."

Peter was all set to kiss her back, just as hard, just as rough, to try to stir up some response in her, but he remembered the Bartons. Glancing from the corner of his eye, he saw that they were still there, big grins on their faces. He settled for a squeeze of her waist.

"I can take care of myself," he murmured.

Merry stared at him, deep blue eyes showing just the hint of mystery. He had no idea what was in her mind, but it didn't seem to matter, compared to the raging hunger for her that swept over him.

She was so beautiful, so vibrant. He ached with the desire to hold her. Yet even as he felt ready to drown in that hunger, other needs pushed themselves forward. The need for tenderness, for softness, for humor. The whole range of human emotions, all of which had been satisfied at one time or another by Merry.

Damn. He was in too deep. No matter how deep the abyss, he knew he'd better run.

Merry gazed around the VFW hall with a frown. Like homes all over Mentone, the hall was fully saturated with the holiday atmosphere, but there sure were differences from the MacAllister house.

Both places had had Christmas carols playing in the background and groups of happy people. But the music at Peter's mother's house had been traditional; the conversation, soft. Here the carols were definitely modern and mocking and warred with loud laughter and chatter for dominance.

Trouble was, none of it was loud enough to drown out her thoughts.

This whole thing was a mess. She couldn't cope with any of it anymore—not with Peter's touch, not with Sean's eyes, not with Jason's grin. She grimaced at the empty glass in her hand. How many of these would she have to drink before it brought strength? Obviously more than she'd had already.

"Merry, I think we should talk," Peter said.

Why? Her life was filled with talk. She suddenly wanted action. She wanted to be held and cherished, to feel as if she belonged to someone, even if only for a few minutes. "I want to dance."

"We can dance later, after we talk."

Merry shook her head. "Uh-uh."

"Why not?"

"We'll just get into an argument."

"There's no reason for us to argue."

"Good." She threw her arms around his neck and leaned heavily against him. Why wouldn't he dance with her? Didn't he find her attractive? He had once, but maybe he was regretting that.

"Let's dance," she repeated.

"Merry." He pulled her arms down but kept his arm around her shoulders. "We had some problems and—"

"Not with everything," she said, laughing low and husky in her throat.

"I'd like us to get to know each other better," he said.

What for? Neither of them was looking for a commitment. All she wanted was some tenderness for an evening. She drew back out of his arms and stuck her hand out. "Hi, I'm Merry Roberts."

"I know that," he said evenly.

"Well," she said. "There you go. Aren't you glad we got that taken care of?"

"Merry."

"If you're not willing to dance with me, I'm going to throw you on the floor and stomp you until you are."

He got slowly to his feet. "Hard to refuse an offer like that."

"Momma always told me that a body could catch more flies with honey than vinegar." She got up also, running her fingertips along his cheek. "Although, I don't know what a body would want with a bunch of flies. They're such dirty things."

"'Lead on, Macduff,'" he said, taking her hand and nodding toward the open lane to the dance floor that lay beyond her.

She didn't move, though. "What's that mean?" she asked. "My name's not Macduff."

"It's a quote from *Macbeth*," he said. Moving beyond her, he led her through the tables to the dance floor.

"Oh." She felt really stupid all of sudden for not knowing. The gap between her and Peter loomed large and uncrossable.

He turned to take her in his arms once he reached the dance floor. It should have felt great. It was what she'd been waiting for all evening, for days, actually, but now it felt lousy.

They swayed slowly to the sensuous beat of a wailing Christmas love song, but she felt as out of place as a worn sneaker at Cinderella's ball. Peter's arms were so strong and safe, but they weren't holding the real her. They were holding the pretend her, the fake Merry that she'd made up.

Not the one who'd grown up dirt-poor, who'd had herself a baby before she had a high-school diploma and who'd scrambled for years to find a new person to be.

The pretend Merry would know who Shakespeare was. The real Merry only knew milk shakes, how to shake a stick and how to shake, rattle and roll. A sour taste rose from her stomach. She missed a step and landed on Peter's foot.

"Sorry," she said. "Maybe dancing wasn't a great idea. Too many people out here."

"It's not that crowded," he said, pulling her a little closer.

His embrace should have melted the resistance in her, made her heart soar, but it only made the pain grow. She was a fraud. She had no right to be here. This wasn't part of their bargain. She'd been lonely and morose and looking for something she had no business wanting. Funny, how fate put you back in your place when you stepped out of line.

"Why'd you get so upset this afternoon when I tried to thank you for helping Sean?" he asked.

"I wasn't upset," she lied. "I guess I was self-conscious."

"Come on, I can't believe you've been self-conscious for one second in your life."

"Shows how much you know."

"Then tell me," he said. "Tell me who the real Merry Roberts is."

"What you see is what you get," she said with a grin that was meant to disarm him.

He didn't seem to notice. "Why won't you confide in me?"

She bumped into another couple and stopped dancing. "Hey, this isn't working. Why don't we try the bar instead? I could use another drink."

"Why don't we go on home?" he suggested. "I'm tired of crowds."

Without a crowd, what would she hide behind when his questions came too close to dangerous ground? "Are you kidding? This is the most fun I've had since I came to this little burg. If you're going to force me to stay out here in the sticks for another two weeks, at least let me have tonight."

He looked as if she'd walloped him a good one. His hands dropped from her, leaving her prey for the cold winds of loneliness to find. His eyes made the wintry winds outside seem downright tropical.

"I certainly wouldn't want to stand in the way of you having a good time," he said stiffly.

She had no idea why she'd said what she had, but she wasn't surprised that it had made her feel no better. Sometimes she just had a perverse way of knowing best how to kill any chance of joy rising in her heart.

Sometimes it was for the best, though, and this was one of those times.

Merry sat up in bed, looking about. She thought she'd heard an animal cry. Was it a dream or was it real?

Blinking, she slowly returned from the land of the living dead and saw that she was in a bedroom. Ah, she thought, as individual brain cells exploded in slow motion. The room that had been Mrs. MacAllister's sewing room. The one that shared the bathroom with Peter. Again, the animal sound rippled through the room. This time recognition replaced fear.

"Sorry, Zach."

The old cat, apparently disoriented, was wandering about the room, softly bumping into furniture. Once he heard her voice, Zachary turned his head in her direction and scolded her again.

"All right," Merry said, swinging her feet to the floor. "All right."

She'd meant to to get right up, but her body wasn't up to the good intentions of her spirit. The room spun and it took some doing to get her feet firmly planted.

"Oh, Zachary," she moaned. "I've got me a whamdoozer of a headache."

The old cat just muttered, probably expressing how little he cared.

"I know it's my fault, and I'm not looking for sympathy. I'm just explaining the situation to you."

Her head's mild protest turned into violent objections as she bent down to pick up the old cat. He grumbled about her clumsy efforts.

"Don't complain," she growled as she hauled him to the bathroom. "If you don't like how I do things, then go ahead and fire me."

Merry watched Zachary as he got carefully out of his litter box, shaking each foot in turn before bumping his way to his water dish. The edges around the skinny old cat blurred as she stared at him, the tiny lapping of his tongue in the water echoing in the empty caverns of her mind.

Actually, there was no need for him to fire her. She was going to be gone soon, anyway. Wasn't anything Old Zach had to do about it. Her usefulness was coming to an end.

He growled that he was done, and Merry picked the old cat up and carried him to the bed. After placing him at the foot, Merry got into bed herself, leaning against the backboard, legs stretched out in front of her. Zachary indulged in some grumbling and spinning around before settling down against her feet.

"I don't know that I was all that useful, anyway, Zach."

Her mind's eye went back to the previous night and her emotions dipped even lower. She'd been into playing a party girl, hoping to get a rise out of Peter. Instead, she'd picked a fight with him. Well, not really a fight, since no angry words were exchanged, just hurt looks and then a real cold kind of distance came between them.

Fortunately, his mother and Sean had been asleep by the time they'd returned home. By then she'd drifted down to the depths of gloom and they'd quietly crept up to their rooms. Peter bade her a good-night, but he hadn't done anything else. Hadn't even given her a good-night peck on the cheek.

"Don't know why I'm moping, old fella. I wanted to be rid of him. And now I am, so why am I unhappy?"

Zachary flicked one of his scarred old ears.

Yeah, she thought, he didn't want to hear about it, either. The whole thing was just too dumb. Why in the world had she ever agreed to be Peter's pretend girlfriend? Should have told him to not let other folks run his life.

A bitter smile twisted her face as the pain twisted in her heart. Good advice. Why didn't she follow it herself? Why didn't she just admit to who she was, instead of playing a thousand different roles, all depending on who she was with.

Like that little gig with Peter's customers from Minneapolis. Sure, she'd fooled them, but what did that buy her? Nothing.

The pain in her heart became so severe that it almost brought tears to her eyes. It was bad enough fooling some strangers, but that was just fibbing. What was really bad was that she'd been fooling Peter all this time. That had been behind her weird behavior last night, a real discomfort at knowing she'd been lying to him all along.

It had been all right in the beginning. After all, he'd hired her to fool his momma. But somewhere along the line all her fibs had become lies. When? She wished she knew.

This time the tears did come. A single river from each eye, winding their way down her cheek like streams down the mountainsides.

She knew exactly when fibs became lies—when you started caring for a person.

"Damn, Zachary!" she exclaimed. "When am I ever going to learn? A body would think that even a poor, dumb girl from the hills would know better than to make the exact same mistake twice."

The old cat sat up and howled.

"What's the matter, old fella? My feet aren't cold, are they?" Merry looked at the clock by the bedside. It was past nine o'clock. "Are you hungry, old buddy?"

Zachary yowled again. Slipping her robe on over her flannel nightgown, Merry carried the cat downstairs and padded into the kitchen.

"Hello, dear," Mrs. MacAllister said. "Did Zachary wake you up?"

"No, ma'am. We just decided it was time for breakfast."

While Mrs. MacAllister opened a can of cat food, Merry poured herself a cup of coffee.

Once the older woman had the cat eating, she turned to Merry. "What can I fix you, dear?"

The idea of food was enough to start the world spinning again. "This is just fine for now," Merry said. "Where are the boys?"

"Peter went to the hardware store. Sean's someplace around. In the living room maybe."

The phone rang as she was speaking and she went to answer. It was obviously either an old friend or relative she hadn't seen recently, and rather than seem to be eavesdropping Merry took her coffee cup and wandered into the living room. Sean was sitting on the floor, staring at the Christmas tree. His whole being sang out dejection.

"Hey, sport, whatcha doing?" Merry sat down next to him, curling her bare feet up under her nightgown.

He turned to look at her, but only briefly. He turned back to the tree with a sigh. "Nothing."

"Doesn't seem like a happy nothing," she said, flicking a brass bell ornament. It had a high-pitched tinkly sound that hurt her head. Didn't do anything for Sean, either, so she didn't ask it for an encore.

"So what did you ask Santa to bring you?" Merry asked.

He shrugged. "Nothing."

She sipped at her coffee. "Nothing? Boy, Santa must like you. You must be the only kid in the world who isn't bugging him for something."

He didn't even crack a smile. "There's no such thing as Santa, anyway."

"You're saying there's no such thing as Santa on Christmas Eve?" She was pretty inexperienced in this area, but she thought he was awfully young to have abandoned Santa. "Who told you that?"

"Nobody," he said. "I just know."

His voice was so low and spiritless that Merry pulled him over into her lap. "Okay," she said. "Spill the beans, sport."

The little boy leaned against her, seeking her strength. She closed her eyes against the hot tears that wanted to flow.

"It's 'cause of Daddy," he said slowly. "What he said last night."

"And what was that?"

He was silent a long moment, reaching down to play with her fingers, touching the red polish on her nails. "I wrote this letter to Santa," he said. "All I wanted was to go live with Daddy again like I used to."

"It can't ever be like it was," she pointed out gently.

"I know Mommy's not coming back," he said, his voice cracking. "But it could be kinda like it was. 'Cept Daddy told Mr. Janisek that I wasn't ever gonna live with him again. That I was staying here with Grandma forever."

"I see."

"So it didn't matter what I wrote to Santa. Daddy said I wasn't going home."

Merry wrapped her arms around him, pulling him close while she rested her chin on his forehead. She could feel his little body quiver as he fought back tears. Jeez, what was she supposed to say? How did you tell a little kid that his father was hurting, too, and didn't know that it would hurt less if they were together?

You couldn't tell the kid anything. You had to tell the father. Which she had tried, a number of times.

"You know what I think, sport?" She wiped away some of his tears with the end of her robe's belt. "I think you've got a basic misunderstanding here."

"Huh?" He was confused enough to stop crying and look up at her.

"What your dad says has nothing to do with what Santa does. You know, dads are just grown-up kids. They've got no idea what Santa's got planned for anybody."

"They don't?"

"Course not. How could they? Think Santa tells all his secrets? Not on your life."

"I thought daddies knew everything."

"Everything but Santa's plans." She smiled down at him. "And the other thing is, sometimes you ask for something really, really hard and it takes Santa a little longer to get it done."

"Is this really hard?"

"Not as hard as some things," she said. "But kinda hard. See, new sleds and bikes and stuff are a lot easier. He just tells the elves to make them and then he brings them. Something like going back to live with your dad is a lot trickier. He's got to have a special kind of magic to make it happen."

His depression came back to weigh him down. "There's no such thing as magic. Not really."

"No magic?" She pretended to be shocked and turned him around slightly to frown at him. "Hey, kiddo. Watch it. Magic's powerful stuff. You just got to know how to see it. If you look real close tomorrow on Christmas, I bet you'll see a sign from Santa telling you that the magic's coming and just to be patient."

His eyes reflected mostly skepticism, with just a tiny trace of hope. "Really?"

"Really." She'd make sure of it. No kid should think his dreams couldn't come true. And as for his wish, she'd do her damnedest to make that happen, too.

Sean turned even more, getting to his knees to face her. He put his arms around her neck and hugged her close. "I'm glad you came," he said. "I like you. You wanta come sledding with me and Daddy?"

"Sure, sport." She hugged him back as she tried to hide the sudden rush of tears. "I love sledding."

He sat back on his heels for a moment and regarded her. His face was solemn. "Is it a little girl or a boy?"

"Who?"

"Your kid."

She stared at him. Her heart sinking suddenly. What was she supposed to say? She'd never told anybody about Jason before, except her mother. Yet if she denied having a child, in Sean's eyes she would have lied. Her need for secrecy warred with Sean's need to trust.

"It's a boy," she said.

"How come he's not here? Does he live with his grandma like me?"

She swallowed hard. "He lives with his daddy and a different mommy."

"Oh." He thought for a long moment. "Don't you miss him?"

"Yes. Terribly."

His eyes were sad, sharing her hurt. "Did you ask Santa to let him live with you?"

If only it were that simple. "He's got a mommy and daddy who love him very much. I think he's happy where he is."

Sean didn't look convinced. "I still think you should ask Santa. Maybe there'll be enough magic for you."

She thought she should concentrate on the possible, not dream about the impossible.

Chapter Twelve

"Sure are a lot of folks here," Merry said.

Peter turned from the vista of rolling semiwooded hills to look at her. Eyes glowing, cheeks a rosy red, Merry radiated robust vitality and good health. She didn't appear to be suffering from the strange mood that had inhabited her yesterday or the effects of the alcohol she'd had.

Either would have been preferable. She was too dangerous as she was, brimming with life and good spirits. She made a person want to laugh and dance and sing out the joy of life. She made a man want to hold her, to feel her softness and know her warmth.

He frowned, instead, at the people around them. "Yeah," he grumbled. "The day before Christmas they ought be out doing their last-minute shopping."

They were at St. Patrick's, a county park up near the Indiana-Michigan border, and the three of them were standing in line, waiting for their turn to go down the tubing hill.

"Boy, you're a cheerful little feller," Merry said.

"Aren't you having fun, Dad?"

Peter looked down at his son's earnest face and pulled the kid's stocking cap down over his eyes. "I'm having a ball, champ. Glad you brought me along."

"I can bring you along lotsa times," Sean replied, as he pushed his hat back up.

"That's good." Peter patted his son lightly on the back.

"He really means that," Merry pointed out, a sharp tone in her voice.

Peter glanced at her, slightly bewildered.

"Like every day," Merry said. "He'd like to take you places every day."

"But I'm not with him every day."

"You could be."

He sighed. "We've had this conversation before, haven't we?"

Merry just grinned at him. "No, not this exact one."

"The way it is is the best way," Peter said. He knew his voice sounded a bit impatient, but he didn't try to hide it.

"Best for who?"

"For everybody."

"Statistically speaking, I doubt that's possible," she said.

He would have laughed if he hadn't been on the verge of being annoyed.

"I mean, what are the chances that the best possible course of action for three people in a given situation would be exactly the same? I can see where it might be good for one, and okay for the others. Or even good for two and lousy for the other. But best for all three? How can what's best for you be what's best for Sean?"

"Give it a rest, will you?" he snapped, then conscious that Sean's eyes were on him, he smiled. "Almost our turn."

Thankfully Merry did drop it. "Who do you want to go down with this time, big guy?" she asked.

"I want to go with my dad," Sean replied. "But you two got to hold hands. Okay?"

"You got it," Merry answered.

They sat down in the huge inner tubes and Peter took Merry's hand. With a slight push from those behind them, they went zipping down the long, iced slope to the bottom of the hill. Sean squealed in excitement. Merry's face shone with a pure childlike joy. The bottom of the hill came up sooner than Peter wanted, and they coasted to a stop.

"Watch to see if anyone is coming behind us," Peter warned as Sean wiggled out of his lap.

"Nobody, Dad."

Peter stood up and helped Merry out of her tube. She lost her balance slightly while getting to her feet and fell against him. It was pure heaven for a moment, her body pressed against his. He wanted to hold her, to keep her with him always, but instead he just steadied her until she could stand.

He was suddenly struck by how life was like a day at the old tubing hill. There were moments of exhilaration, squeezed in between long periods of trudging to get to the top of the hill. Then there were times, like with Kelly, when you couldn't hold on anymore and your partner drifted off to where you couldn't follow her. Then everything changed.

Was Merry right? How could what was best for him also be best for Sean and his mother?

"Are you getting tired, Daddy?"

"He's not tired, honey," Merry said. "He's just getting old."

Peter didn't much care for the snicker in her voice, but she didn't look the least bit sheepish. Instead, she had on that mile-wide smile and her baby blues looked as inviting as a country pond on a hot day in July.

"Dad."

"Huh?" He looked down at Sean pulling at his hand.

"Whatcha doing, Dad?"

"I'm thinking." And he damn well wasn't going to say what he was thinking about.

Peter tried to keep his face inscrutable, but he could feel a frown building. Not wanting his son to think he was mad at him, Peter looked up toward the top of the hill. Figures snaked up the hill, looking like a movie rendition of laborers building the pyramids.

"I think those lines are getting kind of long," Peter said.

Sean looked solemn while Merry's grin just grew even brighter. Peter stared at her broad expanse of joy and told himself that he found it aggravating. For a moment, he considered what he might have done to those smiling lips if he and Merry had been alone. Smash them into submission with his own or rain kisses on them until they drowned.

"We've been here more than two hours, big guy," Merry said.

Sean put a hangdog expression on his face and nodded slowly. The kid was good. Obviously inspiring guilt feelings within your parents was a natural facility. Peter sure as heck hadn't taught him that.

"We can grab a bite to eat," Peter said.

"I get to pick?" his son asked.

Suppressing a smile, Peter nodded.

"I'll show you where it is," Sean said. "It's on the way home."

They turned in their tubes, then slogged their way to the car. Sean bounced ahead, while Peter and Merry walked hand in hand. Even with thick gloves on both their hands, he could feel the warmth of her radiating through. He could feel her heart beating, he was almost certain, and he could feel her energy.

Slow down, boy, he told himself. She had just come because she'd promised his mother and Sean. He shouldn't read things into her natural joy. He unlocked the car, and they all climbed in.

"We're not that far from Mentone, are we?" Merry asked. "They have a lot more snow here."

"Hope it doesn't get warm in the next twenty-four hours," Peter agreed as they drove from the park. "If it does, we won't have a white Christmas."

"Then Santa Claus will have to put wheels on his sled," Merry said.

"Ricky says there's no such thing as Santa," Sean said.

"And you let him get away with that?" Merry said, turning to grin wickedly at his son. "The last person who told me there was no Santa Claus is still in the hospital."

"He's been in the hospital a whole year?" Sean tried to make his voice tough, but there was too much uncertainty hanging onto his words.

"That's right," Merry replied.

From the image in the rearview mirror, Peter could see that his son wasn't fully accepting Merry's words, but he wasn't disputing them, either. He slouched back and stared out his side window.

Peter knew just how he felt, except the dilemma of Santa's existence wasn't what filled his thoughts. No, Merry was doing that quite nicely. He glanced her way, catching her gaze on him and feeling the warmth of her smile as potently as if she'd touched him. He turned back to the road.

What the hell was happening to him?

One minute he was ready to ship Merry packing back to Chicago for interfering. The next minute he could think of nothing but her smile. With just a joking word, she dissolved Sean's worries, knowing just what to say to erase the shadows that a five-year-old feared most.

What about his worries? He wasn't five, but thirty-five. Would she know what fears haunted him? Did he want her to?

"There it is."

Sean's sudden shout caused Peter to jump, but he chose

not to say anything as he turned into the fast-food restaurant's parking lot. He was just hungry, that was all. An empty stomach always made his mind drift into strange areas.

"All right," Merry said as Peter took the box from the closet. "How do we do this?"

"You mean you've never put together a computer on Christmas Eve before? I thought I was getting experienced help."

"Watch it, buddy, or you'll need a bodyguard to protect you from your bodyguard."

He just laughed and laid the box in the middle of the living room floor. Merry pushed the furniture out of the way. There was such a rush of excitement coursing through her. She tried to tell herself it was because tomorrow was Christmas, but she knew it was something much more elemental than that. It was a hunger to be held, a need coursing through everyone to be needed.

"We just have to plug all this in and load the programs," Peter said, plugging the keyboard in. "Want to open that package of disks?"

"Wait a minute," she protested. "What do the directions say?"

"Directions?" He sat back on his heels. "Who reads directions?"

She just laughed and paged through the documentation. "I think I'd better. I didn't know I was dealing with someone who didn't know what went where."

Even as she said the words, Merry felt a delicious fire spread through her. She wasn't surprised when Peter was there at her side, pulling the direction sheet from her hands.

"So I don't know what goes where?" he said, his voice quiet and deadly.

A tension gripped the pit of her stomach, a wonderful tightening of her nerves that spread warmth over her soul.

She looked up into his eyes, and that tension grew into hunger. Needs and longings all raced together to throw caution out the window.

"I don't know," she teased. "Do you?"

"Care for a demonstration?"

"Sure, I'm always willing to be proven wrong."

Peter'd been ready for her challenge and ready to meet her fire head on, for without any dancing about, she was in his arms. His touch was blazing, consuming everything. His lips devoured hers, his hands found every pulsating spot that awoke even deeper hungers in her.

It felt so good, so right. She didn't care about tomorrow or any of the silly things they'd said yesterday. She just wanted to be in his arms, to feel his longing match hers. The night was so silent. Her hungers so strong.

"Oh, Peter," she sighed, lying in his arms and longing for the night to never end. "I've never felt like this. Never knew it could be like this."

"It gets better," he vowed and smothered her lips with his.

There was no time for breathing, for thinking or dreaming. There was only now, only their hungers and the silent, empty night. His hands awoke a scorching need in her. Without words, they slipped out of their clothes and met again. Hunger to hunger. Need to need. Fire to fire.

They clung together—lips, then hands, then hearts. They were one with the stars and the night, soaring into the peaks, then floating down to earth, the voice of ecstasy still echoing in their ears.

The blind old cat stood up and growled at her.

"I'm sorry, Zachary," Merry said. "I'm just not up to sleeping."

He muttered something under his breath, and Merry felt her cheeks grow warm. Her body remembered Peter's warmth, but so did her mind.

"I know I should be all relaxed, but I'm not."

Still muttering, he turned in circles, trying to find a comfortable spot. Merry knew that she wasn't going to sleep for a while, so she sat up in bed.

"Here," she said, putting the old cat up by her pillow. "I got a spot all warmed up for you. I'll be back before it cools."

Zachary's words weren't very accepting, but Merry decided that that was the best she could do for the moment. She pulled the covers up over his skinny old body. All the poor old guy wanted was warmth.

After taking care of her feline roommate, Merry walked over to the window and looked out. It had started to flurry early that evening and now the flakes were getting larger. The weatherman had forecast a white Christmas for Mentone. She was happy to see that the promise was going to ring true.

A blurred image of Sean's solemn face floated up in the frosted edges of the window. Poor little guy. He was too young to have so many disappointments.

The picture outside her window blurred somewhat as she flipped through her scrapbook of Christmases past. There was never much, but she remembered how the excitement would build in the days before Christmas.

Bittersweet memories brought a lump to Merry's throat. There were times when she had just plain hated her momma. The woman couldn't keep her kids' daddies straight. But then there were other times when love would fill Merry's heart. Momma had always made sure every kid had something special on their birthday and Christmas. It wouldn't be anything expensive and was usually handmade, but it would be unique and individual.

In the end, the only measure of worth was how well a person did with what they had. The more years that passed, the higher the grade Merry found herself giving Momma.

She wasn't quite ready to lay aside the resentment she felt toward her mother, but Merry found she was getting closer. Maybe it was because she was more and more conscious of her own inadequacies.

And the more she thought of them, the more inadequacies she discovered in herself.

Merry closed her eyes and leaned forward against the window, savoring the cool glass against her forehead. She was a triple-A, number-one fool. She had pretended to be so motivated, so focused, and what had she gone and done?

She had fallen in love with Peter.

It was such a mind-boggling example of her stupidity that she couldn't sit still. The room suddenly seemed confining, the walls closing in on her, suffocating her with the warmth and acceptance of the whole family. She had to get where she could breathe.

She pulled on a pair of sweatpants and a sweatshirt, then opened her door slowly. There were no sounds in the hallway. She tiptoed out. Belle came to the door of Sean's room and watched her.

Merry pressed her finger to her lips, as if the dog could understand her desire for silence, and crept down the stairs. Belle followed. By the backdoor, Merry slipped into her boots and coat, pulling her stocking cap over her hair before letting herself out. Belle whined softly.

"All right," Merry whispered. "But no barking, you hear?"

Belle raced out into the snowy night, frolicking like a puppy across the yard. Once Merry headed toward the front of the house, though, she raced along after her. The streets were all deserted. The night was all silence, the magic of the softly falling snow weaving a spell over the darkness.

"I'd never do this in Chicago," Merry told Belle. "Course, you'd never find a time when the streets were as empty as this."

Belle looked up, wagging her tail as if she agreed that Mentone was in every way superior to Chicago. Merry just stared ahead. Right now, she'd have to agree that Mentone was superior. In a few weeks, though, when Peter was back in Chicago, her opinion was quite likely to change.

Merry sighed as they headed toward the downtown area. "What the hell am I doing?" she asked the dog. "It doesn't matter where Peter is, since we are not going to be seeing each other by that time."

Belle didn't seem to have any answers and just raced across a lawn, nose down, plowing a path through the snow. Merry stopped to watch her, fighting back a smile at the dog's antics. Belle stopped, and catching Merry's gaze on her, wagged her tail.

"That's the goofiest thing I ever saw," Merry scolded. "All you do is end up with snow in your nose."

Merry sighed. "I know. I'm not one to talk. Snow on your nose melts. A crack in your heart takes a lot longer to heal." If it ever did.

They crossed the street and came to the giant egg. Its top was covered with a blanket of snow, but there was no denying it was a giant egg.

"An egg is an egg is an egg," she told the dog. After brushing the snow off the edge of a nearby planter, she sat down. "Do you know that even if you change into a bug, you're still the same person inside?"

Belle was more interested in sniffing around the base of the egg than discussing Kafka.

"So I guess that means that even if I'm in love with Peter, I'm still the same person I've always been. A liar."

There was no way her relationship with Peter could progress. No way at all. A relationship that wasn't based on mutual honesty was based on nothing.

"How do you think he'd feel about me if he knew everything?" she asked Belle. "Think he'd mind that I'd been lying all along?"

She got to her feet and brushed the snow from her butt. "What a stupid question, huh? Like asking a body if they minded being swindled."

They started back toward the house. The snow was already filling in their footprints. In another hour, no one would know they'd been out.

In a short time, Peter would forget she'd been in his life.

Chapter Thirteen

"I think you ought to get changed," Peter told Sean. "We should be leaving for Aunt Emma's soon."

"Aw, Dad," Sean moaned, but trudged toward the stairs, dragging his giant snake behind him.

Peter watched him with a smile, then put his arms around Merry. "You were right about little boys and snakes. He really loves that thing."

Merry smiled, or tried to smile. Her expression hung heavy with fatigue and there wasn't any sparkle in her eyes. "I'm glad."

"You all right?" he asked. She'd been quiet all morning, showing some enthusiasm when she opened the crystal egg he'd given her and the snowman sweatshirt from Sean. She even laughed aloud when she saw the furry chicken slippers his mother had given her, but somehow he'd known her heart wasn't in it.

"I'm just a little under the weather," Merry said.

"Can I get anything for you?"

Merry shook her head.

"You sure?"

"If there was anything you could do," she said, "you can be sure I'd tell you." Merry smiled up at him, a strangely mysterious smile, then pulled away.

He let her go, watching as she walked over to the sofa and sat down. His arms felt so empty and useless, but his heart felt even worse. There was something in the air that made him worried, frightened almost.

He watched her staring at the snow-draped Currier and Ives scene outside, a feeling of melancholy surrounding her. Maybe it was his silly imagination, but he could almost feel her drifting away from him. If she didn't look at him soon, she'd be too far away to ever get back.

"Is it something I've done?" he asked.

Merry turned slightly and gazed at him. Her eyes held such sadness. "It's nothing you did or didn't do, Peter." She went back to staring outside.

Peter sighed quietly. It wasn't anything he did or did not do. Hell. That didn't leave any room for maneuvering. In fact, it pretty much left him sitting out in the cold.

"Is there anything I can do to help?"

"Nope." She didn't even bother turning around to look at him.

Peter dropped his lanky frame into a chair. Hell's fire and damnation. Merry was a woman of many moods, but this one really scared the hell out of him. What was wrong?

Things had been wonderful last night. And not just for him. He would have sworn on a stack of Bibles that she'd felt that way, too. So what happened in between?

A good night's sleep, opening some presents and then breakfast.

"Peter." Merry had turned from the window and was facing him. "If you don't mind, I think I'll stay here today."

Panic suddenly clutched at his stomach. He didn't know what to say. He just knew that something was terribly wrong.

"I really don't feel all that good."

"Is it something you ate?" He asked, though he seriously doubted it.

"I don't know. I just have this terrible headache."

"Want me to stay with you?" Christmas dinners and family parties had paled to insignificance compared to the fear consuming him.

"Heavens no," Merry said.

"Aren't you two ready yet?" His mother had stepped into the room.

"Merry's not going," Peter said.

"Oh?"

"I really don't feel well, ma'am."

"Oh, dear," his mother murmured. "Maybe one of us should stay here with you."

"Oh, no. You can't." For the briefest of moments, panic seemed to take its turn on her face. "I mean, Christmas is for families. Dinners and stuff like that. I'd feel just awful if you missed that because of me."

His mother looked hard at her.

"And there's so much food in the house," Merry went on to explain. "I'll be just fine."

His mother's face softened. "The Millers down the street will be staying home today," she said. "I'll tell them to keep an eye on you."

"Oh, don't do that," Merry said. "I'm a big girl. I can take care of myself."

"Don't be so proud," his mother said. "A person can always use the help of another."

Merry looked down at the floor. Peter tried to steady his panicking heart. They needed to talk, to open up and be honest with each other. Whatever was so wrong, they would work it out. But how would he get her to believe that?

"Daddy," Sean called down the stairs. "I can't get my shirt right."

Peter sighed and glanced back at Merry, afraid if he took his eyes off of her she'd disappear.

"Can't Grandma help you?" he called up to Sean.

"Grandma's a girl," Sean said. "I've got a guy's shirt."

Peter bit off his irritation, or tried to. "I don't know what's with that kid lately," he grumbled. "I've got to do everything for him. He suddenly thinks his grandmother is totally incompetent."

"Oh, for heaven's sakes, Peter," Merry snapped. The anger in her tone was obvious and heavy. "What's the big deal? You're hardly ever around for him, anyway."

Peter just stared at her—angry, hurt and more than a little confused. Where had all that come from? He wanted to demand she explain, demand that she stop shutting him out. But Merry looked more than ready for a fight. And his mother just looked hurt.

The hell with it, he decided. Then he turned and stomped up the stairs. It wasn't as though this was some kind of lasting relationship anyway.

Merry stood at the window a long time after Peter, his mother, Sean and even Belle had left for Aunt Emma's. The house was deathly silent. There was no more need for pretending happiness, and tears suddenly welled up, flowing down her cheeks. Sobs quickly followed.

There was so much pain and agony bottled up inside her. So many hopes that had been smothered. So many dreams that would never see the light of day. Peter, Jason, Sean. They were all part of some distant star that she could never reach. That she was stupid to have even been looking toward.

There was so much misery in her soul that Merry couldn't stop the crying even if she wanted to. And she didn't want to.

It wouldn't cleanse her, but maybe it would give her a moment of relief. Just a moment to be free of guilt and fear. Just a moment to not be haunted by memories. Images from the past that pulled and tore at her.

She should never have started any of this. It was like the Christmas Eve she and Cassie had peeked in the window of the mayor's house to see all the lights and ornaments and presents spread out. All it had done was made them dissatisfied with what they had at home. Showed them what life could hold, but never would. Momma'd told them they'd been stupid, that looking at what others had was like looking into the sun and would make you blind.

She'd been right.

Eons later the tears finally ended. Merry was drained, exhausted, sucked completely dry of all feeling. No good feelings, no bad feelings, just numb.

Although she knew it wouldn't last, she savored the moment of no pain. She looked out the window. The day was still cloudy and the snow covering the small, quiet street didn't look any fresher. Realistically, she knew that she'd been crying only a few minutes, but she felt as if she'd returned from another world and another time.

She turned and saw Sean's snake, curled up where he'd carefully left it under the tree once Peter had told him it was too big to take to Aunt Emma's. But instead of the plaid skin of the snake, she saw the hurt look in Sean's eyes when he'd said she wasn't going with them to dinner. It was for their own good, his and Peter's, that she was doing what she was doing, but that didn't make it any easier to bear.

Maybe she ought to stop moping about, then, and get it done.

She went to get the bag of silk roses and floral tape that she'd brought. Then, after putting on her coat and boots, she went outside.

The Christmas rosebush stood straight and tall just outside the kitchen door. Squatting down, she fastened her silk roses onto the bare branches. Her fingers got pricked by occasional thorns, but she almost relished the pain. Maybe if she used up enough, there wouldn't be any left in the air for Peter and Sean.

Once all the roses were attached to the bush, she sat back on her heels to look at the result. Not bad. Six red roses in full bloom amid the snow. Granny said that a body should always let things follow their own course, unless they weren't working out the way you wanted them to. The magic here just needed a little help.

Merry collected her things and went inside, up to her room. As usual, Zachary was sound asleep on the bed they had shared. His heart-shaped face, liberally covered with gray, rested in peaceful repose. Whatever dreams the old cat had, came from pleasant memories.

She bent down and kissed him on the head. "You take care of yourself, old feller."

Zachary's reply was a short grunt.

He grunted again when she put her suitcase on the bed, but that couldn't be helped. She had herself a train to catch and had to pack. Tears bubbled behind her eyes but Merry held them back, saving them. The trip to Chicago was a long one, and she'd need something to fill her time. Crying would do as well as anything.

"Peter," Aunt Emma said. "It's your neighbor, Joni Miller."

"Oh." There was a sinking feeling in his stomach. He knew that it was about Merry. It had to be.

"Joni said she'd talk to you or your mother."

"Sure, Emma." Peter struggled to put a smile on his lips. It felt as if he had an anvil hanging off each corner. "I'll take it."

He followed his aunt to the little den off the front door. The phone was on top of an old rolltop desk. Taking a deep breath, he picked up the receiver.

"Peter MacAllister."

"Peter? This is Joni Miller." Her voice was filled with concern. "Your Merry hired our Luke to drive her to the train in South Bend. They just left."

The heaviness in his heart told him it was what he had expected. "Yeah," he said slowly. "She has some things she has to take care of in Chicago. Family business."

"I didn't know she had family. Isn't she an only child and aren't her parents deceased?"

Lord, they couldn't have done better if they'd published Merry's bio in the *Akron-Mentone News*. Peter considered asking Joni if she knew Merry's shoe size, but he stayed polite like always.

"It's a distant cousin," he said. "An emergency came up."

"Oh, that's too bad. Your mother said Merry wasn't feeling well. So we were just keeping an eye on her."

"Thanks, Joni," Peter said. "Thanks a lot for your help."

They exchanged farewells, then Peter hung up. He stood there for a long moment, the murmur of voices steeped in holiday cheer hung around him like the rotting stench of a dead carcass. Turning quickly on his heel, Peter strode for the back door. He needed air.

There was no one out on the back porch, thankfully. He leaned his hands on the railing, staring out at the snow-covered backyard that sloped down into a cornfield. He could see for miles. Acre after acre of barren land, covered with a frozen blanket of snow. No life, no promise of warmth or sweet sunshine. Just like his tomorrows.

Damn Merry and her smile. Damn her laughing eyes and teasing voice that made him care.

He blinked away an unwanted wetness in his eyes and stood up. She bounced into his life with all sorts of promises, then when he started feeling alive again, she disappeared.

Damn her and the sunshine she'd brought.

Peter breathed a sigh of relief once they turned off Aunt
Emma's property and onto the county road. It had taken
them forever to get out the door what with all the kisses,
wishes of happiness for the remainder of the holiday and
the God-willing-see-you-next-years. If any more happiness touched him, he'd have barfed all over those damned
happy relatives.

They rode in silence, his mother in the front with him,
Sean dozing in back with Belle. When they came up on the
south edge of town, over by the trailer park, Peter knew
that he couldn't wait any longer. It wouldn't be right for
them to go into an empty house when his mother and son
were expecting otherwise. He cleared his throat.

"Merry left," he said softly.

He'd just wanted to tell his mother, hoping that Sean
wouldn't hear. But his mother remained silent.

"Where did she go?" Sean asked. "How come she left?"

"She had to go back to Chicago."

"How come?"

Peter concentrated on crossing the railroad tracks. He'd
lied once, he might as well do it again. "She had some
family problems."

"I thought she said her mommy and daddy were dead."

Peter sighed quietly.

"Maybe she went to see her little boy," Sean said.

"Her little boy?" Peter's mother turned around to stare
at Sean. "What little boy?"

"She doesn't have a son," Peter said.

"Don't you remember, Daddy? She said she could talk
to the tree because she was a mommy."

Peter exchanged glances with his mother and shrugged.
"Kelly always talked to the tree before we cut it. We needed
a mommy to do it this year."

His mother nodded and patted his hand. Peter had the feeling that Merry's leaving didn't come as a surprise to her, either. She must have had her suspicions when Merry announced herself ill. He should have let his mother fix him up with Daphne or Denise or whoever.

They were all quiet as he pulled the car into the garage. No one said a word as they got out of the car. Sean was leading the way to the house when he suddenly stopped. His mother gasped, and Peter pushed ahead, wondering what was wrong now.

"Oh, my goodness," his mother said. "That bush is blooming."

Peter's feet froze. There, up ahead in the soft glow from the outside door light, the Christmas rosebush was covered with flowers.

Sean walked slowly to the plant and gently touched a flower. "It's blooming!" he said, his voice filled with wonder. "It's magic, just like Merry said."

Peter found the ability to move had returned. "Merry couldn't make the roses bloom," he said impatiently and went over to the bush. He pulled at a flower. It came off, along with a piece of green tape. "It's not real."

Sean just ran over and grabbed the flower from his hand. "It is too real," he cried and tried to put the bloom back on the plant. "Merry made it real."

With a definite glare at Peter, his mother joined Sean at the bush, stooping down to put an arm around his thin shoulders. "Sometimes the real magic is finding somebody who loves you so much that they'll put silk flowers on an old rosebush," she told the boy.

Peter had heard enough. He unlocked the back door and went storming inside. She walked out on them, abandoned them all without a thought for their feelings, and yet she was some wonderful person who supposedly loved them all. Right.

Peter stomped through the house and up to his room. What about all they'd said last night? Had it all been a lie? Or just part of the pretense? Maybe he should find her and offer her a bonus for acting like she cared about him so convincingly. He slammed his door shut, noticing an envelope on his dresser as he did.

His heart fell into the pit of his stomach as he walked over to get it. His name was written on it in Merry's big, bold handwriting. He stared at it for the longest time, desperate to know what it said, but terrified to find out.

Finally he ripped open the back and took out the single sheet. Her words barely filled one side, not nearly enough to answer all the questions in his heart.

Dear Peter,

I'm sorry to be leaving without a word like this, but I thought it best. Things were getting out of hand, something neither of us wanted. We started out with the best of intentions, so I think it's best we return to them. Thanks for all the fun you showed me. Give your mom and Sean a big hug from me.

Love,
Merry

P.S. Sean is really hurting. He lost his mother and feels rejected by you. Find some way to keep him with you. Kelly died trying to find the perfect life for you two. Honor her memory by making your lives as perfect as you can. Together.

P.P.S. Give Belle and Zachary a big hug, too.

Peter read the letter, then read it again. What the hell did any of this mean? Just that she was tired of them all and had left. He crumpled the letter in his hand and threw it across the room.

He went over to the window to stare down at the backyard. Just below him he could see the stupid roses taped to a frozen rosebush. He wanted to close his eyes, to shut out the sight, but for some reason he couldn't.

Thank God, he hadn't fallen in love. All this escapade had done was prove to him that he was right to keep his heart protected. Right to stay as far from love as possible.

Chapter Fourteen

"Why do we have to go see Aunt Rosa anyway?" Sean's tone was pouty and he was hanging back, shuffling his feet as they they made their way to the car.

"Because she hurt her knee," Peter's mother said. "And she hasn't been able to get out much. And it's our Christian duty to visit the infirm."

"What's infirm?" Sean asked.

"Sick," Peter replied. "Those who are so sick or hurt that they can't do a lot of things for themselves."

His son glared at him, then took his grandmother's hand. He'd been that way, ignoring Peter whenever possible, since yesterday. Since Merry had left.

When they reached the car, he opened the back door for Sean. He was about to open the front for his mother when Sean paused and turned toward them.

"Can you sit back here with me, Grandma?"

"Certainly, dear."

Peter tried to hide his grimace as he watched his mother get into the back seat next to Sean. Great. Now his son was relegating him to the position of chauffeur. Peter didn't think it was a promotion, but the job sounded easier and the benefits appeared to be the same. He slammed the door shut on them, then walked around to the driver's side and got in himself.

"There was no need to slam the door like that," his mother said.

"Sorry," Peter murmured as he fastened his seat belt.

He really wasn't sorry. In fact, he was getting darn sick and tired of being the bad guy. Maybe he wasn't really the bad guy, but he certainly was the sandwich filling. Caught in between his elderly mother and his young son. It was a lose-lose situation no matter which of them he argued with.

Hell with it. He'd be back in Chicago soon. Alone, but at least no one would be bugging him, blaming him for everything bad that happened. Clenching his jaw, Peter put the car in reverse and began backing out of the driveway.

"What if Merry comes while we're gone?" Sean asked.

"She won't," Peter snapped. He spun out into the street, stopped, put the car in first and made his way down toward Main Street.

"How do you know?" Sean's voice was just as sharp as his own.

Surprisingly, Peter's mother made no move to correct the boy. When Peter looked up into the rearview mirror, he saw that she was looking at him, her blue eyes hard like cut glass.

"She has some family problems," Peter said. "Those kind of things aren't solved in a few minutes."

Now two sets of eyes stared at him. Hard eyes, almost disbelieving.

"She explained it all to me."

"Did she call?" Sean asked. "How come you didn't let me talk to her?"

"She didn't call," Peter said tiredly. "She left me a letter."

Neither of his back seat passengers replied, but Peter was happy to see that he made them blink. He turned his attention to the road before him.

The way to Aunt Rosa's farm was down a series of county blacktops, stretching out over the flat Indiana landscape like interconnected straight lines. None of the lines contained even the hint of a curve. They didn't require much attention and his passengers, sitting and staring out their respective windows, called for even less. His mind drifted. Drifted to Merry, her letter, Sean and the whole sorry state of Peter's existence.

What was he supposed to do about Sean? Did Sean want him to live in Mentone? Or did he want to come to Chicago to live with Peter? If his son agreed to come to Chicago, was he really able to understand what that meant? Even if Peter explained it to him, could his son conceive what it would be like living with a single parent?

The big question would be who would take care of Sean while Peter worked. Fortunately, his salary didn't make money a problem, but that still didn't help all that much. Should he hire a live-in nanny? Or would day care be better? But if he chose day care, what would happen when he had to travel?

Hell! He almost missed his turn and took a sharp left. Apparently, he took it a little too fast.

"I know I said Aunt Rosa wasn't well," his mother protested. "But I don't think she's at death's door."

"Sorry," Peter murmured.

"Even if she is, I don't know as we could do anything about it."

"I said I was sorry."

Cold icicles of anger filled the car. They each retreated to their own corner.

Maybe he should move back to Mentone. That way he could spend more time with Sean and his mother could still help care for the kid. His son wouldn't have to leave his friends and would still have the freedom he was used to.

Sean would lose a great deal if he moved in with Peter on Lake Shore Drive. Of course, they could move to the suburbs, but that wasn't all that much better. Peter's commuting time would go out of sight; he'd spend even less time with Sean. Plus, the suburbs were built around the automobile so Sean would still lose his freedom.

Hell's fire! Peter didn't see any kind of viable solution to the problem. And, although he didn't like to put Sean second, Peter didn't see a solution. The one that presently colored his whole world gray. That was loneliness.

He hated to admit it to himself, but even though he'd managed to avoid the snares of commitment, Merry and her mile-wide smile still haunted him.

Little things snuck into his thoughts at the strangest times. Her smile, her laughter, her eyes. He looked up and saw Tippecanoe Valley High School. The time he and Merry had gone to his cousin's basketball game.

Worst of all was the emptiness he felt. As if the very core of him were hollow and barren. His heart was gone, as was his soul. All that was left was just pain and desolation, rattling around inside. He tried to put aside his melancholy thoughts and read the announcement sign in front of the high school complex. Boys' basketball was in full swing.

"That's where Daddy went to school," his mother murmured in the back seat.

Sean's response was a grunt. The kid probably couldn't care less what Daddy did.

"He played baseball and basketball."

"Didn't he play football?"

"A little bit," his mother replied.

The snow-covered football field came up next. Peter'd always made the team and earned his share of bruises, but football had never been his game. Along with the bruises, most of which came during practice, Peter earned his share of splinters from riding the bench.

"Death Valley's all covered with snow," Sean said.

"What?" Peter screamed. His foot went out and hit the brakes. They began fishtailing all over the slippery road.

"Peter," his mother shouted. "What in the world are you doing?"

Trying to keep the car on the road, he wanted to shout back, but he didn't say anything. Because, first of all, the skidding was his fault. And secondly, it took all his skill and attention to keep them from sliding into a snowbank. He was finally able to ease the car to a stop. After putting it in neutral and locking the emergency brake, Peter turned around.

"Don't ever say something like that again," he said, glaring at his son.

Sean stared at him, bewildered.

"Peter," his mother said. "Have you lost whatever sense you were born with?"

"Death Valley isn't covered in snow," he said, speaking slowly and carefully. "It never snows in Death Valley. It's usually the hottest spot in the whole United States."

Shaking his head, Sean turned to look out the window. "It's all covered with snow," he said, pointing at the football field.

Peter stared at the field.

"Land sakes," his mother said. "Everyone calls that field Death Valley. They have for the last ten years, at least."

"Yeah," Sean said. "'Cause our football teams play real good there."

"I didn't know that." Peter could feel a weakness waiting to fill his body. He gripped the steering wheel hard, trying to hold back all his unnameable fears. His words about love were not coming back to haunt him. "But, anyway, that's not the real Death Valley."

"Is that true, Grandma?"

"I don't know what your father means. Folks around here call it Death Valley, so Death Valley it is."

"But it's not the real one," Peter insisted.

"Just about every town in America has a Main Street," his mother said. "Does that mean only one of them is real and all the others are fake?"

"Mom, you just don't understand."

"You're absolutely right, Peter. I don't understand you."

He shook his head. She really didn't understand. It didn't snow in Death Valley. It couldn't snow in Death Valley. Death Valley was a hot, barren desert.

He had to get ahold of himself and get going. He slowly eased the car into gear. She just wouldn't understand. But it didn't matter. No matter what the folks around here called it, the Tippecanoe Valley High School football field wasn't the real Death Valley. It could be Death Valley to the high school's opponents but it didn't count anywhere else.

It didn't count where Fate was concerned. Or Love.

"Are you and Mr. Browder friends, Daddy?"

"Yeah, sort of." Peter quickly checked the total for their breakfast, then left three dollars for a tip. "We went to school together. But he's older, so we weren't in the same grade."

They walked over to the front of the pancake house, where a short teenager with a long black ponytail and a big smile waited behind the register.

"Hi, Sean," she sang out loudly. "Is this your daddy?"

"Yeah."

"Hi, Mr. MacAllister," she said. "How was everything?"

"Just fine—" he paused to look at her name tag "—Wendy."

Peter paid his bill, then Wendy returned his change with a thank-you and an even brighter smile. Sean was already waiting at the door, so Peter nodded and turned away.

"Goodbye, Sean," Wendy said.

His son just hung his head and gave an offhanded wave over his shoulder.

"Do you know her?" Peter asked Sean as they walked to the car.

"Yeah. She's Robbie Hatfield's big sister." His son's tone definitely wasn't congenial. "She's always saying hi to me and stuff."

"She's just being friendly."

"I think she's got the hots for me."

Peter stared at his son for a moment, who was now shuffling along, kicking at ice chunks. He didn't know whether to laugh or be worried. Sean was growing up, though, that was for certain, and at a much faster rate than Peter had. If he weren't careful, he'd have no place at all in his son's life.

"I think she should chase older guys, don't you, Dad?"

"Ah, yeah. Definitely."

"Do you think you could talk to her?" Sean stood looking up at him, his hands on the door handle.

"Sure."

"Thanks, Dad."

Peter opened the door and held it while Sean hopped in. Then he fastened his son's seat belt before going around to the driver's side. Maybe it was time Sean and he lived together again. Maybe Merry was right.

Merry. Just thinking the name hurt. Though the hurt was there whether he thought it or not. It would just take practice putting it farther into the background of his thoughts.

Just as it took a little work to calm down after his shock about Death Valley yesterday. It was such a silly coincidence. How was he supposed to know the nickname of the high school's football field? It was laughable really. Peter headed toward the Browder's farm south of Mentone.

"Did you ever live on a farm, Dad?"

"No." Peter fastened his own seat belt. "I've always lived in the same house you do."

"Except now."

"Right, except now I live in Chicago." He turned on the motor and pulled out of the parking lot onto Route 30. A couple of wide-open miles passed before Sean spoke again.

"Farms are fun," he said. "But I like living in town better."

"They both have pluses and minuses."

"I like being able to walk to my friends' houses."

"You wouldn't be able to do that if you came to live with me."

Sean thought for a minute. "Are there kids where you live, Dad?"

"Some," Peter replied.

"Do they ever go outside and play?"

If an adult takes them. "Sometimes."

"Do they have subways in Chicago?"

"Sure." Peter glanced at his son and saw he was staring out the window. "You rode on one when you came to visit in the summer. Remember. We went on one to see the dinosaurs."

"Oh, yeah."

Oh, yeah. The words and tone sounded so easy. Was that really how Sean felt? Peter wished he could say the same about himself.

"Grandma will like it in Chicago."

"Grandma?"

"Yeah," Sean replied. "She'll like riding the subways. She doesn't like driving anymore."

"She doesn't?"

"Nope. She likes it when other people drive her."

Peter slumped down in the seat. Should he bring both of them to Chicago to live with him? Was his mother the one who needed care now? Even more than Sean? Should he hire someone to live with his mother?

Sean was staring out at the brown-and-white patterns of snow and dirt covering the fields on either side of them. "You know what I'd like best about Chicago?"

Peter shook his head. "What, champ?"

"I'd get to see Merry a whole lot."

"Merry? How—"

"Doesn't she live close to where you live?" Sean asked, his brow wrinkled in question. "She said she did."

Peter felt tired, so very tired. "Yeah, she does." So close, yet so far away. How did he explain that to his kid when he couldn't even explain it to himself? How, even though he lived a short walk from Merry, he couldn't even speak to her?

"There's Mr. Browder's farm," Sean shouted.

They turned up a narrow lane and pulled to a stop by a rambling farmhouse, as large dogs came charging out to greet them. Their barking brought Matt and a girl, probably one of his daughters, who looked a little older than Sean.

"Oh, oh," Sean said.

"What's the matter, champ?"

"That's Missy Browder. She's really mean."

"She is?"

"Yeah," Sean replied. "She'll kick you if you spit on her. I mean, really hard."

"Well, I guess I won't spit on her, then."

The words just spilled out and Peter wished he could retrieve them. No, he wished Merry had been here to hear the whole conversation. She would have thought it so funny. It was frightening just how much he missed her. But it would pass. Love might not, but attractions like he'd felt for her would. As long as it wasn't love, he would recover.

Sean was already out of the car and bouncing up the drive, shouting greetings at Missy as she shouted them back. Relieved that no one kicked or spit at the other, Peter released his seat belt and eased himself out.

"Hey, old buddy," Matt said heartily. "How ya been?"

"Fine," Peter answered, trying to match Matt in joviality. "Yourself?"

"Fit as an old boar hog."

"One of our pigs is going to California," Missy said, jumping up and down.

"He is not," Sean said.

"Is so," Missy replied.

"How's he gonna get there?" Sean asked.

"He's gonna fly, nerdface."

Fear exploded in the pit of Peter's stomach, but he told himself he was just being silly. Overly sensitive. The mention of pigs flying the day after the snow in Death Valley was just a coincidence. Another thing he'd laugh about some day.

"Pigs can't fly," Sean said.

That's right. You tell 'em, Peter thought.

Matt leaned down, putting his arm around Sean's shoulders. "Sure they can, little buddy," he said. "They can fly just as good as you and I."

Sean stared at him. So did Peter, his stomach lurching in sudden disagreement.

"They fly in an airplane, dummy," Missy said. "But that's still a pig flying."

Peter could taste his apple pancake souring in his stomach. No, it didn't mean anything. Not one damn thing.

"Missy," Matt said. "Why don't you take Sean and show him our little traveler?"

The two kids went racing off down to the pig sheds while Peter just stood there by the car.

"Peter?" Matt was staring at him. "You don't look too good, old buddy. What you been doing? Hitting all the joints since your little lady isn't here to keep an eye on you?''

Peter shook his head slowly. Snow in Death Valley and pigs flying. But it didn't mean this ache in his heart was love. It didn't mean anything of the sort. It just meant that the gods had a sense of humor. He just needed more time and he'd get over Merry.

"You staying up tonight to ring in the New Year?'' Jim Rogers asked Sean as they paid for their light bulbs. "Got yourself a hot party to go to?''

Sean looked hopefully at his father, but Peter just shook his head. "You need your sleep.''

Actually, Peter was the one who needed his sleep. This past week had been awful. He hadn't thought he was doing all that much, but he was exhausted most of the time. Then at night, when he should have collapsed, he tossed and turned, unable to get comfortable. He took their bag from the clerk with a nod and he and Sean walked with Jim toward the door.

"Better watch it,'' Jim said. "What you do on New Year's, you do all year long!''

"Golly, Daddy,'' Sean said, his eyes still on their neighbor as he left the store. "Are we going be at the hardware store all next year?''

Peter shook his head as he bent down to help Sean with his mittens. "No, Mr. Rogers meant what you're feeling at midnight, when the new year starts, you'll feel all year. If you're happy on New Year's Eve, you're happy all year long.''

"Oh.'' Sean pulled his hat over his ears. "So I'm going to miss Merry all next year?''

"Of course not.''

"Is she gonna be sad all next year?''

Peter just shoved the door open and led Sean out. That old saying was nonsense. No one was going to miss anyone for the whole next year. Still, when Sean immediately turned to his right, Peter stopped him.

"Hey, champ," he called. "Let's go this way."

Sean stopped and asked, "How come?"

Peter stared for a long moment at the giant egg sitting in the parking lot up the street.

"Because," he murmured.

"Because why?" his son persisted.

Because he'd already had snow in Death Valley and learned that pigs could fly. He was not going anywhere near that damn egg. He didn't want to see a giant chicken in any shape or form whatsoever.

"We always walk home that way," Peter replied. "I want to go a different way."

"Okay," Sean said. He shrugged and came back, skipping past Peter and going west on Main. "You're kinda weird, Dad."

"Thank you."

Sean turned around and walked backward.

"Be careful you don't fall on your head," Peter said.

"I never do."

Sean tried hopping backward but soon gave up on that and fell in by Peter's side, reaching up to take his father's hand. Peter sighed. They were buddies again. It eased part of the ache in his heart, but not all of it.

"But you're not as weird as Mickey Frame's dad."

"Oh, no?"

"Nah. Mickey says he gets all dressed up before he eats breakfast."

"I think Mr. Frame works in an office in Warsaw," Peter said. "He's just getting dressed for work."

"He does other weird things," Sean assured him. "When do you think Merry'll be back?"

"She won't be."

"Yes, she will."

Peter just let the subject drop and looked around them. The street was empty and quiet. It wouldn't be bad to move back home to Mentone. It would be good for his mother and Sean. And it would work out nicely for him, too. He could turn one of the spare bedrooms into an office and put in some extra phone lines so he could connect his computer into the office network. If he needed to, he could go back to Chicago every couple of weeks.

He doubted his managers would see any problems. Most of his work was solitary. With the computer and communications technology available now, working in Mentone would be no different than working a couple floors down from where his office was now. And if his managers didn't agree, then he'd look into options of his own. Do a little consulting. Maybe set up a newsletter. There were a lot of things he could do.

"Hi, Peter." A woman stood in their way. "And how are you, young man?" she asked Sean.

"Fine, Mrs. Warren," Sean replied.

"Hear from that young lady of yours, Peter?"

His jaw clenched momentarily. Oh, the joys of living in a small town where everyone knew everyone else's business. "No, I haven't," Peter replied. "I imagine she has a lot on her mind."

"Yes," the woman said. "I understand one of her cousins is sick."

Peter moved his head slightly, noncommittally.

"You going to spend New Year's with her?" she asked. "Wouldn't want the two of you to spend the whole next year being apart. Well, give her my best when you see her. And say hello to your mother for me."

"We will," Sean said. "Bye, Mrs. Warren."

Peter just nodded, and they continued on their way home.

Damn. The whole town thought Merry was coming back. If he moved back here, would he spend the rest of his life answering questions about her?

"Daddy," Sean said, plodding along thoughtfully at his side. "'Member how we visited Aunt Rosa 'cause she was firm?"

"Infirm," Peter said.

"And Grandma said we were supposed to."

"Right. It was our Christian duty." What was Sean getting at?

The boy sloshed through a puddle. "Well, I think you gotta go see Merry."

"Sean." Peter bit back his impatience.

"'Cause I think she's maybe firm, too." His words raced along as if he feared his father would stop him. "You know, she's so sad that she can't do anything for herself. And if you don't make her smile at midnight, she's gonna be sad all year long."

"Sean, it's not that easy." Peter scrambled for wisdom, but none appeared. He couldn't tell Sean the real reason Merry left, because he had no idea what it was.

"But she talked to the tree for us. We gotta do something for her."

"Maybe we could write her a letter," Peter suggested. "You know—"

"Daddy, look!" Sean screamed. "There's a giant chicken!"

Peter's heart wanted to stop. Fear clutched at his stomach, but he followed Sean's eyes and found what his son was screaming about. There, over across the street from King's Memorial Home, stood a concrete statue of a rooster on a pedestal.

"That's not a chicken, Sean." Peter forced his heart to start beating again. "It's a rooster."

"Roosters are chickens."

This whole thing was so silly. "No, they're not. Chickens lay eggs and roosters can't."

"Dad!" Sean was taking this all seriously. The boy sounded practically in tears. "Hens lay eggs, but they're both chickens. The giant chickens are back!"

"Sean, it's just a statue."

"You don't understand." Sean was almost screaming, his face frantic. "The magic's here. Daddy, you got to go get Merry."

"Get Merry? Why?"

"Because the magic's here." Sean was grabbing at Peter's hand, tugging at it as if it would make him see the urgency. "She said the rose would bloom and the chickens would come back and then the magic would be here and it would let me live with you. You got to get her so that the magic can give her her little boy back."

Peter stooped down, taking Sean's hands in his own. He didn't understand everything Sean was saying. Okay, the rose sort of bloomed and he was seriously trying to figure out how to have Sean live with him, but what was all this about Merry and a little boy? There was no doubt, though, that Sean really believed some sort of magic was here. How did Peter convince him that there was no magic, just . . .

Snow in Death Valley.

Pigs that flew.

And giant chickens back in Mentone.

Chapter Fifteen

"Come on, Merry," ZeeZee pleaded. "It's New Year's Eve. Come with us to Georgie's party."

"Yeah," Sandi added. "It'll be a lot of fun."

"There'll be a lot of stray studs."

Merry had tried ignoring her roommates, sitting in bed and staring at the book in her lap. She'd been reading *The Brothers Karamazov* for a month now and getting nowhere. Maybe she wasn't meant to be smart and successful. She'd never be anybody somebody could be proud of.

"Leave me alone," she said with a sigh. "Can't you see I have a lot of work?"

"You're between semesters," Sandi said quietly.

"Well, I'm tired from working at the restaurant," Merry said. "And I want to get a head start on the next semester."

"Jeez, Merry, you're no fun lately," ZeeZee said. She and Sandi left the room, closing the door behind them.

Merry stopped pretending to read and threw the book onto the floor. She lay back on the bed and covered her eyes with her arm. Why, oh, why, did she have to be so stupid? She was always getting involved with these guys who were out of her class. Then she'd make up these big lies about who she was. Why couldn't she just get involved with someone from her own station? Like a guy who went to school with her.

Better yet, why did she have to get involved at all? The single life wasn't bad for her. A lot of women did it. There was no reason why she couldn't take care of herself. She might get a little lonely once in a while, but that would pass.

"Merry. Phone call for you."

"I'm not here. I told you that before."

"It's Mona, from the restaurant."

"Tell her—" Aw, heck. Mona was one of her close friends at work. She might as well see what she wanted. Merry got up from bed and pushed past Sandi to the phone. "Yeah, Mona. What do you want?"

"Nice to see you're still your cheery old self."

"Mona, please."

"Okay, okay." Mona shifted her ever present gum to the other side of her mouth. "How about working with me tonight? It's a New Year's Eve party at that retirement home on Wilson. It's good money."

"No, I—"

"You ain't doin' nothin'," Mona snapped. "Except maybe slitting your wrists."

"I got some reading I need to do."

"Hey," Mona said. "Work with me tonight. You'll still be down, but at least your wallet will be a little fatter. Besides, they're nice folks. I worked there last year."

Merry sighed. She'd avoided taking a New Year's Eve gig because she was afraid that the sight of happy young couples in each other's arms would send her off the edge and she would wind up beating the bejeebers out of all of them.

But this would be different. It would be elderly folks, most of them probably women.

"Okay, okay," Merry said. "What time?"

"Great, kid. Great. I'll pick you up at seven."

"Isn't that early?"

"Merry, these are old folks. Two minutes after midnight and they'll be in dreamland. They gotta get their partying in early."

"All right, see you then."

She hung up the phone and went back into her room, shutting the door firmly behind her. She really couldn't just sit around and mope. That wasn't healthy. What she needed was a full slate. Fill her time with work, work and more work. Eventually Mr. Peter MacAllister would fade away into a distant past. He had to. One dark memory was load enough for her.

Peter found a parking place just two blocks from Merry's, a record for him, and hurried along to her apartment. It was a little after seven-thirty, Chicago time. Eight-thirty, Mentone time.

Something really weird was happening back in Mentone. Sean said it was the magic. Peter wasn't sure, but he wasn't taking any chances. Sean was right when he said Merry'd been unhappy, and if happiness was in the air in Mentone at midnight, Peter wanted her there to get her share. And he had just enough time to do so.

The lobby door was open so he raced up the stairs, but no one answered his knocking at Merry's door. Damn! He looked at his watch again. Even if they had a big evening planned, they should still be home dressing.

He knocked at the next door. Maybe they were at a neighbor's or told someone where they were going. No answer.

He tried the next apartment.

"Yeah?" a surly voice called out.

"I'm looking for the residents in 2 B," he said. "I really need to find Merry or ZeeZee or Sandi."

"They ain't here."

"But do you know where they are? I really need to find them."

"Get lost 'fore I call the cops."

Great. No one answered at the next two doors, and Peter was getting really frustrated when the manager came home. Peter hurried to her door.

"I really need to find Merry or ZeeZee or Sandi."

She glared at him as she slipped through her door. "It ain't my business to keep an eye on three adults who aren't bothering anybody."

He stuck his foot in the doorway so she couldn't close the door. "But I really need to—"

She kicked his foot out of the way. "Beat it before I call my boyfriend." She slammed the door.

Damn. He sank onto the top step. What was he supposed to do, just sit here on the stairs until Merry came home? If he didn't find her soon, they'd never get to Mentone even close to midnight.

He supposed he could fight with the neighbors until they called the cops. It would make for some excitement, but he didn't want to spend New Year's Eve in jail, especially if the old saying was true. The thought of a year in Cook County Jail didn't thrill him.

"You got the door?"

"Oops, catch that will you?"

Peter stood up and stared down the stairs. He couldn't believe it. ZeeZee and Sandi had just come in.

"Uh-oh." ZeeZee stopped midway up the flight of stairs. "Trouble ahead."

Sandi peered around her roommate and frowned. "What do you want?"

"I'm looking for Merry."

"Well, tough. She's not looking for you." ZeeZee brushed past him and unlocked the apartment door.

"I just want to talk to her," he pleaded to Sandi.

She pushed past him also. "She's not here."

"I know that. Just tell me where she is." He followed them up to the apartment door.

"Why? So you can wreck another party for her?" Sandi asked. She went past ZeeZee into the apartment.

"I need to see her."

ZeeZee went into the apartment, too, but her eyes seemed uncertain. "If she wanted you to know where she was, she'd have told you."

"She didn't know I was coming. I drove in from Mentone because—"

"You drove in tonight just to see her?" ZeeZee asked and glanced over at Sandi. "It is New Year's. Maybe . . ."

Sandi sighed. "She's working a party with Mona over at the Wilson Towers."

Peter fought the urge to hug them both. No use tempting fate. "Thanks. I really appreciate it." With a grin, he turned to race down the stairs.

"If she's mad at us for telling you, we'll find you and make you sorry," ZeeZee called after him.

He just waved his hand in acknowledgment. If he failed in his mission, they wouldn't be the only ones after him. Sean, his mother, Zachary. Hell, the whole town would make him suffer.

He jumped into his car and sped to Wilson Towers. There were no parking places immediately visible, and he didn't waste time cruising the neighborhood for one. He just double-parked in the curved drive, then bolted toward the doorway. A uniformed doorman gave him a hard stare over a newspaper but let him in.

The Wilson Avenue Retirement Home was a refurbished hotel, and Peter easily found the high-ceilinged old ballroom in the back. Tonight, it was gaily decorated with streamers and balloons, with music coming from records manipulated by a deejay. Residents, most of them women, milled about the large room so that Peter couldn't see more than a few feet ahead of him.

He came farther into the room. Damn it. Where was she?

Some party guests encircled him, smiling.

"Hi, honey."

"You come to our party?"

He smiled but edged along, trying to see where the serving tables were.

"Wanna dance, sugar?"

"Actually I'm looking for somebody," he said. "One of the servers."

"What's her name?"

"Merry, Merry Roberts."

"Merry," one of the old women called out. "Where are you?"

"Merry, Merry Roberts!" another one shouted.

Peter grinned at them and put his hands to his mouth. "Merry. Are you here?"

"Merry?" someone else asked. "Who's Merry?"

But in moments, it seemed that most of the room was calling her name. Magically, a few seconds later, a red-faced Merry was pushed forward. She stopped moving when she spotted him.

"Peter." She frowned. "What are you doing here?"

The crowd got deathly quiet.

"I'm not sure," he said, and looked around them. They were encircled by the elderly party goers, all with rapt expressions on their faces as they watched.

He turned back to Merry. "There's snow in Death Valley."

"Oh," someone sighed.

"Ah," another said knowingly.

"What'd he say?" someone from the edges cried out.

"There's snow in Death Valley," someone else repeated.

Merry bit at her lip. "Peter, please—"

He saw no anger in her eyes so he took a step closer. "And pigs can fly."

"No, they can't," a watcher argued.

"That's not possible."

"What'd he say?"

"They can fly in an airplane," Peter told her. "Just like you and me. But they can fly."

"I guess."

"He's got a point there."

Merry just shook her head. "Peter."

"And the three-hundred-pound chickens have returned to Mentone."

"Three-hundred-pound chickens?"

"They've come back to Mentone?"

"Where's that?"

"What'd he say?"

Merry looked away from him briefly, as if gathering strength. She folded her arms over her chest and faced him once more. "Peter, this is all nonsense."

"A three-hundred-pound chicken don't sound like nonsense to me," someone shouted.

Merry closed her eyes briefly. She was weakening, he could tell.

Peter turned to the crowd. "We have an egg in the center of town," he said. "It's about six feet tall."

"It would take a three-hundred-pound chicken to lay that kind of egg," someone agreed.

Merry opened her eyes. Her look bordered on a glare.

"All right." Peter grinned at her. "It's just one rooster, but there's got to be more coming."

"Oh, sure."

"You find one chicken, you got a flock."

"They don't like to be alone."

Merry stared hard at him. She should be smiling by now, or trying to fight back a smile. All he saw was sadness in her eyes. He took a giant step forward and grabbed her hands.

"Sean told me what this means," Peter said. "He says the magic has arrived."

She remained silent and staring.

"He said you said it would come and it has. The rose bloomed, the snow came to Death Valley, pigs are flying to California, the chickens are back and he's going to live with me. We all got our share of the magic. Now you have to come back so it can work its spell on you."

A collective, satisfied sigh erupted from the crowd. Merry's face quivered, then tears started from her eyes. "I don't deserve it," she said.

"Every woman deserves a warm bed," someone called out.

Merry's hold on Peter's hands tightened. "I lied to you," she said.

"What else do you do with a man?"

"They can't handle the truth at all."

"They're too fragile."

"They're like poets."

The hurt in her eyes was just too deep. He wanted to hold her, to kiss away the pain and shelter from it forever. "I don't care," he said.

She shook her head. "I didn't grow up in Atlanta. I grew up in a little town in the hills of Tennessee."

"So?"

"So?" someone in the crowd echoed.

"I have a bunch of brothers and sisters," Merry rushed her words out.

"You didn't seem selfish like an only child."

"Listen to him, honey."

"My mother worked as a waitress in a bar on the only paved road in town." Merry's voice was growing more defiant, as if daring him to not be shocked and turn away.

But he wasn't, he didn't. "It isn't opportunities that make a person, it's what the person does with their opportunities."

"I never knew who my father was. My mother had a hard time placing him."

"That's not under your control."

She took a deep breath and looked him straight in the eye. "I've got a son."

Peter just nodded. "Sean told me."

"He's gonna be ten, come next April." All that strength in her voice was suddenly gone. She bit at her lip as if it could stop the flood of tears that was threatening.

"Who's taking care of him?" Peter asked gently.

"His father," Merry replied. "And his mother."

"He was adopted?"

Merry nodded, all her walls suddenly tumbling down. Peter gathered her into his arms. He felt her resist at first, a token challenge, but then she just let go and clung to him.

Peter buried his face in her hair and breathed in the wondrous scent of her. "I didn't believe Sean the first time he told me," he said softly. "But I began to wonder with all this magic stuff. He obviously knew more about everything than me."

Merry pushed herself away slightly. Her eyes were teary, her face flushed. "Oh, Peter, you can see why—"

But the magic had given him powers, too, and he wouldn't let her finish. Not when it was going to be such a silly statement. "All I can see is that you're badly in need of some magic, and I know just the place where it's at its strongest tonight."

She stared up at him. "But I've just told you everything. You can't still—"

He brought her hand up to his lips. Suddenly everything was very clear to him. The real meaning behind all the magic. "A very wise woman once told me that love was seeing the holes in someone else's underwear and loving her anyway."

"Oh, Peter."

"We can work anything out," he told her. "Just as long as we love each other."

"But—"

"He's right, Merry," someone called out.

Peter pulled her back into his arms, afraid that the return of the crowd's voice would spook her. "As long as we're together, we can fix anything," he told her. "And I want us together. I'm tired of being alone."

"Are you asking her to marry you?"

"Yes." Peter smiled down into Merry's eyes.

"Should get down on one knee," someone advised.

"They don't do that anymore," someone else argued.

"I think they should."

"All right." Peter let go of her and got down on his right knee. "Merry Roberts, I love you with my whole heart and soul. Will you please marry me?"

New tears were flowing down her cheeks, but Peter had a feeling that they were happy tears. He waited. But the crowd wasn't as patient.

"Go ahead, dear. He's a nice-looking fella."

"Does he have a job?"

"He looks like a professional. Probably a doctor or something like that."

Peter was waiting. "Merry, please."

Either unable or unwilling, she didn't reply.

He prodded her. "I want to spend New Year's Eve in the Egg Basket of the Midwest."

"He wants to live in a basket?"

"I thought you said he looked like a professional."

"Come on, Merry," Peter urged. "I want to get to Mentone by midnight."

Merry frowned in thought. "Do you think there's enough time?"

For the first time in weeks, Peter felt his heart dance. "If not, I'm sure we can make Bourbon."

"What did he say?"

"He wants to make Bourbon."

"What for? Why doesn't he make love instead?"

"Merry?"

She pulled him up and slipped into his arms. "Yes."

"Yes, what?" Peter asked.

"All of the above."

Epilogue

Dear Santa:

Grandma's writing this for me. She says you don't have to write thank-you notes to Santa, just to people like Aunt Rosa and Cousin Cheryl, but I wanted to thank you, anyway.

Everything came out just right. Both Merry and I are going to live with Daddy, and she's going to be my new mommy. For now, we're going to live part-time in Chicago and part-time in Mentone, and that's great 'cause I like both places.

And guess what? I'm getting a new cousin! His name is Jason and he's really Merry's little boy, but that's a secret. Daddy got Mr. Anderson to help him 'cause Mr. Anderson's a lawyer, and they got Jason's mommy and daddy to let Merry be his aunt. I don't know how a mommy can be an aunt, but Merry cried and cried when Daddy told her. I could tell it was 'cause she was so happy. Jason's going to come visit us on his spring break from school. I'm going to show him the egg.

I don't think any more giant chickens are coming to Mentone. Grandma said the only reason the big rooster is here is 'cause people kept backing their cars into the pedestal in that parking lot. They couldn't get the pedestal out, so they saw this big rooster on sale someplace and bought it to sit on top of the pedestal so people can see it. Merry says that's still magic, but I think she's just kind of weird lately. She and Daddy are talking about painting Zachary's room either pink or blue, and I keep telling them Zachary's blind so he doesn't care what color the room is.

Ricky still says there's no such thing as Santa, but me and Missy made a deal, and he doesn't say it too loud any more.

Anyway, thank you for all the trouble you went to this year, and I promise next year I'll ask for something easy like a bike or sled.

Your pal,
Sean

* * * * *

HARDHEARTED
Bay Matthews

Chantal Robichaux would rather die than call on Dylan Garvey again, but now she desperately needed his help. Chantal's newborn baby—a baby Dylan didn't know was his—had been kidnapped. If anyone could find their son, it was tough cop Dylan. Dylan's heart, on the other hand, would be hard to reach...and only Chantal's love could soften his defenses.

Share Chantal's loving reunion in Bay Matthews's HARDHEARTED, available in January.

THAT SPECIAL WOMAN! She's friend, wife, mother—she's you! And beside each Special Woman stands a wonderfully *special* man. It's a celebration of our heroines—and the men who become part of their lives.

TSW194

Silhouette

SPECIAL EDITION

™

WHAT EVER HAPPENED TO...?

Have you been wondering when a much-loved character will finally get their own story? Well, have we got a lineup for you! Silhouette Special Edition is proud to present a *Spin-off Spectacular!* Be sure to catch these exciting titles from some of your favorite authors.

FOREVER (SE #854, December) *Ginna Gray*'s THE BLAINES AND THE McCALLS OF CROCKETT, TEXAS are back! Outrageously flirtatious Reilly McCall is having the time of his life trying to win over the reluctant heart of Amanda Sutherland!

A DARING VOW (SE #855, December) You met Zelda Lane in KATE'S VOW (SE #823), and she's about to show her old flame she's as bold as ever in this spin-off of *Sherryl Woods*'s VOWS series.

MAGNOLIA DAWN (SE #857, December) *Erica Spindler* returns with a third story of BLOSSOMS OF THE SOUTH in this tale of one woman learning to love again as she struggles to preserve her heritage.

Don't miss these wonderful titles, only for our readers—only from Silhouette Special Edition!

When the only time you have for yourself is…

STOLEN *moments* ™

Christmas is such a busy time—with shopping, decorating, writing cards, trimming trees, wrapping gifts.…

When you do have a few *stolen moments* to call your own, treat yourself to a brand-new *short* novel. Relax with one of our Stocking Stuffers—or with all six!

Each STOLEN MOMENTS title
is a complete and original contemporary romance that's the perfect length for the busy woman of the nineties! Especially at Christmas…

And they make perfect **stocking stuffers**, too! (For your mother, grandmother, daughters, friends, co-workers, neighbors, aunts, cousins—all the other women in your life!)

Look for the STOLEN MOMENTS display in December

STOCKING STUFFERS:

HIS MISTRESS Carrie Alexander
DANIEL'S DECEPTION Marie DeWitt
SNOW ANGEL Isolde Evans
THE FAMILY MAN Danielle Kelly
THE LONE WOLF Ellen Rogers
MONTANA CHRISTMAS Lynn Russell

HSM2

 W⊕RLDWIDE LIBRARY®

If you've been looking for something a little bit different and a little bit spooky, let Silhouette Books take you on a journey to the dark side of love with

SILHOUETTE® Shadows®

Every month, Silhouette brings you two romantic, spine-tingling Shadows novels, written by some of your favorite authors, such as Heather Graham Pozzessere, Anne Stuart, Helen R. Myers and Rachel Lee—to name just a few.

In October, look for:

THE HAUNTING OF BRIER ROSE
by Patricia Simpson
TWILIGHT PHANTASIES
by Maggie Shayne

In November, look for:

TREACHEROUS BEAUTIES
by Cheryl Emerson
DREAM A DEADLY DREAM
by Allie Harrison

In December, look for:

BRIDGE ACROSS FOREVER
by Regan Forest
THE SECRETS OF SEBASTIAN BEAUMONT
by Carrie Peterson

Come into the world of Shadows and prepare to tremble with fear—and passion....

SHAD4

Silhouette Books
is proud to present
our best authors,
their best books...
and the best in
your reading pleasure!

Throughout 1993, look for exciting
books by these top names in
contemporary romance:

DIANA PALMER—
The Australian in October

FERN MICHAELS—
Sea Gypsy in October

ELIZABETH LOWELL—
Chain Lightning in November

CATHERINE COULTER—
The Aristocrat in December

JOAN HOHL—
Texas Gold in December

LINDA HOWARD—
Tears of the Renegade in January '94

When it comes to passion,
we wrote the book.   BOBT3

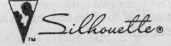

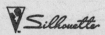